The Company

Bill Kidd

AmErica House
Baltimore

© 2002 by Bill Kidd.

All rights reserved. No part of this book may be reproduced in any form without written permission from the publishers, except by a reviewer who may quote brief passages in a review to be printed in a newspaper or magazine.

First printing

ISBN: 1-59129-192-5
PUBLISHED BY AMERICA HOUSE BOOK PUBLISHERS
www.publishamerica.com
Baltimore

Printed in the United States of America

1

Saturday night!

Washington shook loose from the pomp and the power and – chased the pizzaz.

For Marty Price that meant a seafood grill at Georgetown Harbor and jazz on U Street. He also intended to catch up on his relationship with Lisa Page. That was going well until Lisa glanced across the restaurant.

"Oh, no…" she said, her lazy smile turning into a sultry frown.

Marty turned to see what had caught her attention.

It was Jack Watson, Marty's ex-business partner. Wearing a dark leather coat, the thirty-year-old man with the black hair, strong jaw and Santa Monica tan, had gotten past the Riverview's maitre d'. As he pressed through the crowd at the zebrawood-paneled bar, he moved like he was on an urgent mission.

"I love you," Lisa said, "but I don't know if I can handle your world."

Marty's turquoise-blue eyes flashed fire. He didn't need this, the past walking in on him. Not when he had a ring in his pocket and was hoping to give it to Lisa. Dressed in a white suit with a lavender shirt, the twenty-nine-year-old man stood straight on his lithe five-eleven frame, saying, "I'm sorry, I'll get rid of him."

Turning, Marty faced Jack. The man had a frosted stare, was breathing hard like he had been running, and his fists were clenched as if he was under duress. "Are you okay?" Marty asked.

"We've got to talk," Jack huffed. "It's real important."

Marty forced a gentleman's smile across his angular face. "Can it wait until morning?"

Jack shook his head.

Marty ran a hand through his dirty-blond flattop. He hadn't seen Jack in six months, and it had been three years since they worked a case together. But now he burst in on him like a tropical storm. Still standing, Marty said, "I'm in the middle of something. Can you call me in an hour?"

Jack's face welled with pain. "I don't how to say this, but I need help … now."

"What's wrong?" Marty asked, extending a hand, inviting Jack to sit down. "You know Lisa."

Jack nodded to her as he sat on the edge of a chair. Leaning towards Marty, he whispered, "They're trying to kill me."

"Kill you?" Marty said, disbelief ghosting across his face.

"They've been following me for a week. I don't know how to shake them. They could be here already." Jack's eyes scanned the room as if he was looking for someone.

Marty looked too. It was after nine, and most of the tables were empty. The chef had stepped out front to meet a couple who had left a generous tip. Senator Bancroft sat at the bar, fiddling with a snifter of brandy. His muscular bodyguard had his back to the counter and was looking at them. "Who?" Marty asked.

Jack's mouth stretched into a sweeping grimace. "I don't want anyone to hear this. Can we step outside?"

Expressionless, Marty stood and glanced at Lisa, saying, "I'll be back in a minute."

Jack headed out the door and trudged through the puddles left by the chilly, spring rain. When a mist swept up from the river, he didn't seem to notice. Rather, he appeared dead to his sensibilities, ghostlike and pale, until a boat flashed its spotlight on the dock, and he flinched, ducking, like they were shooting at him.

Stepping onto the boardwalk, Marty glanced at the Coast Guard cutter plowing through the dark waters of the Potomac River. "You're really on edge," he said.

"Yeah, I was shot." Jack pulled back his coat. Under the shoulder holster with the automatic, the shirt bulged from the bandages.

"Shot?" Marty exclaimed.

Jack eased the gun out of the holster as if he was waiting for an intruder. "Yesterday, in L.A. I couldn't think of anywhere else to go, so I came here. You've got to help me."

Marty could see the man was clearly over the edge. He turned slowly about, his hands out, expressively showing Jack that it was safe. "Look, no one is here. You have to put the gun away."

Jack stuck the black pistol in his belt, ready for a quick draw.

"Who shot you?" Marty asked.

"That's the hard part. It's the feds."

"Huh?"

"They ripped off Professor Rose for the Hydrogen Accelerator, then killed him. Now, they're going to kill me."

Marty's eyes wandered downstream, across the empire of lights shining on the white, rectangular Kennedy Center and the curvilinear Watergate Apartments. Jack must be pressured, killers on his tail. Something truly awful. No sober-brained P.I. would talk this way. "What do you mean saying it's the feds?" Marty asked.

Jack pulled a thin diskette case from his pocket and stuffed it into Marty's hand. "It's all right here."

Marty knew Jack to be a proud man. He had never heard him sound so afraid. "What is a Hydrogen Accelerator?"

"An energy generator. The feds stole it to keep it off the market. You know, to prop up the oil prices."

Marty didn't want to hear another conspiracy theory. That was the stuff of smear campaigns and movies. He tried to act calm and professional, the way he would react to a flustered client. "Tell me some more about it," he said.

Jack moved away from the lamppost and headed down the boardwalk where it was darker. "Professor Rose retired out of the Jet Propulsion Laboratory. He had the patent papers right there in his hand when he broke the news to his family. He'd invented a device for making cheap energy. They'd all be rich. Billionaires, he said. Then someone figured it out. Rose's machine would put the traditional energy companies out of business. So they came, and they took it, then covered it up by killing him."

Marty felt a sudden shameful feeling that if Jack continued telling his conspiracy theory, Senator Bancroft would hear about it and make this moment come back on Marty where it hurt the most, his contract to do investigations for the Senate Commerce Committee. But realizing Jack's sanity was hanging on a thread, he said, "Covered it up?"

Jack glared ashen-faced past Marty. "They work out of the FBI office. My hunch is that the director is in on it. Who knows? It might go all the way up the food chain to the president."

Marty liked the new president, and the FBI had testified with him at the computer-crime hearings. He felt an urge to poke holes in Jack's theory. But he knew that his former partner was suffering from posttraumatic stress and needed a shrink. Not criticism. People didn't kill people over patents. Certainly not the federal government. Marty worked for them. He was moving up in the world and didn't need this, Jack all crazy, bad-mouthing everyone. "I've got to think about this for a minute," he said, putting his arm on Jack's shoulder and nudging him towards the restaurant. "We'll pick up

Lisa, and then go over it later at my place. Okay?"

"Thanks."

Down the stairs from the boardwalk, they strolled around the fountain on the lower plaza.

"I'm sorry to dump this on you, but –" Misty-eyed, Jack stopped and stared at Marty. "They're going to kill me, tonight, I know it."

Marty blew out a sea of air and resumed walking, going past the restaurant door. Jack would have to cool off a bit if they were going to pick up Lisa. She was tired of detective stories, and she surely would not want to hear the rest of this one.

At the edge of the fountain, Marty watched the jets squirt water up into the night air. He didn't want to sound patronizing by offering advice, so he turned to his ex-partner and said, "You're scaring me, man."

"I'm sorry," Jack said, "but it's real."

Yeah, sure. Marty wanted to give Jack a piece of his mind.

When something moved above them, he startled. But looking past the balustrade marking the edge of the upper plaza, Marty didn't see anything but shadows. That made him realize that Jack's story had put him on-guard. "Real or not," he said, "you can't take care of business while you're acting so paranoid."

"Listen to me, that's all I ask."

"Fine. But stop the dramatics."

"If you'd let me finish, you would understand."

Something moved again. Above them. A man at the edge of the upper deck, pointing a pistol with a sound suppressor on the barrel.

"Get down!" Marty grunted, grabbing Jack and throwing him onto the pavement.

They tumbled topsy-turvy as the bullets whizzed past.

Bull-headed, Jack jumped up. "Run!" he yelled, his pistol pulled, taking aim at the intruder.

2

Marty ran straight for the wall and burst through the door leading to the underground parking lot. When a gruff voice reverberated through the maze of cement posts, he instinctively crouched behind a sports utility vehicle in order to hide. Peeking around the fender, he watched a tall, sinewy man storm around a corner, trailed by a stampede of men.

Ah, the cops are here.

Sighing with relief, Marty started after them as they raced through the door and out onto the lower plaza. But suddenly he stopped. How did these men know what was going on? There weren't any sounds of guns shooting. Not that he heard. The intruder had a silencer on his weapon. And as far as Marty could tell, Jack didn't shoot, but raced after the gunman. There hadn't been time to call these people, so who were they? Why were they even here? To get Jack? Or were they after the shooter?

He moved into the shadows and tried to think it out. He knew that crooks didn't run in gangs, not in Washington. No, the District was a lady, and you respected her. These had to be the feds, one group or the other.

Marty saw someone coming. It was a brut-of-a-man dressed in a Hawaiian shirt. He had a security communication's plug in his ear, and he looked to and fro, searching for something. Realizing that this was a government professional, Marty knew that he should stand up and identify himself as a private investigator who worked for the Senate Commerce Committee. Stepping out of the shadows, he approached the man from behind. "Excuse me –"

In a quick, cold turn, Mr. Hawaiian Shirt reached behind his back and pulled a pistol.

Marty's instincts went on autopilot, and he kicked the man's gun hand.

The weapon flew out of the man's grasp. But reacting with calculated malevolence, Mr. Hawaiian Shirt swung a perfected-executed, flat-knuckled punch towards Marty's throat.

Marty stepped to the side and kicked the man in the knee, knocking him down. Then he turned and sprinted away, knowing that winning the fight would be a pyrrhic victory. When he reached the stairwell at the end of the garage, he glanced back and saw that the gunman had retrieved the automatic and was following him.

Marty hustled into the landing, and taking a risk, he headed down instead of up. After all, he believed that these people – part of the group trying to kill Jack – were waiting for him outside. When he reached the lower landing, a gunshot echoed from the far side of the parking garage. Marty rolled behind a car and waited.

Following a profound silence, he stole through the shadows. Towards the other end of the garage, he spotted a group of men next to a white van. FBI Special Agent George Harrington was with them.

The FBI?

Marty wondered how these thugs could be agents. He watched them talk until Harrington got in the passenger seat of the vehicle. After the van took off, the men stood around for a moment, then fanned out, continuing their search.

He crept further into the shadows, wanting to get close to the other exit, maybe risk getting shot as he left the building. He also wanted his gun, and he wanted to know if they had shot Jack and stuffed his body into the vehicle. And most important, he wanted to know if Harrington had ordered these men to kill him. And why?

Suddenly, he could curse. He didn't get the license number of the vehicle.

He thought about tackling one of the men and beating the truth out of him, but he had to think about Lisa. They both needed to get away from here. But how?

He looked about. Under the floodlights, a red BMW was leaving, shrouded under a symphony of soft music. He had the urge to step in front of the car and stop it, say to the driver, excuse me, these men, they shot Jack, and they tried to kill me.

He knew no one was going to help him, not like that. So he crept back to the stairwell and went up the stairs. Approaching the street-level exit above him, he heard voices coming from outside the metal door. Figuring it wasn't safe to go that direction, he ducked back down into the first basement level of the garage and waited.

Knowing how the feds worked, Marty imagined that they would throw in waves of officers until he was flushed out. And hell, maybe there was some truth to what Jack was saying about the FBI crossing the line. Didn't they shoot him back in Los Angeles? And they shot him again now. That was what had happened. And Harrington was leaving with Jack's body hidden in the van.

Marty got close enough to watch the ramp leading out of the garage and up to the street. While the cars stopped at the pay booth, men in suits were glancing inside. Marty knew they were looking for him. When a couple of men approached the spot where he was hiding, he ducked under a car.

Looking around, he noticed he was lying a couple of cars over from Lisa's. The possibility of salvation raised hope up from the pits of doom. He pulled out his cell phone and dialed her number. She answered on the first ring.

"Hi, honey, it's me," he said.

"Marty? Where did you go? I'm outside, but I don't see you."

"I'm waiting for you at the car. We've got to get out of here. Jack's been shot. Now they're trying to catch me."

"Catch you?"

"Yes, there's been a mix up. They tried to kill me. We've got to go – fast."

"Not wait for the ambulance?"

"No, I didn't call one. The people who did the shooting took Jack with them. At least that's what it looked like."

"I didn't hear any shooting."

"Well, no, the jerks had silencers on their guns."

"I don't understand."

"I don't understand either. The FBI is here. Well … at least I saw Agent Harrington. But they think I'm one of the bad guys."

"Marty, how could you joke about this?"

"Honey, baby, listen … pleeeeze…"

"It's true?"

"No. The Bureau has mistaken me for one of the people who shot Jack. Or mistook Jack for someone who shot at them. I don't know. But they're running around with their weapons pulled and shooting whatever moves."

"I'm calling the police."

"No, these guys won't hurt you. They want me, or someone that looks like me. We have to get out of here right now. We can call the cops later."

"Where are you?"

"I'm lying under a car in the parking lot near your car. Can you come here and help me? I know anyone with any sense wouldn't want to get involved. But honey, it's my life we're talking about. Jack's dead. I know it, I just know it."

"I'm calling 911."

"No, I'll be dead by the time the District gets a cop over here."

"Are you saying the government is after you because you were with Jack?"

"That's probably it. My suit. They saw someone dressed in white standing with Jack. They took a few pot shots at us and missed. We got away, but they cornered Jack in the parking lot. Now they want me, I guess, so they can cover it up. I know it's impossible to imagine, but that's what's happening."

"I don't see you under my car."

"Huh?"

"I'm standing next to my car."

Marty twisted and looked around the tire. He watched the back side of her sleek, black, strapless dress as she opened the door and hopped into her silver Mercedes.

"Honey, listen," he said into the phone, "start the car, pull back a couple spaces, and pop the trunk. I know it sounds ridiculous, but I'll jump in the back and pull down the lid. That way we can drive out the gate, and they won't see me."

"Marty, walk over here and get in the car. Right now."

"Listen, they don't understand. They think I killed Jack, or somebody, or something."

"You're going to get us into trouble. Why don't you stand up, take a deep breath, and we'll go tell the police –"

Marty saw a couple pairs of feet – men's shoes – running behind Lisa's car and heading off into the distance.

"They have guns," she whispered into her phone.

"That's what I'm saying. I had to fight one of these thugs to keep him from killing me." He watched the car roll back. "That's it, keep it coming. A little more. Oh, yes, c'mon, that's it, pop the trunk."

"I can't believe we're doing this."

"I know. We'll talk about it when we get over to your place."

Marty heard the trunk latch thunk, and he rolled out from under the car and raced over and jumped in. He pulled down the lid and tucked his head in next to the hard rubber tire.

Back on the phone he said, "Smile when you stop at the toll booth, and they won't worry about you."

"What do you mean they think you did it?" Lisa said over the phone.

Listening to car engine purr, Marty reached under his back and pulled out a wooden coat hanger that was jabbing him. "I don't really know who they are or what they think I did. But Jack told me about a wild case where the people killed his client's father, a professor who invented an energy device. Now they want to kill Jack before he takes the information to the police."

"It's a murder case, and they think Jack told you who did it. Now they want to stop you from revealing that information. Is that it?"

"I think so."

"Are you okay?" she asked.

"I'll make it."

"Hang on a second."

He felt the car stop, and in the darkness of the trunk, he could hear the attendant at the pay booth tell her the charge.

A baritone voice interrupted. "I'm officer Barr. We're looking for a fugitive."

"Oh, my…" Lisa said.

"Are you by yourself tonight?"

"No," Lisa said.

Hearing this, Marty held his breath.

"Does that mean you left someone here?" Barr continued.

"My friends from the office. We had dinner. I'm driving my car home."

"Oh, I see. Did you see anyone who looked suspicious tonight?"

"No."

"What about a man in a white suit?"

"I'd like that."

Marty listened to them laugh.

"Have a good night," Barr said.

Marty felt the force of the car slowly accelerating.

"You were right about the white suit," Lisa said, back on the phone.

"Yes. This Barr character – could you tell what agency he worked for?"

"No. I figured it was FBI because you mentioned it."

"What was he wearing?"

"A polished-gray suit."

"Did you see a gun?"

"No."

"Do you think he wrote down your license plate number?"

"I didn't notice if he looked at the plates. What were you saying about a professor getting killed?"

He found Lisa's sports cushion and stuffed it behind his neck, trying to get comfortable on the cold carpet. "It's bizarre. He invented a way to make cheap energy. Jack said the feds appropriated it for themselves by killing him. Some sort of alliance with the traditional energy people who don't want the competition."

"Sounds preposterous."

"I know the story is unbelievable, but Jack had already been shot in L.A. Then they shot him again just now. So you know they're trying to shut him up, whoever they are … some sort of government gangsters."

"Government gangsters?"

"Jack said it was a group using the FBI as a cover. Then I saw agent Harrington here. When I approached one of the men, he pulled a gun and tried to shoot me."

"What did you do?"

"Kicked the gun and ran."

"That's why they want you."

"He was going to kill me."

"How did you know that?"

"This guy had the look of the devil in his eye."

"That's a lot to go on." She paused a moment. "Let's start over and figure it out. There has to be a logical reason it happened."

Phone to his ear, Marty wanted to talk about getting out of the trunk, but let it go for the moment. "Okay."

"Where was Jack, and what was he doing when he got shot?"

"I didn't see him get shot."

"Then how do you know that's what happened?"

He huffed out his disappointments. "Okay, from the beginning. We were talking on the plaza, and a man shot at us. All right?"

"Why didn't I hear it?"

"He had a silencer on his gun ... Then, in the garage, a man tried to shoot me, but I kicked the gun out of his hand."

"Before you spoke to him?"

"Well, yeah, he was going to kill me!"

"You knew that? You looked into his mind and saw his intent?"

In the darkness of the trunk, Marty held the phone away from his face and silently counted to five.

"How did you know he was going to kill you?" she continued.

"Believe me, you know by the way a person grabs their gun. There's an urgency in their body movements."

"Really?"

"Kind of like the way you know a guy is going to get sexual."

"I see."

"Can we pull over so I can get out?"

"We'd better go all the way home, just to be safe."

Believing there was nothing he could do to stop this from being a long, endless night, Marty laid back and said, "Good idea."

3

Twenty minutes later, they were in the black-walnut-paneled second-floor study of Lisa's home. She sat at the cherry wood desk; he stood by the window. Soft jazz drifted in from the next room.

"The FBI believes I'm a criminal," Marty said. "I can't call them."

Lisa pulled the diamond-studded clip from the bun in her long, golden-hued hair. "Okay, then what would an ordinary person do in your situation?"

"An ordinary person wouldn't have known Harrington –"

"Or Jack," she said.

"And would have called 911 from the restaurant like you suggested."

"You could still call," she said, "and see if they report what you saw, or something different."

"I suppose." He scrutinized her for a moment. With fine facial features, artful pouting lips, a hint of natural blush on her cheeks, and cloudy-blue eyes, she was a supple woman. Her attention was directed to a stack of dark-green journals she had brought home from the office. He waited for her to look up. When she didn't, he turned and gazed through the glass doors which led to the balcony.

Outside, the illumination from the spotlights shimmered through the misty drizzle falling over the semi-circle of rounded-top yew trees. Beyond that was the dark forest at the northern-end of Rock Creek Park near Chevy Chase, Maryland.

"I'm calling the District Police, first," Marty said, pulling his phone off his belt and dialing. When the police dispatcher came on the line, he said, "I was at the Riverview Restaurant tonight, and I thought I heard gunshots. Did you get a report on a shooting over there?"

"Nothing came this way," replied the dispatcher. "Do you want to file a report?"

"No, that's okay," Marty said.

"Anything else?"

"Did you have an ambulance going to Georgetown Harbor within the last hour?"

"Not for a shooting."

"What for?"

"Can't say."

Marty shifted his weight back and forth, one foot to the other. "Look, I'm a local P.I. Price is the name. Commander Nelson said to call if I ever ran into trouble. Is he on duty."

"You know Nelson?" said the dispatcher.

"Yes, my office is in the Second District. I helped out during the inauguration."

"The call concerned the FBI. One of their agents had been injured."

Marty smirked. "But it wasn't a shooting."

"No. They had a swat team practice at the harbor. A man fell and was hurt."

"But it could have been something else, right? And they said it was a swat team exercise as a coverup."

"Look, Price, I can't use the word coverup, not while I'm on duty."

"I'm sorry." Marty thought for a second. "Was anybody killed tonight?"

"Not that I heard about unless ... No, you're talking the District, not Arlington."

"What happened over there?"

"Body in the water near the cemetery."

Marty thoughts swirled. He imagined the FBI hiding Jack's killing, saying it was only a swat-team practice at the Riverview, and then dumping his body on federal lands out of the investigative reach of the DC Police Department. "When did that happen?"

"Just now."

"Where are they taking the body?"

"That's a federal matter, I wouldn't know."

"What about the injured officer?"

"Off the record I'd say you'd have a good chance of finding that person at Quantico."

"Quantico?" Marty couldn't imagine driving a bleeding officer 40 miles to the FBI training center when they could have gone a mile east on K Street to the emergency room at George Washington University. "That's stupid."

The dispatcher snickered. "*Feds* and *brains* is an oxymoron."

"I guess."

After hearing that there wasn't much else happening that Saturday night at the Capitol, Marty hung up. He looked at Lisa sitting at the desk. "No report of a shooting, but mysteriously, an FBI agent was injured at Georgetown Harbor." He held out both arms. "What? Zorro got him with a sword?"

She shook her head.

He said, "There was a body dumped across the river in Arlington, conveniently on government park lands. It's got to be Jack. They took him there in the van. Still think I should call the FBI and tell them I know about the shooting?"

"Not unless you shot Jack."

"Good one."

Marty watched the drizzle outside the window turn into sheets of rain. He thought about how Jack was the brother he never had. Actually, his only family aside from his grandmother. She raised Marty after his parents were killed in a car accident on the Pasadena Freeway in L.A. He could still remember that night, grandma telling him to go back to sleep. Everything would be all right. The woman was in such shock she didn't know what else to say. He was four, but he knew something was wrong. The phone calls, the crying. Tonight was like that, but he was too angry and too old to cry.

He moved towards the computer workstation. Picking up the disk case that Jack had given him, he said, "Maybe this explains something."

"Let's hope so," Lisa said.

He opened the small plastic box. There was a single floppy disk inside along with a metal key. Marty recognized it as the U.S. Post Office key from the box they used when they ran the agency together in L.A. He held it up so that Lisa could see it. "Jack must have sent something to himself. That's the only way he could guarantee I'd get it after the feds made a search of his office. Talk about desperate, or what?"

"I don't know," Lisa said, getting up to watch what he was doing. "Does Jack have a history of going ballistic?"

He pretended to smile. "Yes, but we lock him up twice a year and force Prozac down his throat. It beats sex."

"For you, or for him?"

"It's safe sex for both of us."

"You should have been a comic – a sit down comic."

"Good one."

Marty pushed the diskette into the floppy drive, opened the file, and looked at the screen. It displayed a title and an introductory note:

The Rose Case
This is a copy of my daily log. The notes chronicle the activities of a racketeering-orientated, criminal conspiracy run by the government. Professor Rose came into contact with the organization when he applied for a patent. The application was confiscated. The government

is withholding it from the public, using the technology themselves. They murdered the professor to cover it up. David Rose, his son, opened the case. He can be reached at his home in Beverly Hills.

I hope that you will review this case and pursue it to a just end.

Best regards, Jack Watson.

Marty scanned the document, quickly heading to the end. Then he studied the professor's summary of how the Hydrogen Accelerator worked. Finally, he said, "It sounds like you split the water into hydrogen atoms, and then bring it back together, making power. Finally, you end up with water all over again."

"If you believe in miracles," Lisa said, turning and heading for the adjacent sitting room.

"What's that supposed to mean?" he said, watching the delicate muscles of her backside undulate under her silky evening gown as she sashayed out of the room.

Her voice filtered back to him. "It sounds too simple, like it was written to beguile the innocent ... maybe use it to set up a Ponzi investment scheme."

He studied the notes. "David Rose suffered a seizure and his father suffered a stroke. The old man died. Is that a little too coincidental, or what?"

"Huh?"

He got up and went through the arch into the sitting room. Located between the master bedroom and the study, it had a used-brick-covered wall facing a contrasting, spotlessly-white plastered wall on the opposite side of the room. There were two, tall glass doors opening to the balcony. At the center of the room, a light-grey overstuffed sofa and chair were surrounded by coffee and end tables made of dark, African sapele wood. Lisa was circling the room, spraying a mist from a plastic bottle onto the houseplants.

He said, "I'm thinking, how did they induce a stroke? That's how they killed the professor."

"Who are they?"

"I told you, I saw an FBI agent that I knew."

Lisa stopped to pick a few dry leaves off the Mini English Ivy vine that hung in a pot from the ceiling. "Jack says there's a criminal conspiracy, and he's basing it on the fact that a professor had a stroke near the time his son had a seizure. You, in turn, are buying into the theory because you saw an FBI agent that you knew."

"Not just that. They shot Jack. Then shot him again tonight."

"But you didn't see it happen either time."

"I heard it tonight."

"I thought they had silencers."

"Right, upstairs on the plaza, we were almost killed. But Jack chased the shooter and returned fire, somewhere inside the garage. I heard that ... that was when they killed him."

Lisa stared hollow-eyed, until she said, "If it is a conspiracy, and if it is the FBI, you're outnumbered, and you'd better find a way to back out of this thing. Or you had better find overwhelming evidence to support Jack's theory. What you have, including the disk, doesn't support much of anything. Does it?"

He shrugged.

"Are you willing to risk your life over this?"

Marty flopped onto the deep, lazy sofa. She had a point. He didn't have any evidence supporting a conspiracy. It could only sign Marty's death warrant if he stirred up the rogue agents and they came after him again.

She said, "Maybe you need to forget about this, at least until Jack's body turns up."

"How do I let it go?"

"First thing is relax."

"Okay."

"Next thing, take off all your clothes."

He chuckled.

"Third thing, do the horizontal bop until you're as rummy as a fruitcake and wimpy limp as a noodle. Then –"

Marty sat up. If there was anyone who could make him rummy as a fruitcake, it was Lisa. He wondered if they'd ever be that way again. "Then what?"

Lisa walked over and poked the bottle in his face, then squirted him.

He flayed the air with his arms. "*What?*"

"Forget the whole thing."

He knew that friends and family of police officers and private investigators often turned cold from constantly hearing stories of danger. But this was ridiculous. "Jack was murdered, and I'm supposed to forget it? You knew him. You saw him tonight. Alive. Real. A beautiful human. Doesn't the loss of his life matter to you?"

"Yes, but I didn't see what happened, and the story is hard to believe, unless Jack murdered someone, and the FBI has evidence pointing at him. Maybe at both of you. It's possible. You're his ex-partner."

She had gone beyond her usual psychologizing and was sounding like a lawyer. Blistering now, he said, "If I hear you right, you're saying that you don't have to get involved here emotionally because the feds have evidence that makes an appearance – rightly or wrongly – that Jack and I did something pretty darn evil?"

"What do you think?"

"I think I'm the only one who gives a damn about an innocent man being shot."

"Let's say that's what happened, even though we don't know it is the truth. Okay?" When he nodded, she glanced around the mansion, saying, "Should I get involved with you on this case and risk losing everything?"

Hmmm. He knew that she had given up her career while she managed her grandfather's affairs. He was senile. Authoritarian. Angry. It wasn't a cake walk. When he died, he left her his estate.

She said, "The house puts me on par with my friends who went to the big schools. I don't want to throw it away because you and Jack met a man with a gun on the dock. Besides, you're always meeting someone strange, and there's always a question of who is right or wrong. Well, this time, I'm scared." Her eyes opened wide, and her mouth tucked down into an painful frown. "Really, really scared. That's what's happening."

She moved point blank and pointed the spray bottle at his nose. "If you weren't the nicest man I know, I would have left you on the pavement back there at the Riverview. I'm sorry, but I don't need this. You don't need it either. I thought you'd gotten out of the midnight-caper business and were working for the Senate. What's going on? Do you and Jack have a pact with the devil?"

He stared in her cloudy blues and mulled it over. A woman who carried herself in a proud fashion, she was a psychologist, and her clients placed their lives in her care. Oh sure, once in a while he would like to tell her to turn off the doctor-talk and get real. But tonight, despite it all, he felt he was lucky enough to get her bottom line. "I'm the nicest?" he said.

She set the spray bottle on the coffee table and padded across the thick carpet towards the door to the hall. "I'm going to bed. You can join me if you want."

"I'll be there in a minute," he said, looking at the empty doorway. His head sank back into the sofa as he gazed up at the dusky paneling on the vaulted ceiling.

He could lose Lisa over this.

And his job.

Maybe his life.

He regurgitated the events of the evening. There were no questions asked, they simply starting shooting. He couldn't believe it even though he had been there. And he would have been dead, too, if the shooter hadn't flinched, then run, when Jack counterattacked.

His thoughts turned to the call he made to the police. Didn't the dispatcher say the FBI had a man injured at the Riverview? It had to be the guy who had shot at them. Jack got him. That was the wounded – actually, dead – officer who was shipped off to Quantico, a scheme to keep it out of the news. The details of Jack's death would emerge tomorrow. The news would say that the U.S. Park Police at Arlington Cemetery discovered a body in the river. That would be the spin.

He considered the data on the disk and wondered about the government stealing energy patents. How did they think they could cover up something like that? Surely Professor Rose worked on a team with other scientists. One man couldn't put together something so cutting-edge, single-handedly breaking the laws of traditional physics. It had to have been something he researched at work, a new method to power spacecraft.

But it didn't matter if the thing worked or not. The issue was that the government stole the Accelerator and suppressed the knowledge of its existence.

But wait a minute ... Jack had been shot, and Marty hadn't called the emergency rooms. What was he thinking? That District dispatch had the whole story?

He pulled his phone off his belt and called Greater Southeast Community Hospital. That's where people without identification or insurance were sent, which would be Jack when the feds got through with him. After questioning the emergency room receptionist, the admission desk, and the billing office, he was sure Jack had not been shipped there.

He called the District of Columbia morgue.

Same story, no Jack.

Same thing with the Arlington, Virginia, morgue and the one in Prince George County in Maryland.

He buzzed the ER at George Washington University Hospital over on the West End, the place where they saved Ronald Reagan's life after the senseless shooting.

Jack wasn't there.

Just to be sure, he called the emergency rooms at the Howard University and Washington Hospital Center.

No Jack.

He thought for a moment. Finally, he remembered Sibley Memorial Hospital there in the Northwest corner of the District, not all that far from Lisa's.

Still no Jack.

He paced the floor.

He became fraught with questions.

In the early morning hours, he flopped onto the sofa, exhausted by the whole mess.

Thoughts turned to images.

Images turned to dreams.

FBI agents in a tug boat were hoisting Jack out of the water on a gigantic stainless steel hook when –

Wham! Something punched Marty in the gut, and reflexively, his arms reached out to grab whatever it was.

He had to laugh. It was Nikki, the monstrous white ball of fur which paraded around Lisa's home pretending to be a cat. Marty knew better. This was a sorcerer's companion. Not an ordinary feline. And it was up to something.

The cat purred, kneading Marty's chest with its claws.

"Okay," he said, "I'll get you some food."

4

The FBI Academy at Quantico, Virginia, shared 400 forested acres of land with the Drug Enforcement Administration. Inside that space were a dozen glass-and-steel buildings, state-of-the-art forensic laboratories, computer rooms, gun ranges, classrooms, and theaters. There was even a mini-city staffed with actors where the bank was staked out and robbed on a regular basis. In the bowels of the Behavioral Sciences Building in one of the underground laboratories, a knock rang out from someone hitting the other side of the metal door.

With a strong jaw, sharp nose, hollow cheeks, and high forehead, Commander John Krocker had the stern-lined face of a Puritan minister. Marching across the spotlessly antiseptic white office, he opened the door and saw Special Agent George Harrington. The man was dressed in a grey suit and looked disgruntled. “I thought you were going to call,” Krocker said.

“We got Jack Watson,” Harrington said, “but shit rained down from heaven.”

“Huh?” Krocker said.

Forty-year-old Harrington had an oval face, protruding brow, thick black hair, and an endless five o’clock shadow. He hustled into the office, stared up at the twenty-foot-high, metal-beam ceiling, and finally said, “Tucker got killed.”

The commander’s steely gray eyes burnt red like fire. “On a routine operation? What the fuck happened?”

“Tucker picked up the lead on Watson at the Riverside Restaurant. He called, saying he was covering the dock and needed us to come in and squeeze Watson out. When we got there, they were in the basement of the parking lot firing at each other.”

“I don’t believe this.” Krocker knew that Tucker Johnston was one of the few people who would do whatever he ordered without questioning it. Sitting on the corner of his massive executive desk, he glared at his alligator-skin boots and mumbled, “How did we screw up?”

“If you want the truth, the screw-up was not shooting Watson the first we heard he was investigating the Company.”

"Yeah?"

"Well, sure, pull the plug on the guy before he ran." Harrington eased onto the deep, peach-colored sofa. "Maybe Buddy should be running the team. He wanted to do a hit on Watson in L.A., not talk to the jerk and see what he had on us."

Krocker's glum face twisted with a hint of a smile. "Buddy's solution for everything is a hit."

"I guess."

"How much publicity did you stir up at the Harbor?"

"Not much. We said an agent was hurt on a swat team practice, and we got one of our ambulances down there." Harrington grinned mischievously. "We brought Watson in ourselves. They're patching him up at the clinic."

"You're telling me Watson is alive?" Krocker said.

"Still hanging on. So you'll be able to question him yourself" – Harrington inhaled lustfully – "if you don't kill him first."

Krocker stared off into space. He was an old-fashioned man of steel who had made a profession out of solving government problems, the sticky ones where militant, American groups had weapons and were willing to die for their cause. He would cool the freebooters down, then cover up the operation. At one time, his position was classified top security and he had unrestricted license. But he went too far in abridging constitutional freedoms, and his special-operations budget was eliminated. So these days, when he created hell for someone, he was acting on his own, raising his own money, promoting his own cause. "What's a perpetrator from L.A. doing in DC?" he asked.

"He was trying to bust our operation. Talk to the higher-ups. Expose the Company."

"That's my hunch, too. Better tear the Riverview apart. Get the guest list. See if anybody important was meeting with him."

"Senator Bancroft was there."

"Coincidence. He's a silent partner in the harbor development. Owns half the place."

"Watson did meet someone – we think."

"You think?" Krocker grumbled. "What does that mean?"

"A man in a white suit. We tried to nab him, but he disappeared. No telling if Watson passed information to him or not."

Six-foot-three, and well-muscled at forty-five, the reddish-blond haired Krocker stood expressionless and stared at the other man. Finally, he said, "What the hell do you mean the man disappeared?"

"When Tucker called, he said Watson had walked out the door of the restaurant talking to a man in a white suit. The guy bumped into Mack, but he got away."

Krocker sounded incredulous. "This jerk got away from Mack?"

Harrington nodded.

"Find this guy and get the story out of him. Actually, send him to me. The happy-time truth serum makes for a clean confession."

"Clean confession – sounds like a book."

Krocker chuckled. He had hired a Russian, Dr. Yurinkovitch, to lead the team that was developing exotic drugs at a covert lab in Azerbaidzhan. Using pharmacological secrets from the mordant U.S.S.R. neuropsychology program, he produced a fast-acting, receptor-specific, sedative-hypnotic drug that would loosen people up so they would become completely uninhibited. Then they couldn't help but yack about their hidden agendas. "Hey, while I've got your attention –"

Harrington groaned, "Uh-oh."

"How did Watson get all the way from L.A. to DC before you apprehended him?"

There was hesitation in Harrington's voice. "We don't know, not yet."

"Put someone on it. I want a report on my desk in two days. We're going to learn from this lesson, right?"

"Right."

"You think it's a fluke, or do you think Watson's the Houdini we made him out to be … picking up and leaving when we had him surrounded? "

Harrington grew defensive. "He didn't exactly waltz his way out of there. He was shot, managed to get bandaged up, got by us at LAX … disguised, or something … then got to National Airport and took a cab. That's when he made a phone call, which was how we nailed him. He used his cell."

Krocker stood and turned to the computer workstation. Leaning over the chair, he punched a few keys and tied into the mainframes on the first floor of the J. Edgar Hoover Building. He said as a way of explanation, "It almost sounds like he dared us to shoot him."

"What?"

"He thought we were helpless, that we couldn't shoot him so near the Capitol. Especially if his contact had clout."

"You're saying he's got an ally on the Hill?"

"Let's face it. He's got someone in the District. If he didn't, he sure wouldn't have come here, not knowing what he knows about us."

"We'll find him."

"No doubt in my mind."

"I'm sorry about Tucker, but I honestly don't know what went wrong.

You've been to the Riverview Restaurant, haven't you? With the underground parking lot?"

"Uh-huh."

"We drove inside and parked, then headed out to the boardwalk. At that same time, Tucker and Watson were going down the stairs, one chasing the other. That's the best I can figure. As we spread out to look for them, they started firing."

"How many witnesses were there?"

"Just the man in the white coat."

"How are we going to account for the intrusion?"

"We spread the word that the FBI had a swat team practice, and people felt good about it, like they hope we could make the District safer to live in."

"Good. Keep that rumor going until you believe it yourself."

"Got it."

Krocker's eyes ferreted this way and that. "It's too late to bring Tucker back. What kind of spin do you think we should put on his death?"

"You can blame it on Watson's partner, if we find him."

"When you find him."

"Right. That's what we'll do."

Krocker stood still for a moment. Tucker Johnston was a civilian posing as an FBI agent. In that capacity he had a Bureau I.D. "If we have to, we'll make Tucker a full special agent. Then people won't care if we shoot Watson's partner. He would be held guilty of killing a federal man."

"Okay, then I'll keep a lid on Tucker's death until we find this guy."

"Good. What kind of shape is Watson in?"

"Critical, but he's going to make it."

Krocker stared momentarily at the computer screen. These integrity kooks like Jack Watson never beat him, yet they fought some good battles. Watson was one of the toughest. Fortunately, he didn't die, and wasn't going to die. Not yet. He had to be kept alive until he told everything. Then, it didn't matter what they did with him. Krocker pointed at the monitor. "L.A. Self Defense Academy. That's where Watson trained."

"They did a good job."

Krocker smiled. "Not good enough."

5

Golden rays of sunshine filtered through the leaves of the giant, white ash trees, laying a lustrous, filigreed mesh of light across the green lawn.

The gray squirrel sat back on it haunches.

The black-faced, red cardinal whistled *cheer … cheer,* then took to flight.

It was Sunday morning. Marty stood before the picture windows in the livingroom gazing into the Arcadian setting. He didn't know how long he had been standing there when Lisa came up silently from behind and interrupted him.

"Latte?" she said.

He turned. "Thanks."

She handed him the drink. "I'm sorry I talked so harshly last night about Jack's death."

"I'm sorry I dragged you into this. I should have told you to go home. Handled it myself."

"Do you still think they would have killed you?"

"Yes, unless I took the man's gun and fought back."

Her eyes grew serious. "How can you put this away without ending up floating in the river like Jack?"

He studied her momentarily. She was his friend, and he listened to her for advice. But now, he felt a chilly foreboding that nagged at his heart, warning him to get used to the cold silence of tragedy. Yes, the feeling cautioned him that their lives had been permanently changed by the evil which followed Jack to the Riverview. In fact, they would be lucky if they survived the clutch of death that reached out for them even as they stood here and chatted on this lustrous morn. When he finally spoke, he said, "I honestly don't know how to solve this case, or how to move beyond it."

"That worries me," she said. "You can't sit still. You always have to be fiddling, finessing, calculating, doing something. Well, fine, but your usual modus operandi won't work here." When his eyes met hers, she said, "What can you do besides tracking these people yourself? Something at home. Calling somebody. Someone who will take over the investigation into Jack's disappearance."

"Maybe Jason Wells," Marty said. "He works on the Undercover and Sensitive Operations Unit for the FBI."

"Good."

"Well, maybe not. He knows Harrington. If he checked out the story with him, the whole team of jerks would be over here, and we'd have the same situation we had last night."

"Then don't call him, call someone else."

"Hey, Derek Walker. He could run it past the senator." He watched her face brighten.

"Great idea," she said. "It's only 8 o'clock. Why not come for a jog with me? Afterwards you can call Derek. Then we'll go out for breakfast."

He couldn't imagine jogging when a special FBI team was gunning for him. His single motivation, rather, was a yearning to get his gun and stay alive. "I don't want to run."

They studied each other until she said, "I'm going to do the short loop. Then we'll go to the Joint, okay?"

The Joint was their pet name for a coffee shop over in Chevy Chase.

He nodded.

After Lisa left, Marty went upstairs to the study. On the computer, he wrote some notes, outlining what he had seen at the harbor as if it were a case he was investigating. He hoped that by getting the material in a form that was manageable he would see something he had missed.

By nine he had the case outlined and had gone over the notes. He had a fair description of two of the men in the garage. He was impressed by how the group operated as a team. The deft coordination. But what concerned him most was George Harrington. He might be able to identify Marty from the description that Mr. Hawaiian Shirt gave him. But it didn't stop there. If Harrington was leading a team, it was a covert FBI operation. And if the FBI tried to suppress Jack's investigation of a stolen patent, then the operation was authorized by the director. And if the director knew –

No way.

It didn't go all the way up the food chain like Jack had suggested. Not to the president. He was a man who evoked civility and kindness in others, even in his detractors. He would have no part in this travesty. In fact, he was working to bring a new standard to all the federal police forces, especially the FBI. That meant that Harrington had taken the law in his own hands.

Marty picked up his cell and called Derek Walker. He was the young, bulky lawyer who was chief aid to Senator Stanton. The man answered, and Marty said, "I didn't wake you, did I?"

"No, who is this?" said Walker.

"Marty Price."

"What's going on?"

"My partner from the L.A. days … you remember, Jack Watson?"

"I've heard you mention him."

"He was shot at the Riverview Restaurant last night."

"You're kidding."

"No, and it get's worse. I believe the FBI did it, at least I saw an agent I knew, George Harrington." Marty listened to Derek moan, then he added, "They tried to kill me, too. Silencers on their guns."

"Have you been drinking?"

"No, Derek. Not at all. And you know I don't allow drugs in my presence."

"I didn't see anything about the Feebies on the news."

"Derek, think about it. Silencers on their guns. Hiding the body. That's not going to make the news."

"You're talking conspiracy, is that it? Run by Harrington?"

"Yes. Will you discuss it with the senator?"

"Yeah, but why should he believe your story? It's preposterous."

"Because he used my recommendations to put the computer-crime bill together. He knows I'm on the up-and-up. I work for him. For you, remember? I received the most-valued contractor award."

"The senator is out of town. When I talk with him today, I'll let him know what you said."

"Thanks, Derek."

"Not a problem. Are you okay?"

"I have to tell you that after what I saw last night, I'm scared."

"Hang in there, buddy. I'll look into it. It has to be some kind of a mistake."

"They're calling it a swat team practice. That's the spin I got from District dispatch. But they chased me through the parking lot trying to kill me. They want to retrieve the information Jack has on them … a federal agency stealing patents."

"Marty, I have to tell you that I would let it go if I were you."

"No, they fired at us, and Jack has disappeared. He was with me at dinner. You understand? A friend gone. Vanished. I had to fight a man to get his gun away from him in order to save my life. How do you let that go when you had planned a quiet dinner, hoping to ask your girlfriend if she would marry you."

"I'm really sorry. Is Lisa okay?"

"She is quite upset. She even talked like she might end our relationship.

You know, as if I brought this on myself."

"That's really too bad. I'll talk to the Senator, and tell him what you said. We'll get it straightened out."

"Thanks for listening."

When Marty clicked off, he realized that Derek didn't understand the seriousness of the situation, or he was politely disconnecting from him. Then again, if someone called him with this story, he'd run from it too.

At the café, they ordered coffee and croissants, then sat at one of the round, wooden tables. Wary-eyed, Marty watched the slow-moving Sunday-morning crowd. Casually dressed in jogging outfits, or jeans and sandals, they seemed to have been poured like water from a bucket into the sofas and chairs, and were now practicing the art of muttering inanities.

Marty's demeanor was serious. He had already scanned the Metro section of the paper. There was no mention of a disturbance at the waterfront.

He looked across the table. Lisa was reading her favorite column in the Post. She was living on Cancun vacation-time like the rest of these people. How could she really believe Derek Walker and Senator Stanton would fix his problem with the FBI? Hell, Walker was only interested in covering his own butt. He might not even talk to the senator. And that meant that if this situation was going to get fixed, Marty would have to do it himself. Otherwise, no one was going to take the rap for killing Jack. No. Harrington and his buddies had pulled off a near-perfect crime.

"Honey," he said, "I'm going to look into this shooting. At least go to the Riverview and look for clues. I have to do it while the trail is fresh. Maybe fly to L.A. and talk to Jack's client, David Rose. I also want to look in Jack's mail box." He watched her set down the newspaper. "I'm sorry. I can't let it go. If the Senator instigates an investigation, I'll have the information ready to hand over to him."

Doe-eyed, she reached across the table and took his hand.

"Jack would have done it for me," Marty said. "He was like my own damn brother. Oh, yeah. He dragged me into this mess, pulled me back down to hustling in the street, nearly got me killed last night, but I was the only one he trusted."

The corners of her mouth hold a ghost of a smirk. "I'll let you go if you promise me one thing."

He cocked his head to the side. "Yeah?"

"No more shootouts."

It was a little after noon when Lisa dropped him off at his Georgetown home. Located near a park on a tree-lined street north of the business district, it sat in a group of Federal-style row houses. Built of red brick, his home had three floors and an attic. Out front, a paneled, hardwood door dwelt under the arch of a fanlight window. The double-hung windows facing the street were topped with flat brick arches and encased by shutters. Two chimneys and a dormer cut through the gabled roof.

He stopped and stared at the house before entering. What were the chances, he wondered, that Jack's killers had traced Marty to this address and were waiting inside to kill him? That wouldn't be too hard, seeing how Marty and Jack had been partners.

Knowing he couldn't cover all his bases, he shrugged, took a deep breath, and marched up the brick stairs leading to the porch. Opening the heavy wooden door, he stepped into the foyer and entered the code on the security keypad. The green light came on, and it appeared that the safety equipment hadn't been breeched. Still, he wondered if someone had figured out how to bypass the security system.

Stepping into the parlor, he glanced around. White marble surrounded the fireplace. A yellow-pine-and-glass, three-cabinet Chippendale bookcase sat near the opposite wall. A mahogany-and-leather Biedermeier Scandinavian sofa graced the end of the room. A red-and-black Persian rug lay on the polished-hardwood floor. Nothing had changed here. It was antique heaven. Which was what he had planned to own ever since his grandmother showed him the books on American history when he was a kid.

He went to the dining room. His digital camera sat on the maple-wood table where he'd left it. He headed for the hall and went up the carpeted stairs, going past framed pictures of his parents. The photos were cheerful shots, taken when the couple was in their twenties, a year before they died.

At the second-floor landing, he went into his office which was situated between two bedrooms. Part of his house security system was a couple of hidden e-cams. They downloaded their digitalized film onto a dot-com memory-storage server in Maryland. A copy could be kept here in his office on the laptop if it was plugged into the docking port. Sitting down before his desk, he entered some data into the computer, then hit the playback symbol. The computer raced though the digitalized security film, showing in a few minutes what had happened in his house for the last twelve hours. He didn't bother to slow it down and run it at normal speed. There was nothing but an uninterrupted split-screen view of the kitchen backdoor and the front-room foyer.

Now that he was comfortable that no one had made a forced entry into his home, he showered and shaved. In the bedroom, he tossed the towel onto the floor and put on a pair of chinos and a sweater.

He glanced around. The room was painted light-yellow with long white drapes. The palms in the colorful glazed pots caught the daylight coming through the window. A fireplace with an ornamented white mantel faced the bed. A roaring black panther cast in bronze was bent ready to jump across the zig-zag-patterned hardwood floor. He wondered if he would ever be safe here again. Not if he didn't act. Not if he didn't track down the group running wild with Harrington.

Problem was – he wasn't going to get any help on the investigation. No. The Senate was hung up by dowdy procedures, and it spent a quarter of the year taking holidays. It would be arrogant to think that Marty's case would move anyone on the Hill to get in a hurry. No, more than likely, Stanton wouldn't get the message about the shooting until Walker had mulled it over, maybe even researched it. It could be days before Marty heard back from him, if he heard back at all. And who knew? Stanton might be out of the country.

Marty's best option would be to go talk to David Rose. But he really wanted to put that off and solve the case here in the District – where Jack was killed. Where the FBI headquarters was located. Where this crazy mob ran wild.

But wait. If Rose brought the case to Jack, why wasn't he leaking it to the press? Why wasn't he on TV? Maybe the FBI had threatened to kill the rest of his family if he talked? Marty had better go find out.

Back in the study, he logged onto the Internet in order to book a flight to L.A., but he sat there staring at the computer instead. Why hadn't he searched the FBI data banks for leads on Harrington? Discover who he really worked for. Find out what operations he was assigned to. Who was on his team.

He immediately connected with the data storage server he used in Maryland and brought up the program he had employed in the past to hack into government mainframes. Interfacing with District Police, he used their tie-in to enter the FBI main computer banks on the first floor of the Hoover Building downtown. But that's where the connection ended. Someone had build another layer of firewalls between the two systems, and he couldn't figure out how to get through them. He backed up, tried to access the FBI mainframe through the Maryland State Police. Same thing – a new firewall, another layer of codes. Fortunately, there was another way, a backdoor to the FBI high security files. He had established that surreptitious portal when he was left alone with the Senate Intelligence Committee's computers. He hesitated to use it because it put his job at risk. But he accessed it, anyway. His screen flashed the word *GOTCHA!* spelled out in big white letters on a green page. He blinked, stared at it momentarily, then looked down in the corner. It was signed by *The Phantom*.

He got the joke, but he didn't know whether to laugh or to cry. The Phantom was Monty Bradshaw's hacker name. He was one of the other geeks who testified at data-fraud hearings. Marty didn't know how Monty had discovered Marty's backdoor to the FBI system, nor did he understand why Monty would be monitoring those computers. Whatever had happened, the backdoor was closed, and Marty couldn't get into the FBI security files.

He picked up his cell and dialed Monty's number. When the man answered, Marty said, "Is this the Phantom, or just another lookalike?"

"This is the man," Monty joked. "Is this Marty?"

"Yeah, I was talking to a friend … well, an acquaintance. And he said he was hacking around a bit downtown, and ran into a page signed by the Phantom. I was wondering what was going on."

"Wondering, huh?"

"Yeah."

"I won the contract to plug up the holes in the FBI system. You know, after Albert Spear was caught trading in secrets."

"Congratulations."

"Thanks. Listen. There's another contract begging for someone to set up an auditing system to track who's accessing what material. You could get it if you wanted it. Twenty-million bucks begging for a taker."

"Whoa."

"You can tell your friend that my warning signs are coming down tomorrow. After that, my assistant will be coming at him with the Carnivore Program, followed by an arrest warrant. And I have to tell you, Marty, I'm glad you called. I'm sworn to uphold the law. If I catch you on my system, I'm going to bust you."

"That's a friendly thing."

"No more kid stuff. I've got to bottoms-up and go with this one. It's too much money to play games with old-time hacker buddies."

"I understand."

"What's with you? You still working for the Senate?"

"Got my contract renewed, but I'll consider your offer. I'd better let you get back to work."

"Spread the warning."

"Will do."

"Come by and talk when you're downtown."

"Okay. See you in a bit."

Marty clicked off.

Great, just great. If he went after data on the FBI system, he had the best hacker on the Atlantic Coast coming after him with the Carnivore Program and a warrant. He'd better think about going and talking to Rose instead. See where that led.

Back on the computer, he connected to the Internet and found a first-class seat available on an afternoon flight to LAX. He bought the ticket. Then he packed his bag, called a taxi, and stepped outside and waited. When the cab came around the corner, he moved off the curb and hailed it. He had a few hours to kill before the flight, which was plenty of time to do what he least wanted to do – search the harbor and the parking lot where Jack had been killed.

Marty stood on the dock above the pale, green waters of the Potomac River and looked back at the balustrade on the edge of the upper plaza. The gunman had waited up there, watched him and Jack while they stood here on the boardwalk. The shooter probably called his buddies from there, maybe as he stood behind one of the tall, white columns. When the gunman thought that Jack and Marty were leaving, he got rushed, knowing they would get away. That was when he took advantage of his ideal location and shot at them as they came forward to the fountain and stood below him.

Marty stepped down from the boardwalk and crossed the lower plaza. He stood where he and Jack had been when the shooting started. Hand to his chin, he wandered about looking at the ground. There were fresh chips hacked out of the brick plaza. Bullet impressions. He found a twisted hollow point slug and quickly pocketed it. Over by the wall, he found another.

After going up the stairs, he stood where the shooter had stood. It was a good location to watch the boardwalk and lower plaza, even the restaurant. He turned. You could also see across the upper plaza from there and watch the door to the Harbor View Hotel. It was even possible to see the archway where the sidewalk passed between the office building and the hotel, going westward to the park. What an ideal place to wait for the backup team to arrive.

Marty turned slowly about and noticed that the upstairs entrance to the underground parking lot was only a few feet away. Was this the direction that the gunman traveled when Jack pulled his gun and charged?

He went over to the glass door and entered. No, he realized, that didn't work. There weren't any stairs. Only an elevator. Jack would have shot the gunman as he waited.

Marty would have gone from there straight to where he saw the van on the lower level of the garage, but he knew from experience that if you started at the logical hotspot, you would miss something important about the crime scene. He decided to walk around the building.

The designer had used post-modern spaces, domes, tubular facades, art deco curves, and contemporary arches to create a colorful and boisterous structure. In that atmosphere, Marty expected to find redundant stairwells leading to the underground garage. But no, there were only two staircases going down from the upper level. One was near the hotel. Another was around the west side of the building, letting out into the park. He didn't think someone trying to be inconspicuous would have run past the glass lobby of the hotel to get to the stairs. No, the gunman had to have turned down the passageway leading to the park. And if the intruder had made it that far, why would he have gone downstairs into the garage? Why not run?

Marty took the passageway and stood before the park. He glanced around and saw that there wasn't any place to hide. No significant tree, no concrete block, only a dumpster. Any large-caliber pistol could penetrate that. If the gunman had gotten this far, and then decided to keep running, he would have had to make it all the way to K Street and hide behind a car. Otherwise Jack would have killed him. Surely he knew that Jack was an excellent marksman. That was why he ran when Jack pulled his gun. And that was why he took the stairs and went down into the concrete maze.

But Jack also knew something about the gunman. He knew the shooter was coming. That's why he pulled his weapon when he and Marty reached the dock. That was also why he kept it tucked in his belt, ready to draw.

Why didn't Marty listen when Jack waved the gun?

The same reason Derek wasn't going to listen: These rouge agents were utterly galling.

He opened the door to the stairwell and went down the steps. These were the same ones Marty had been on last night, first racing down to second basement floor to hide from Mr. Hawaiian Shirt. Taking the stairs to the lower landing, now, he searched about, looking for bullet casings, but didn't find any. That meant that no shots were fired on the stairs. At least not from semi-automatic pistols which discharged their bullet casings after every shot.

But he had been to a dozen murder scenes. They were never clean. People forgot about footprint impressions, carpet damage, stuff on the ceiling. There had to be something here the feds overlooked when they cleaned up the mess.

Wait a second.

After the initial shooting, Marty had burst through the door on the lower plaza and took refuge on the first basement floor. That was one flight up from where he was now. While he had been up there last night, hiding behind the SUV, the herd of men had come from the direction of the elevator. That meant they had parked on the lower basement floor, then rode up one flight, got out, and rushed past him and onto the lower plaza. That's how it had to have happened. They could not have gotten in the elevator on the upper plaza level and come down a flight, or Jack would have seen them there and fired.

Marty went to the elevator and walked completely around its bulky housing. On the backside wall – facing away from where the van had been parked a hundred feet or so in the distance – he spotted a shiny area about six feet in diameter on the floor. He got on his knees and examined it. The area had recently been mopped up with chemicals. He could smell them. He wondered if this was where Jack went down. Otherwise, it was the spot where Jack had killed the shooter. No way to tell which one of them died here, not yet.

He made a sweep of the area, looking under cars and in corners for another cleaned-up space. There simply had to be another one. Jack had been killed, but he also shot the gunman.

Marty was coming around a corner when he saw the letter *M.* It was at eye-level, on the wall, barely visible, scribbled with a finger into the dust.

His heart sunk and a tear welled in his eye. The *M* represented the first letter in Marty's name. This had to be Jack's last message to him.

He glanced around making sure no one was watching, then he reached up and ran his hand along the concrete ledge above the wall where the letter had been written. He felt something smooth and latched on to it. He nearly choked when he saw that it was a leather wallet.

He stuck the wallet in his pocket, then knelt, looking at the concrete. There wasn't anything noticeable on the floor. That meant that Jack hadn't been shot here, but had shot the perpetrator back at the cleaned-up spot, then grabbed the man's wallet, and put it on the ledge. Then –

Marty could see the other set of stairs. If he went directly to them, he would have crossed the spot where the van had been sitting last night. That meant that Jack had run that way as he tried to escape from the garage, but before he made it to the stairs, he had been shot. Then the van pulled up and snatched his body.

Marty went towards the stairwell and found a clean spot on the floor with the same chemical smell. He thought about Jack and all the good times and all the crimes they had solved. This was the spot where it came to an end. Jack died here. If not that, this was where the van stopped and picked up his bleeding body.

Marty took the elevator upstairs and walked down to the river. He gazed at the Memorial Bridge, gracefully arching over the Potomac a mile downstream. On the Virginia side of the waterway, trees lined the river. On the District side, the river wound around the Lincoln Memorial and its backwater entered the West Tidal Basin.

Why couldn't he be a tourist, here to enjoy the view?

No. He was a P.I., and Jack had come to him because there was nowhere else to turn.

Marty pulled the wallet from his pocket. Inside was a plastic identification badge. The shooter's name was Tucker Johnston. The deep-blue background indicated that he had high-security clearance with the FBI.

Geez!

They were feds. Maybe the conspiracy did go to the top of the Bureau.

Under normal circumstances, Marty would have been on the phone to the U.S. Attorney's Office. They were the ones who were supposed to keep the FBI in line. But this wasn't normal. No. Johnston had killed Jack to stop him from exposing a federal crime.

He instinctively felt for his gun, under his coat, where it would have been if he were still tracking down thugs in L.A. Feeling the empty spot where the weapon should have been, he was stung with ambivalence. He longed for the gun. Even right now a fed could pop around a corner and start firing. But he was going to be on an airplane momentarily. He knew he didn't want to go through the hassle of declaring the gun at the airline counter and letting them handle it until he got to Los Angeles. It might not even arrive on the same flight. He decided to leave the gun in his office for now. If things hadn't settled down by the time he got back, he would start carrying it again.

The cab crossed the Memorial Bridge into Arlington, Virginia, and headed downstream towards Ronald Reagan National Airport. Inside the terminal, Marty killed a few minutes walking about under the arched, multi-domed structure. He knew he didn't want to leave town, not now, not when he had the name of the gunman. But what could he do? Go to the FBI headquarters and show them the wallet? No. He needed more evidence. He needed David Rose to give him a signed statement.

Four hours later he walked inside the terminal at Denver Airport, making his way up the glass-and-steel covered isle towards the McDonald's. He carried his laptop over one shoulder and his sports bag on the other. He clutched a paperback in his hand, a detective story he was determined to finish before he got to L.A.

He stood in the fast-food line behind a couple with kids. A toddler in a fuzzy, pink outfit was pointing a finger at the glass near the ceiling, saying, "Sky." The older kid wanted daddy to help him with an electronic game.

When he got his order, Marty put the tray with the burger and coffee on the plastic table and looked at his paperback. *P.I. in Paradise*, the book jacket exclaimed over a backdrop of green island foliage and white sandy shoreline. That's where he'd like to be. In paradise. But no. He felt like he was in-hiding, which was the usual prelude to feeling all alone. Cold, tired, alone. It was as if this damned mess Jack had dragged him into triggered the orphan thing again, the lonely-needing-someone-anyone feeling.

Every time he thought he was over losing his parents, something like this happened. Sure, he had tried turning a cold shoulder to the ugly feeling. When that didn't work, he tried to assimilate it into his character. To grow. But hell. How much harder could you try? He'd given it his all to move on. Yes. He had established a profitable career; learned etiquette, such that Senators were comfortable with him; practiced martial arts until he knew no fear. Aside from that, he faced his problems as if they were challenges and learned to focus steady on the task before him. Like being a pro golfer, he would concentrate so hard and so clear that no thought would come between the club and the perfect swing. In fact, he had found that any problem could be put in those terms – getting a good shot down the greenway. That's all it took to make life work. But that wasn't enough, apparently, to numb the pain of losing his family. In a crowded airport, he could still have a moment where he felt sorry for himself, a few minutes where life had no purpose.

His ruminations turned to Lisa. She was all he had except for his grandmother. And, well, you never had anyone for real, not nowadays, not the way the old folks did. He suddenly wished he had done what Lisa had said. Simply forgotten what had happened at the Riverview, not taken off post haste to L.A. in order to talk to David Rose. If he had stayed in bed, it would have been so simple. No feeling of being nobody lost among strangers at airports. No fear of retribution from the FBI. Maybe hang around her home. Chit chat. Play with Nikki the cat. Go out to dinner. Hold Lisa's hand. Talk about living together and getting married. Hey, maybe she wanted to have children. Did he ever ask? Somehow he knew he would never get the chance.

6

Six-six, broad-shouldered, with greying hair, Dr. Rolland Archer flopped onto the broad-armed, stuffed chair. Wearing a white lab coat over a pin-stripped, button-down shirt, he glanced at Tanya Burns sitting in the chair across from him. They were in Dr. Archer's office in the basement of the Behavioral Sciences Building at the Quantico Training Station. Burns, a neuropsychologist, had her angry eyes glued on FBI Commander John Krocker.

"Doctor Burns," Krocker said in a grandiose formal tone as he paced the floor before his captive audience, "if you're thinking about taking over the Behavioral Health Clinic when Rolland retires, you will have to learn to go by the book."

With Roman nose and silky skin, Tanya puffed her pretty face into a blowfish frown. She glanced from Krocker to Archer, then back. Her head moved quick enough to make her thick, brown, braided ponytail lash across her back.

The reddish-blond-haired, grey-eyed commander continued. "And that means doing what your commanding officer tells you. You know, as if we were situated on a Marine Base." Krocker pretended to chuckle. They really were on one. "As if everyone here at Quantico answered to a higher power, to the Commander in Chief." He made a quirky, thin-lined smile. "Surely Rolland has discussed this with you during your tenure here."

Tanya stared blank-eyed at Krocker. "Yes. But aren't you misconstruing what I said? The patient's medical condition is unstable. That means we could harm him, maybe kill him if he is moved from the clinic. Can't the country wait twenty-four hours?"

Krocker averted his eyes when his wrist phone vibrated his arm. He pulled back his sleeve and pressed the button on the phone. "Krocker here," he said into the tiny cell that looked similar to a watch.

A voice as smooth as Kentucky whiskey came over the line. "John, I'm not interrupting anything, am I?"

It was the Director of the FBI, James Franklin. Krocker's bully-face melted into a sugar-coated smile. "No. What is it, sir?"

"They're saying some of our men left a very bad impression at the Riverview Restaurant last night. Tell me that didn't happen."

"Who said that?"

"Senator Stanton from the Oversight Committee. We weren't over there, were we, John?"

"Yes. We had some people testing an emergency procedure."

"With live ammo?"

"No, way."

"Did you have permission to be on the property?"

Krocker had gotten it after the fact. "Yes, sir."

"What is it going to say in the media when this breaks?"

"This isn't going to break. I talked to our friend at the Post. He took it to the editor. No one really cares that an FBI agent fell off a dock and nearly broke his neck. If the exercise had Secret Service or President written on it, it might be a different matter. What's the deal with Stanton? Is he after our budget?"

"There's always a catch with him. But tell me. Off the record. What were you really doing, John?"

Krocker puffed up straight. "The special operations team was demonstrating an active-response strategy to a hostage situation. You know, a Congressman is abducted in the District, at dinner, say, and we decide that negotiations with the perpetrator won't work. What is the FBI's response? Well, we're formalizing it, making it snappy, no rough edges, no room to fall apart when the real thing happens."

"That's important."

"I know, and I'm sorry I didn't call you beforehand."

"No, I've told you, I only want to know about a government operation when it looks like we're going to take a hit from the media. If this isn't going to the press, forget it, unless of course you can put a good spin to it. Something to please Stanton."

Krocker thought about it a moment. He had people he paid in every media organization in DC to spin the news before it broke. "Give him the truth. And why not go public with it? Have someone talk to a columnist ... the FBI testing emergency procedures that we would use against rogue nations. Korea, Sudan, Libya. Any one of them could have a team in the Capitol and grab one of our people, which is why we were out there, Jim. It's a crazy, mixed-up world."

"No kidding. I'll mention the active-response idea to Senator Blabber Mouth, and the whole Hill will know by tonight."

Krocker chuckled. These fools fell for everything he spun to them. "Will

I see you at the conference in Vegas?"

"Last I heard I was the keynote speaker. Preparedness is the topic. Sounds like what you were doing yesterday fits right in. Can someone get over here and brief Pete on it, so he can get it into the speech?"

"Sure, I'll send Harrington."

"Anything else we need to talk about?"

Krocker glanced at Tanya, and an obscene word ghosted across his lips. He wanted to say he didn't like the idea of shattering the glass ceiling and allowing women to replace the retiring instructors. In fact, women shouldn't be in the FBI at all. They were like his ex-wife. She wouldn't obey him. Krocker kept his misogynous complaint to himself, saying, "Not that I can discuss right now. See you in Vegas."

"God willing." Franklin clicked off.

Krocker turned to glare at Tanya. He believed that her emotionalized flak flew in the face of his penchant for swift, high-tech solutions. He held out his finger, pointing, but before he could issue a reprimand, someone pounded on the metal door. That was followed by deep-throated laughter.

Krocker marched to the door and jerked it open. "What the –" he bellowed, catching himself mid-sentence.

In the hall were two well-muscled, crew-cut brutes who looked to be in their early thirties. The short, husky one wore a Hawaiian shirt and a Panama hat; the tall, handsome one was dressed in a skin-tight pollo shirt. A thick gold chain hung around his neck.

"Buddy … Mack," Krocker exclaimed. "You're here."

Buddy, the one who wore the gold chain, massaged the palm of his hand like he was itching for a fight. "What the – what?" he said, mimicking Krocker in an exaggerated, scruffy, nasal tone. "You don't like my date?"

Plain-faced, with a weight-lifter body, Mack laughed.

Krocker stared at Mack, saying, "What? Can't you speak for yourself?"

Mack grinned as big as a wolf. "Hey, old man –"

Krocker's swift kick hit Mack's knee, knocking his leg out from underneath him. He was catching his fall when Krocker issued a stern reprimand. "Don't call me old man … Ever."

Buddy had stepped back from the horseplay. "Damn, you're touchy about your age."

"With jerks like you for friends…"

"Jerks?" said Buddy. "Who does your cyberspace tracking?"

Krocker knew the men had a point, that he was temperamental about his age, and that someone like Buddy, who was younger, who had quick muscle *and* wide-ranging computer literacy, left him feeling jealous.

"Yeah, yeah ... hang on," Krocker said. He stepped back inside the office and shut the door behind himself. Once he was alone again with Tanya and Rolland, he brayed, "The tests are going to be completed within the next two hours."

"Not a problem," Rolland said, watching his angry-eyed commander watch him.

Krocker studied the older man. If Rolland ever got into the top-secret intelligence files and learned that Krocker had lost his authority to do most of what they were doing, the doctor would be the one to come after him. Why couldn't he hurry up and retire? "The report is going to be on my desk tonight," Krocker finally said, not deigning to look at Tanya as he opened the door, stepped though, and shut it behind himself.

After a moment, Tanya's eyes settled on Rolland. "He's such a --"

Rolland smiled sympathetically. "Go ahead, say it. John's a prick. He also doesn't remember this isn't the Army, and that it's our day off."

"Is he personally involved in this case? That's the way he's acting."

"It's my fault for not explaining a little more about how this works. When you do an interrogation, or anything else for Krocker, you do what he says even if it can't work. And when the operation falls apart, you send him a memo. Then you do it your way."

"Fine. But it seems like he is taking revenge against Jack Watson. Is he trying to kill him?"

"Don't know."

"How do you get away with having criminals on a training base?"

"After the big hijacking, the attorney general issued a special order which allows us to teach interrogation techniques using live subjects."

"That's a good one. Who were those men?"

"Operatives. I don't know what they do."

"They act like a wolf pack, with Krocker as the leader."

"Forget Krocker for a moment, all right?" Rolland watched as a frown twisted across Tanya's lips. When she finally nodded, he continued. "This isn't quite what it seems down here." He spread out his arms and looked around the room, his eyes passing the framed diplomas on the wall and stopping on the water fountain. It was making soothing gurgles from over in the corner where it sat among the tangle of green, indoor plants. "I picked you to be my successor because I knew from your profile that you would bring a new level of integrity to the Behavioral Sciences Program. We're begging for it down here. That said, I also knew you wouldn't like it here when you found out what we really do. But I knew that over the years –" Rolland knuckled his fists in an expression of intense emotion. "How do I say this?"

He had recruited Tanya Burns from one of the nation's top medical schools where she was ranked first in her physiological-psychology doctoral program. Her testing showed she wanted to make a difference in the world; she also liked power.

Finally, he got the words. "You're only thirty. You'll be here after Krocker and I are dead."

Tanya's big round eyes flashed hot like molten lava. "For God's sake. I've been here a year, and you're telling me I don't know what we do."

The fifty-five year old doctor rubbed a hand though his long, salt-and-pepper hair. "We are working under the presidential finding on terrorism ... reviewed by the Chairmen of the Joint Congressional Intelligence Committee. And in that capacity ... well, aside from training forensic specialists, we force confessions from criminals when the nation's security is at grave risk."

"Just wonderful," Tanya said.

"There's more. We're doing cutting-edge research, stuff that others have only proposed is possible." He squinted as his forehead wrinkled. "Your doctorate is on positron emission tomography, right?" She raised a brow, and Rolland continued. "I picked you because you're thinking about what the laboratory is actually doing." He grinned modestly. "It's live, it's real ... the stuff in your dissertation that you hypothesized would be possible at the other end of the twenty-first century."

Her angry eyes grew hollow, and the corners of her mouth turned up into a bewildered smile. "Not the PET-scan, free-radical auto-tracing? You don't have that? No way?"

Rolland nodded.

"C'mon, you can't trace a free radical."

"We can trace brain activity without injecting radioactive dyes. Now we're looking at making a portable brain scanner."

Tanya's face flushed white. She had proposed that the breakdown process of glucose being metabolized in the active parts of the brain gave off its own characteristic negative charge, and that in thirty or forty years the scientific community would have instruments sensitive enough to detect it. But that was the future, and Dr. Archer was asking her to believe it was here, now. "Where did you get the equipment?" she responded.

"That's the ethical problem we need to talk about."

"Huh?"

Rolland leaned forward on the sofa. "I want you to be my successor. I believe in you, okay?" She bit her lip, and he said, "I have to tell you a few things that you cannot repeat to anyone."

Tanya flopped back in the chair and stared at the ceiling. "Now what?"

"This is high intelligence, high science. And you heard the man, you're going to have to do what Krocker says, when he orders it done, or you're not going to head this department when I retire. That's the Faustian bargain you will have to make with the devil in order to be here working on the cutting edge of science."

Her laughter cut through the room like a coyote baying at the moon.

"Ah-ha, I think you're getting the picture. This is a tragicomedy. Do you want to hear more, or do you want to call it quits, resign your position?"

Tanya sat up and leaned towards Rolland and whispered. "Where did you get the equipment?"

"I take it you're buying into what I said."

"Maybe."

"Krocker is the boss. If we slide down the slippery gray slope of questionable ethics, the FBI covers for us. It's all done in the name of national security."

"With extremely lax Congressional oversight," Tanya interrupted, "so lax that only you and Krocker know what's going on, right?"

"Harrington and Krocker."

Hand to her chin, Tanya looked to be stuck in the middle of a thought. Finally, she said, "Was it the ATP? That's it, right? Your machine detects a charged particle when the brain cell activates."

"That's right," Rolland said, knowing that the machine detected the activity at the center of the cell when the enzyme ATP converted glucose into energy.

"I knew it, I knew it!" Tanya exclaimed, hitting a fist to a flattened palm. "How do you measure it?"

Rolland got up and went to the workstation and punched a few keys. "You didn't see this, okay?" When she nodded, he said, "Chris Walters brought me a copy of the blueprints for the Eraser Project. Krocker and Harrington are guarding the data with their lives. Actually, the potential is so great that they're vying for control over it. Chris felt there had to be some accountability. With the pilfered copy of the data, I can always take it to the director if their fight gets out of hand, or if they use the Eraser for their own ends ... It'll take a second, here; I keep the data at another location. Krocker doesn't know that I am aware of the project. So keep a lid on this, will ya?"

Squint-eyed with perplexity, she gripped her hips and said, "You withhold information from him?"

"If I have to."

"You called it the Eraser? What did you mean?"

"You tell me. Look at the diagrams." An engineer's blueprint came up on the screen showing the parts of a machine shaped like a football helmet. A flexible conduit connected wiring to a metal case which accompanied it. Rolland pointed. "That's the advanced model the lab will start working on if the prototype functions properly."

"Where are they building it? They can't be doing this on the base. Not under my nose."

"The Annex. It's a secret facility."

"Where?" Tanya said.

"Widewater."

Studying the computer screen, Tanya gasped. "This technology is impossible ... utterly impossible. Where'd it come from?"

Rolland frowned. "Chris thinks we might have a lab in Russia."

"Oh, please..."

"Well, somewhere in the territories of the old U.S.S.R."

Tanya sat down and took the mouse and scrolled down the page. After a bit, she said, "It does a functional M.R.I.; it monitors metabolism; it pinpoints brain activity; it ... Wait a minute." She glanced up at Rolland who was sitting on the edge of the desk. "I've studied a lot of machines –"

"Yes, you have."

Clicking to the next page of blueprints, she said, "This is set up to stimulate the site in the brain where the highest ATP activity is taking place." She pushed the chair back from the workstation. "What are they doing? Preparing to cut people's brains apart?"

He smiled politely. "It won't hurt the cells. Chris says that it will only wiggle them. Shake them on a molecular level, like a microwave oven shakes the water molecules and warms things up. But with this, there is no heat. No cell damage. Try to imagine what happens. Let's say the patient is concentrating on seeing someone getting killed. What happens when the positive charge from the machine meets the negative charge at the brain site where the painful memory is stored?"

Dr. Tanya Burns let out the biggest cackle her130-pound frame could muster. Rolland laughed with her. Catching herself, she said, "They cancel each other out, and you erase the memory."

"That's why it's called the Eraser Project."

She looked deep into his watery amber eyes and shook her head. "Rolland ... Rolland ... Rolland..."

"Tanya, Tanya, Tanya," Rolland replied.

"Does the guy forget about the crime, and then go about his merry way?"

"You are quite intuitive for a science person." She faked an acknowledging smile, and he said, "Walters says the psychological potential is staggering." He pointed at the monitor. "Krocker should have this machine for us next year. Want to be in on it?"

Tanya bent the black computer chair back on its hinges and stared at the ceiling. "No damage to the cells?"

"No damage. Which means what?"

"There is a high potential for abuse."

"Right. And this is James Franklin's FBI."

Tanya knew that the president had appointed a good-old-boy to the director's post to appease the conservatives who backed him in the election. She shook off her grimace and grinned mischievously. "What if I put this on Krocker and had him think about his anal-retentive parents who twisted his mind so he thinks he is perfect?"

Rolland chuckled. "If you were to ask someone like John questions about the problems of his childhood, and then hit the erase button when the screen showed that his brain metabolism was at its highest rate – that he was concentrating fully on the abuses rendered by his parents – within the week, he'd come in and sit down with us and chew the fat."

She spoke like they were collage chums. "Get out!"

"That's the potential of this thing. Which is why I wanted someone with integrity to take over when I retire."

"Are you saying I'd use the Eraser for interrogations?"

"Yes, provided we actually pry it loose from Krocker and Harrington. They may want it for their own projects."

Watching him rub the back of his neck, she said, "As in – illegal, personal projects?"

He nodded. "Yeah, I think they've crossed the line, but I can't prove it."

"And if you could prove it?"

"I'd have to take it to the director, or to Congress."

She watched him stare at her until she said, "You're telling me about the Eraser in case Krocker and Harrington silence you, is that it?"

Rolland huffed out his frustrations, paced in a tight circle, then said, "You've got the politics figured out. Now you've got to figure out if you want to risk the danger of getting involved in this with me. It's not what I would want for you on a personal level, but for the good of the country, I need you here to keep an eye on things."

She smiled with fake enthusiasm. "Great, just great."

"That's a worst case scenario ... silencing me. I can't imagine it happening."

"The whole lab must know about the Eraser, right?"

"No, it was being built in pieces with Walters doing the final construction. Then Krocker hired another engineer to manage the project. The rest of the people are mercenaries who don't give a crap."

"Mercenaries?"

"The scientists from Russia. You know, the kind who believe that good science is whatever begets money and privilege. Krocker brought some over here and gave them jobs."

"Not send them to my grad school?"

"They are pretty mercenary, aren't they?"

She looked at him askance. "But if Walters suddenly disappears, he's stolen it, or he's been silenced. Right?"

"It won't come to that. Walters is as tight-lipped as Krocker is retentive."

"But Walters spoke to you."

"He was feeling uneasy about being replaced on the project by the new hire. It made him think he needed a back door in case something went wrong. Like being fired."

She plopped into the sofa and glared into space.

He watched her a moment. "You would have learned this sooner or later."

"What do you want to do if he lets us use the Eraser?"

"If I had it my way, after an interrogation, I would erase the data, so to speak. That means they would bring us one of the top-ten, most-wanted offenders for a truth serum interview. Let's say he knows something we've got to have to stop a terrorist attack. He tells us, then we erase the crap from his mind. Now, he is no danger to the public. He doesn't even remember his life of crime. We can send him on his way." He stood over her. "The Eraser could create a whole new human. A beautiful one. That is, if it's used right."

Tanya got up and paced the room. "Is there anything you do down here that's legal?"

Rolland chuckled. "Ethical or unethical, that's the question. I still come down on the ethical side each night when I go to bed. That's why I'm still here and why I hired you. This is going to be your baby." He flopped onto the sofa, slouching down with his lanky legs up on the coffee table. He watched her staring at the water fountain until he said, "What are you thinking?"

"This is the most vile government operation I've ever heard of."

Rolland held his breath momentarily, then said, "What's that mean down here at ground zero in Behavioral Sciences?"

She looked deep into his eyes without flinching. "I'll take the job."

7

It was Monday morning.

While half the people in Los Angeles jumped into their cars and raced to work, Marty ventured out onto the old pier at Santa Monica Beach. Watching the waves roll gently along the white, sandy shore, and the seagulls buffet on the salt-air breeze, he felt at peace with himself. He hoped he could hold on to that equanimity, that fullness, and not let his outrage throw him off kilter as he delved into the case against the government.

Looking across the endless stretch of beach, his thoughts bounced through the memories. This was where he jogged the loop, starting from the golf course along San Vincente Boulevard and going to Ocean Avenue. Then he would venture up or down the coast, plodding along in the wet sand. Maybe come back and do the stairs up the cliff. This was also where he and Jack had come for dinner and a drink three years ago when Marty told him he was moving to DC. Now, he would have liked to stay and spend the day, shoes off, feet in the cool water, strolling through the memories, but it was time for him to go to Jack's post office box and root out the next clue.

An hour later, he was across town, where Beverly Boulevard met Fairfax Avenue. He parked the rental car in a lot and entered the post office. Opening Jack's business-sized box, he found a thick stack of mail. He took it to one of the waist-high tables and sorted through it. When he found a large white envelope, his heart sunk with breathless trepidation. Jack had sent a letter to himself just as Marty had predicted.

He tore it open and pulled out a standard fill-in-the-blanks contract. Where the client's name had been written, it said: *David Rose*.

Pay dirt.

He had his hands on the key piece of evidence which proved Jack had not flipped out, but really did have a client named Rose.

Marty grabbed the stack of mail and headed towards the car. Instantly, he had it reeved up, and almost as if the vehicle had an autopilot system, he found himself heading towards the nearby Jewish deli. He knew that the procedure of driving there and going inside and ordering a toasted bagel with cream cheese would create a sense of normalization. That's what he needed now more than anything. Yes. To stop, to pull it together, to reconnoiter, then nail down the case. With his hands on the first piece of real evidence, he knew exactly what he should *not* do – go ballistic. That's where Jack got hung up, he suspected. Making a fuss. Waving the Rose contract in people's faces and shouting: *feds! feds! feds!*

Keller's Hollywood Deli was a brash convergence of tempest and taste, where howling Jewish food met the tongue of wannabe stars, movie moguls, tramps, has-beens, intellectuals, and trendsetters on a steady stream going all the way back to the nineteen-twenties. And in its capacity as the after-hours breeder of new ideas, Keller's had become a cultural entity in itself. That meant that even if you were country before it was cool, you borrowed a chopper, spun down off of Laurel Canyon, and headed for the Deli.

The physical establishment did not, of itself, anoint the trendies with a sense of desire or ostentation. The place was, rather, no more than an oversized storefront café sitting on the spot where the grunge of Los Angeles swept up against the painted fantasy of Hollywood. But if looks didn't matter for the wannabes and the trendsetters, they surely didn't matter for Marty. He wasn't into trends, and Keller's, oddly enough, spun his mind in a different direction. It was a place that gave him that old-fashioned, mom's-cooking kind of a feeling. His mother, of course, didn't cook. She was dead. But his grandmother brought him here. They ate cinnamon-raisin babbka, chocolate rugeluch, strawberry cheesecake, sabra salad, and perfectly-assembled four-inch-thick pastrami sandwiches. He also had his first cup of coffee here. And Maxine. He'd bumped into her at the deli, and had kept right on bumping.

Maxine's mother didn't cook. In fact, Maxine was ten the first time Ruth handed her a twenty and sent her to the deli on her own. She was nineteen when Marty met her. Going to UCLA, she was intent on getting a Ph.D. Marty didn't consider college that serious of a project. His only interest was in the night classes he took to learn new computer systems and languages. Maxine didn't seemed concerned. She liked his inventiveness and said it reminded her of her father, a man who prospered designing animation programs for Hollywood. She and Marty were talking marriage at one time, but they slipped apart when Maxine entered a doctoral program at UC Berkeley.

Parking the car across the street from the deli, he thought of her and wondered for the umpteenth time why he hadn't moved to San Francisco, so he and Maxine could have stayed together. He supposed it was the causal nature of their relationship. Pledging that there was no room in his life for another throwaway affair, he crossed the street and headed into the deli.

Sitting down in a large, over-stuffed booth, he ordered, then pulled out the Rose contract. He found that it said exactly what Jack had told him. David Rose complained that his father's invention had been stolen, and he wanted it back. He also wanted his father's murderers found out, tried, and sent to jail. There was no mention of the FBI. Marty reasoned that Jack had discovered the federal connection after a tireless investigation. That took him back to where he started. No one was going to respond to this piece of evidence, not unless Rose was willing to stand behind his accusations and support Jack's contentions that a racketeering-orientated, criminal conspiracy worked out of the offices of the FBI.

"More coffee?" said a young woman with a rounded metal pot in her hand.

He glanced at the young, dark-rooted redhead with the sparkling green stud in her nose. "I'm having a latte –"

"You're out," she said, going ahead and filling the white porcelain cup.

"Well, yes, I guess I was."

"How's business?"

"Huh?"

"Don't you remember me? You and Jack used to sit here until three in the morning talking cop talk. I could have written a book."

"Shanna?" Marty's mind flashed back, recalling the wisp of a girl who used to question them about P.I. stuff.

She put a hand behind her head, slunked her body, and stuck out her chest. "I grew up," she said.

"I'll say."

"It's been a couple years."

"Yeah."

"You back working with Jack?"

"No, actually –" Marty fought off telling the truth. "Jack's sick and I flew out to help him. Did he look ill last time you saw him?"

"He was torqued to the max."

"You mean, worried?"

"Well, yeah, paranoid, like a tweaker. He isn't drying out at rehab, is he?"

"No, it's overwork. Exhaustion. Dehydration. He'll be okay."

"Can I ask you something?"

"Shoot."

"I always wondered why you guys would talk half the night about busting some fool when the place was full of cute bitches." When Marty batted his eyes, she asked, "Is it better doing them in, rather than doing them? You know, getting off on the power trip?"

Marty's head flew back and he cackled.

"I mean, even if you guys were fags, all you wanna do is put people away."

"There's fun in it, sure, but it's tough, challenging work. Nothing sexual, I guarantee it."

Shanna glanced at the front counter. The take-out customers were backing up. "You'll have to tell me about it," she said, walking away.

"Deal."

He drank the coffee and thought about Jack appearing haggard. He glanced at the contract, wondering if Shanna had seen Jack after he'd been shot. He was thumbing through the stack of mail when his cell rang.

"Hi, this is Marty," he said, answering the phone.

"It's Derek," said the voice on the line.

Hearing Senator Stanton's chief aid, Marty sat up straight in the booth. "Did you find anything on Jack?"

"The FBI said they were testing emergency procedures at the Riverview. Imitating a hostage situation. You walked through the middle of it."

"But Jack..."

"Marty, get a grip. I spent all day on this. There is no body. Jack could have walked away for all you know. Right?"

"No, he was shot. I found the place on the ground where they cleaned up his blood. Professional job. They're covering it up."

"Fine. The Senator loves a conspiracy story. But until you have a body, leave us out of it. Okay?"

"I found a slug from the gun."

"Get the body, or get over it."

Marty grew hot. "I found the shooter's I.D. He dropped it, okay. Top security FBI. His name was Tucker Johnston. Jack shot him. They're covering that up too."

"Great. That adds a helluva twist to the story, but like I said, they had a drill imitating a hostage situation. The man moved some muscle, and the wallet fell out of his pocket. That's how the case notes are going to read. Okay?"

"Yeah, sure."

"We're not going to lose our job over this, are we?"

Marty wondered if he hadn't already lost it. "No," he mumbled.

"Call me when you've got the bodies."

"Great."

Walker clicked off.

Marty flipped the cell onto the table and slouched into the booth. All he wanted was his life back. To turn the clock to the night before last when he was holding Lisa's hand and talking about living together. Not this kind of crap where someone was threatening to fire him.

He looked at the jokers backed up behind a clutch of Jewish grandmothers at the cash register. Purple dreadlocks. Panties on the outside of the jeans. Metal studs in the tongue. Men in women's high heals. Pubescent boys, pants hung below the buns. If this was all that freedom could buy, was it worth it?

Calming himself, he picked up his coffee cup and took a sip. His thoughts drifted. When he was young, he was roughed up at school. He told his grandmother that the roughneck had said if he saw Marty's face again he was going to kill him. Marty's grandmother didn't seemed shocked. Life wasn't fair, she said. There were bullies even in the finest schools. If the kid threatens you again, you threaten him. If that doesn't work, you hit him. When Marty complained he didn't know how to hit someone, his grandmother took him to watch the people practicing martial arts at the L.A. Defense Academy. They can teach you to stop bullies, she said. He joined the Academy, and ever since, when someone threatened him, he hit back – hard.

That was what he intended to do now.

Marty had been to the Los Angeles coroner a number of times over the years, enough that he knew who to call when he had a question. He left the deli and went to the West L.A. office. Soon Charlie Jackson was out front waving him to come on back. He was black, handsome, and nattily dressed. He was also the man who seemed to know everything about anyone who ever died in L.A.

"What's going on?" Charlie said, walking down the narrow, lime-colored hall.

Marty followed him into his cramped workspace where stacks of old manila files competed with science books for a place to sit. "It's working out great in DC, but I'm back in town helping Jack on a few cases."

Grave doubts wrinkling his forehead, Charlie glared at him. "Has he cooled his jets?"

"What do you mean?"

The two men sat down on either side of the grey metal desk, and Charlie said, "Didn't he tell you?"

Marty wondered what was going to rap him on the head next. "You mean, the Rose case?"

Charlie nodded. "He went off on me, demanding that I take his hit on the Rose's death upstairs to the boss. But I'm telling you like I told him. You can't order an autopsy without the family's consent. Not unless something big is coming down."

"What was the reported cause of death?"

"The old guy had a stroke. It killed him. These things happen, okay?"

"Well, yeah. Did you hear anything about David Rose having a seizure about the same time?"

"Marty, we've been doing business for what, seven years?"

"Something like that."

"Don't talk conspiracy. I'll discuss the facts, but if you go off on me like Jack did, you can forget I ever knew you."

"I'm really sorry," Marty lamented.

"Like I told Jack, it was a coincidence that the father and the son had head problems about the same time. But hey, these things run in families. So, is it all that unusual that it should happen?"

"No, not when you put it that way."

"That's right."

"Do you have anything else on the family, I mean, with the father dying and all?"

"Do you really need to talk about this?"

"I think so."

Charlie stared into the distance. "David Rose bought into Jack's conspiracy theory. But when it came down to walking the line, I called out there about getting the signature for the autopsy. Rose acted like he didn't know what I was talking about. You'd think that would have been enough to get Jack to drop it ... David Rose opting out of the investigation of his father's death. But no. On and on Jack went. Non-stop. Did he finally flip? Is that it? The reason you're here?"

"Jack's exhausted and is taking a break. I came out to tie up some loose ends for him."

"Take this one and drop it. That's my advice."

"Did Rose come here with Jack?"

"No," Charlie said, "he came in by himself to pick up the forms."

"Is there anything else that stands out about this case?" Marty asked.

"The mind funk."

"What?"

"Rose acting like he didn't know what I was talking about. I mean, hey, he probably had gotten over his anger and denial and quit trying to blame his father's death on someone. So he didn't want to talk about it anymore. That happens with people. But when I made the call out there, he sounded strange. Like he didn't know what I was talking about –" Charlie's eyes went hollow.

"Like he was afraid."

"Before or after the seizure."

"After."

Marty reasoned that somebody had done something to the man, maybe stimulated the seizure, and if that had caused serious memory loss, maybe Rose didn't know what Charlie was talking about. But whatever had happened, it added a whole new dimension to the case. Especially with Jack knowing that Rose had bailed out. There had to be something that piqued Jack's curiosity for him to stay on the investigation. "I wish I could apologize for Jack's behavior," Marty said, knowing he'd gotten all he could out of Charlie

"Forget it."

Marty stood and stuck his hand across the desk. They shook, and he said, "No hard feelings?"

Charlie waved him off. "Get out of here."

"I'm heading out tonight, or I'd stick around and have a beer with you."

Charlie smiled. "Next time."

Marty left and spent the rest of the afternoon driving around, making calls, trying to find anyone who had knowledge of Jack Watson being shot before he left L.A. But it was always the same. No emergency room report. No police report. No doctor's report. A big zip. Zero.

That's the same zip Marty was feeling when evening rolled around. How could a guy get shot, be bandaged up, and leave town without anyone knowing about it?

David Rose lived at the edge of Beverly Hills in a mission-style house with lazy arches and tan plaster, topped with a red tile roof. Marty parked out front and moved up the curved, shrub-lined walkway towards Rose's door. There was a mezuza on the frame, indicating Rose was a practicing Jew. He rang the bell. It was after seven-thirty, and he expected Rose to be home. He wasn't sure why. Rose could be anywhere. He could even be dead like his father.

A curly-haired boy wearing a white shirt and glasses answered. When Marty asked for the boy's father, the kid yelled, "Dad!" and left him staring through the security door at what looked to be a typical, upper-middle-class home.

Of medium height, thin, with long nose and thick glasses, David Rose wore a coat and tie. He smiled politely and asked, "What can I help you with, Mister –"

"Price, Martin Price." Rose unofficiously opened the security door, so Marty stuck out his hand to shake. "It's about your father."

Rose burst into sardonic laughter. "What the hell did he do now?"

"I work with a local private detective. Jack Watson. You heard of him?"

Rose's eyes drew thin with murderous rage. Then he looked at his son and forced a smile. He extended a hand for Marty to come in. "No. How does my father fit into this?"

"I'm surprised you have to ask. Surely you must remember the name Watson." Marty sat down on the sofa in the livingroom and glanced about at the paintings. Original cubists. He reckoned Rose had a hundred thousand tied up into them. He waved an arm. "Down off of La Brea. About six-two, dark hair, good-looking. Could pass for an actor living in the canyon." He studied Rose's face. His uneasy, faked smile hadn't changed since the man patted the kid on the head.

"No," Rose said. "I'm sorry I can't help you,"

Marty pulled the contract out of his pocket and handed it to Rose. "Do you recognize the signature? It's yours, right?"

Rose studied the document. "Hmmm," he mumbled.

"What's it say, Dad?" said the boy.

Rose faked a gravelly accent. "The feds are hauling us out of here unless we give them your Play Station as ransom."

"Are you gonna pay, Dad? Or should we turn up the heat?"

"We're going to turn up the heat, son." Rose smiled at the kid, then studied Marty for a long moment. "I'm confused. Someone has gone to a lot of effort to look up my family's background and fake my signature ... I mean, hell, *I* can't even tell it's not mine. But I didn't sign this, and I've never heard of Watson. Don't know anything about the FBI, and can't imagine why you'd come here and desecrate the dead." He handed the contract back to Marty. "Sorry I can't help you."

Marty's thoughts spun. Why did Rose mention the FBI? Did he think Marty represented them and was testing Rose to see if he'd talk when they had told him to be silent?

"I meant no offense," Marty said. Seeing the fear in the man's eyes, he knew that Rose knew what he was talking about. But Rose kept a facade of ignorance going for the sake of the kid. The boy's life had been threatened. That's what it had to be. The two of them were now tossing a ball back and forth like nothing had happened. "Can you think of anyone who would try to defame, blame, libel, or extort from your family?"

"What's extort, Dad?" the kid interrupted.

Rose had all the time in the world for the kid, and it showed. He stood, keeping the game of toss going. "Extortion is like when mommy says she isn't going to take you to the soccer game unless you clean up your room. And no, we don't have anyone trying to get us to do anything, Mr. Price. We wouldn't do it anyway," he said, looking at the kid and grinning. "We'd fight for our right to party."

"Yeah," said the boy.

Seeing it was over, Marty stood. The three of them went to the door.

"Is my family in some kind of danger?" Rose asked.

Marty huffed out his breath. "No. I'm picking up some loose ends for Watson, and I stumbled across this." He waved the contract. "I can't figure it. It was in Watson's desk."

"What does he say happened?"

"He's dead." Marty watched Rose flinch, and he knew without a doubt he had met with Jack. When the boy ran into the other room, Marty thought this might be his opening. "I'm Jack's ex-partner. I want to know why he died. I'm not a cop, nor do I represent the FBI. I could run prints on this contract, but I'm betting there would only be yours, mine, and Jack's. Can't you help me?"

His wary eyes betraying grave caution, Rose studied Marty for a long moment. Finally, he said. "I don't know Watson or anything about this contract. I think you'd better go now."

"Thanks," Marty said, turning for the door.

8

Hearing a knock, Dr. Rolland Archer rose from his office sofa and stretched his tall frame. “We’re on,” he said.

Dressed in white lab coat and slacks, Tanya Burns left the workstation and opened the metal door. Staring blank-eyed like robots, two guards in black-and-white uniforms stood behind Jack Watson. One of them said, “We’ll be in the hall if you need any help.”

Tanya momentarily studied Jack. Dressed in jeans, T-shirt, and loafers, he was hunched over. His hands were pressed rigidly into his stomach. Wobbly on his feet, his black hair was mussed up, and his face muscles were taut. He glared hollow-eyed at the floor.

“Are you okay?” she said.

Without making eye contact, Jack mumbled, “Yes, ma’am.”

She didn’t believe that. When they brought him in the day before as per Krocker’s orders, he said he was okay, then, too. That was when he collapsed. Now, with his ashen face and trembling hands, he probably wasn’t much better off. “Take the cuffs off this man, then you’re dismissed,” she said to the guards.

One of the guards protested. “He escaped maximum security –”

“Get the cuffs off of him and get out of here,” Tanya ordered. “I’ll call you if I need you.”

When the restraints were off, Tanya took Jack by the arm and held him steady. “Come in and sit down.”

Head bowed, Jack watched the floor as Tanya pointed to the divan, saying, “Try to make yourself at home, Jack. I’m sorry about all this confusion and pain, but at least it’s over now.”

Jack sat on the edge of the white couch and stared at the Persian rug.

Tanya hit the remote button that turned on the hidden camera, then sat down in the stuffed chair across the coffee table from Jack. “You would think that we had entered an enlightened age,” she said, “and that people didn’t do stupid things in the name of national security. But it still happens. They shot you twice, didn’t they?”

Jack nodded.

"I'm sorry," she said.

Jack didn't respond.

She bit her lip. "We want to hear the whole story from your point of view." She brushed a hand though her mop of long, brown hair. "We also want to know how you were treated here."

A tear rolled down Jack's face.

"I'm sorry about what happened," Tanya said. "But it's over now. Tell us the whole story, and we'll get you out of here." She leaned towards Jack, whose eyes hadn't moved from the floor. "Its all right to talk."

"Please," Jack whispered, "gimme the gun, I'll shoot myself. Let's get it over with."

Tanya gasped. "My God, we're running a torture chamber."

Cold-eyed, Rolland glared at Tanya until he said, "You don't get off that easy, Jack. I'm Doctor Archer, and we're here to rehabilitate you. I know you have seen too much crap, more than the mind can take, and you have had all your ideals crushed. But we're patching you up and sending you on your way. All you have to do is tell us what you saw and promise us you'll never talk about it. That's all we need for our report. Then you can go."

Jack's croaking laugh sounded like a car engine that was turning over and over but wouldn't start.

"That a boy," Rolland said, "there's comedy even during brushes with death. How did this all start, anyway?"

Hunkered on the edge of the sofa, his arms wrapped around himself like he was freezing, Jack said, "You're going to let me go with what I know about the FBI stealing patents?"

Brows raised, Rolland said, "Stealing patents, huh?"

"Yeah, you know I caught you at it. Now you're going to have to kill me to cover it up."

"Not me, no way, I don't kill anyone," Rolland said. "If you've gotten this far, you're going to live. Might be a little trouble at first keeping your mouth shut, but you'll learn how to do it. Besides, now you know you can't beat us. Myself, I'm sorry that you got caught up in this. But if you tell us the whole story, I'm going to see that you walk."

When Jack turned and his gaze met Tanya's, she forced a half smile. "Walk," she said.

Jack's voice was slow and labored. "Where do you want me to start? With David Rose coming to my office?"

"Sure," Rolland said.

Jack's story began with David Rose calling and asking about credentials and confidentiality. When Jack said he had both, Rose came by the office, talking about how his father had been killed by someone who wanted the device he had invented. Jack took the case, leery at first, thinking it didn't make any sense. The big break came when someone at the U.S. Patent Office unwittingly gave Jack the name of the FBI agent who reviewed patent applications on a regular basis. The clerk's assumption was that the FBI agent was tracking down technology thieves.

Jack's story continued for almost an hour and a half when Rolland said, "Thanks for telling us the truth. I have a few mop-up questions, then we're going to do a little therapy. After that, we're sending you off to a hospital in DC, and your life will be yours again. Sound okay?"

Murky-eyed, Jack blinked.

"You still with me?" Rolland said.

Jack nodded.

Rolland leaned back into the stuffed chair. "First of all, my boss wants to know how you escaped in L.A. He thinks you, well ... maybe you're another Houdini. On the other hand, maybe the team was sleeping on the job."

Jack picked up the mug off the table and took a deep swig of coffee. "My ex-partner set the office up with remote cameras. I could watch your people from anywhere via the Web if I had my laptop. My house was set up the same way with e-cams. Also, my car has sensors which tell when it's been tampered with. If it wasn't enough watching your people snooping around, they came in like a parody on Hollywood cops. Your suits and shades. Your big cars. Talk about bozos."

Tanya looked at Rolland. "We still do that?"

Rolland chuckled. "I guess so." He grew serious. "But still, they pulled you over, and you were shot. How did you get from the corner of Pico and Hollywood all the way to DC?"

"I made it into the coffee shop and out the back door to the next block. Then I bought a coat off a stranger, a wig off another, and called a taxi. He took me to old Doc Winters. He'd always told me that if I got shot for God's sake don't go to emergency. You could die waiting in line."

"Okay, Winters patched you up, and you took a cab to LAX, is that it?"

"I knew you'd be watching for me at the L.A. airport, so I went to Ontario and got a flight to Phoenix."

"Then you flew to National and made a call your cell phone."

Jack winced with sour disbelief. "Shit. That's how you caught me, isn't it?"

Rolland nodded.

The gleam in his eyes going blank, Jack said, "You people are everywhere."

"Don't worry about it, no one is going to hurt you." Rolland stood. "Time for therapy." He motioned for Jack to follow him to the door.

Jack clambered to his feet and made it to the hallway on his own.

The guards were outside, and they accompanied the two agents and Jack to a room at the end of the hall, across from Krocker's office.

Rolland punched in the security code onto the pad, and they entered a sterile white windowless room with medical equipment, pull-down lights, and a stainless-steel operating table. A couple gurneys sat next to the wall.

"This is it, huh?" Jack said. "Where you kill people?"

Rolland shut the door, leaving the guards in the hall."No," he said. "This will put you out for a little while, and when you wake up, you'll be in a hospital. One of our agents will call you, and you will think about what has happened to you. You will probably decide to keep your mouth shut." The lines in his face grew tight. "You can't beat these people, Jack. Don't try it. Act like nothing happened, and you'll be able to go your own way. Can you do that?"

Jack raved. "If you hurt Cheryl, I'll kill you. All of you!"

"Nobody's going to hurt Cheryl," Rolland said. He unscrewed the lid off a small bottle. It had an eye dropper poking through the hole in the cap. Rolland squeezed the rubber end and the dropper filled with orange liquid. "Open your mouth, Jack. It'll taste like cough syrup."

Jack opened up, and Rolland squirt the medication into his mouth. It was a fast-acting sedative. Rolland set the bottle on the cabinet and pulled a gurney away from the wall. "Lie down on this."

His eyes growing pale, Jack crawled up onto the stretcher and lay down.

Rolland put a few leather straps around Jack's body, securing him. Then he went to a small refrigerator built flush with the wall cabinets and took out a glass vial. He popped the plastic top and held it under Jack's nose. "Sniff this, and before you know it, you'll be waking up at the hospital."

Jack's ferret-eyes shifted between Tanya and Rolland's faces. Finally, he sniffed and passed out.

Rolland went back to the cabinet and grabbed an aluminum instrument the size and shape of a small flashlight. "This is Krocker's latest piece of crime-fighting equipment. He calls it the END device. That stands for electro neuron disruptor."

"What does that mean?"

"Just what it says. It disrupts the pathways in the brain."

"Great..."

Rolland glanced at her. "It beats the old electroshock for knocking out painful memories."

"How so?"

"If you keep it turned down low, the patient doesn't go into a seizure the way one does during electroconvulsive therapy."

Rolland adjusted the setting and held the END device to Jack's forehead. "Jack won't remember anything about today. I could make him forget more. Turn up the wattage and hold it over the temporal lobe ... creating a massive epileptic convulsion. Then, he would forget blocks of time, but we would also run the risk of killing him. So I'm keeping it set low and leaving it to Jack to deal with the issue of the stolen patents."

"Did you know the FBI stole patents?" Tanya asked.

"No."

"Are you getting closer to busting Krocker?"

"Every day."

Rolland pressed the button on the instrument and touched it to Jack's forehead.

Jack tossed and turned like he was having a nightmare. When he settled down, Rolland put the tools away and leaned against the cabinet. "I've done a lot of these, but I still can't get used to it."

"I don't know why not," Tanya said, mocking him.

"It didn't seem wrong at first, back when it was terrorists, serial killers, spies. You know, psychos. But in the last year, Krocker tossed in a few people like Jack. Their only crime was getting in his way. I didn't understand for a while. But now, you know, it's like you said, that he is personally involved. Has a stake in it."

"What do you suppose that stake might be?"

"I don't know, but there's nothing I can do to stop it, unless I risk losing everything." Hands on his hips he looked at Tanya. "I'm wondering if Krocker is testing us, giving us Jack to interrogate to see if we'll sicken from the job and quit, or go turn Krocker in."

"It sounds like it's time to do both." Tanya's face wrinkled with stress lines. "Why can't you call a press conference and report Krocker's crimes, if it's true what Jack said, that he's breaking the law?"

"I'd be violating my secrecy oath. Besides, Krocker would weasel out of it. He has people who will mold the truth any which way he pleases. He also has allies on the Hill. Armchair, cloak-and-dagger afficionados who believe that the U.S. must push forward the cutting edge of criminal interrogation at any cost. They would all be after me if I interrupted Krocker."

"So you're not going to report the patent theft?"

Rolland shook his head. "No, we didn't use the truth serum and can't prove Jack isn't lying."

She studied him for a hard moment. "How did this operation start?"

"A black budget intelligence unit, specializing in getting information out of terrorists. Then it took on militant movements, then top ten criminals. Now, who knows." His mouth pulled down into a tight-lipped frown. "I don't know where it will end."

"You're starting to scare me," she said, glaring at him.

"I know, but don't jump ship. If anything goes wrong, I'll bail you out, okay?"

"Wonderful."

Rolland went to the phone and dialed. "This is Doctor Archer," he said. "I need an ambulance in the basement of the Behavioral Sciences Building. It is a thirty-year-old white male who is going immediately to the emergency room at Southeast Community Hospital in the District. You drop him off, I'll cover the admission from here."

When Rolland hung up the phone, Tanya was standing next to him. "What is Jack going to think happened to him?"

"He had a flat tire near Quantico. Someone stopped. Instead of offering help, the person tried to rob him. They fought, and Jack was shot. One of our people spotted him, and we patched him up, and sent him to the hospital."

"Why would he believe that crock?"

"The END device will blot out the last twenty-four hours from his memory. Jack will wake at the hospital, and he will learn that his rental car was discovered near here with a flat tire. He will be told that the shock of getting shot made him forget whatever he was doing, why he was even in DC."

She eyed Jack, struggling in his sleep. "This sucks."

"Exactly."

9

Lisa sat across the gold-flake kitchen counter from Marty. They were eating pastries and drinking hot chocolate. It was Tuesday morning. He had gone to her house after arriving in D.C. on Monday night's red-eye flight from L.A.

"David Rose is lying," she said, "and there's nothing you can do about it."

"I guess not," Marty said. "You should have seen the pain in the man's eyes, yet the pleasing smile on his face. What right does the government have to do this to people?"

"You're talking like Jack, dear."

"Is that your reaction? I've gone fanatic?"

"I was simply giving feedback."

He flipped the contract down onto the table. "Rose denied he signed this. Can you imagine the pressure the FBI must have put on him … threatening to kill the rest of his family? That's what it had to be."

Her delicate-featured face turned up into a cozy smile.

"What?" he said, knowing that self-satisfied look of hers.

She made a pointed grimace like a courthouse judge. "This reminds me of the movies. When there's a crisis, the bozo boys run around doing dumb things that lead essentially to nowhere. Half the movie is over but nothing constructive has happened." She studied his long-faced reaction, then said, "If you would have called the FBI in the beginning, this would have been settled by now."

"Is that your plan? Call them?"

Her mouth tightened into a thin line, and she batted her eye lashes.

"Oh, I get it. Not your job."

She nodded.

"So what you're saying is that I'm running about like an idiot when I should be negotiating with the government?"

Lisa smiled. "You're learning."

"Me?"

"Last year it would have taken you a couple weeks to reach that conclusion."

"I've learned to ask for other people's opinions, haven't I?"

She nodded. "If you can't forget about this case, go to the Hoover Building and tell them a group of FBI agents killed your ex-partner, but you can't find the body because they stole it. When they laugh at you, you'll see what I'm saying. For all you know, Jack is in recovery at Washington Medical Center, negotiating with the Attorney General's Office about a settlement for damages."

"If you're laughing at me – sorry. I called all the hospitals and didn't find Jack. He wasn't at the morgue, either." Marty rubbed his fingers though his short, dirty-blond hair. "Jack has ceased to exist."

"I wasn't poking fun at you even if you hadn't made the calls. I'm sad to see you go through this, that's all. But let's face it. If it's a conspiracy, it's a damn tight one, backed by the full force of the U.S. government."

Nikki, the silk-white cat, scratched at Marty's heals.

Marty got up from the tall, high-backed stool and picked her up. Stroking the cat's fluffy, thick hair, he said, "I'd give anything to forget this."

Lisa grinned. "Now that that's settled…"

Driving through the deciduous forest on Rock Creek Expressway later that morning, Marty considered going to his office and getting his gun. Except for helping at the presidential inauguration, he had stopped carrying a weapon after he moved to Washington. Lately he considered weapons vulgar, something you needed in L.A., but not here. No. When you lived in Georgetown, you didn't have shootouts. You negotiated. The need now for a weapon made him feel anything but macho. A failure, really, like he had lost everything he had gained over the last few years. Most of all, his status.

Near his office, he hesitated about pulling into the driveway and opening the metal door to the garage with his cardlock key. What if the feds were waiting inside?

Driving past the building, he went down the hill and under the Whitehurst Freeway, the expressway overshadowing K Street. Looping back up the hill on Wisconsin, he headed for his home. Back there, he went into his study and opened the security file on his computer. He first ran the video of his home taken during the trip to L.A. There were no surprises. Next he tied into the data bank in Maryland and downloaded the digitalized film that had flowed into the security system from the e-cam at his office. He watched as the video showed a mid-sized office wrapped in dark-blond Ash paneling. There was an antique desk with a computer table and a book shelf on one side of the room. On the other side sat two walnut arm chairs along with PJ, the green rubber tree plant. He had viewed twenty-fours-hours-worth of security coverage when he saw a dark figure zip across his office.

"Hey, now wait a minute!" he wailed.

He backed up the tape and went to normal-speed viewing. It showed a well-built, broad-shouldered man dressed in a Hawaiian shirt rummaging though his file cabinet. It was the guy he had fought in the parking lot at the harbor. Only instead of blues and whites, his shirt was highlighted with browns and greens. The man turned his head, talking to someone. Then, another man crossed in front of the camera. Dressed in jeans, shirt, and baseball cap, the second man wore a thick gold chain around his neck. It was another one of the thugs from Saturday night. Marty watched as Mr. Gold Chain pulled up a chair and sit down in front of the computer in Marty's office.

Marty turned up the volume.

"I'll download his hard drive," said the man with the gold chain. He pulled out what looked to be a CD writer and connected it to the PC.

"That's against the law," Marty said, wishing he was at his office and had his gun. Then he remembered that the intruders probably weren't there right now. The digital recording was from Sunday night when he was in L.A.

Calming down, he watched. The men were silent as Mr. Gold Chain whizzed across the keyboard, tying to hack his way into the computer. Marty speeded it up and saw what looked like a short parody on Americana: The man sweeping across the keyboard like it was a grand piano and he was playing Rag Time music. Then, in Keystone Cop fashion, the thug was in and out of his gym bag, plugging in cables, slapping in disks, turning, twisting, slouching, then finally standing and shaking his fists, he blurted out something that sounded like a mouse screaming.

Marty backed up the video and slowed it down so he could understand what the man was saying.

"The fucking widget-head built an impenetrable firewall," said Mister Gold Chain. "He ought to be working for Bill Gates."

"Got that right," Marty said.

The man in the Hawaiian shirt approached the other. "What's that mean to us?"

"I'll have to rip out the hard drive and take it to the lab if we're going to get anything off of it."

"No, leave it. If anything is moved or taken, he'll know we've been here."

The men were silent, continuing their search of the room. Hands covered with surgeon's gloves, they looked like they were professionals.

A phone rang, and the man in the Hawaiian shirt pulled a cell off his belt and took the call, saying, "What's going on?" He listened, then glared at the man wearing the gold chain, saying, "Buddy couldn't download the hard drive."

Mr. Gold Chain – the one referred to as Buddy – interrupted the other man's phone call, saying, "He'd better not blame me if he misses the convention in Vegas. He should have turned this over to us in L.A."

The man in the Hawaiian shirt listened to the phone, then looked at Buddy. "He says he's not missing the convention, because we're going to bury this guy before the weekend."

Watching this on tape, Marty choked.

"Maybe the commander should do it himself," Buddy joked.

Mr. Hawaiian Shirt spoke to the person on the other end of the line: "You've never missed the Vegas conference, have you?" He listened a moment, then said, "We'll know soon enough." Momentarily, he clicked off the connection and hung the phone on his belt. He came over and watched Buddy. "You sure you can't get into that machine?"

"Not with the equipment I've got. But what's the fucking hurry?"

"Price has information exposing the Company."

"Let's shoot him."

"May have to."

Marty couldn't believe they discussed killing him with such a casual air. His stomach churning, he watched the men tidy up and leave.

Angry now, he rolled the video back over the tape and played the conversation again. He had heard right. They called their organization the Company. But what did that mean? While the FBI might on occasion be called the Bureau, it was not called the Company. He mulled over the message Jack had left on the computer disk, that this was racketeering-orientated, criminal conspiracy. Maybe that meant they weren't FBI.

Going to a real time connection, he made sure no one was in his office at that moment. Then he got up from the computer, intent on going there to get his weapon.

Bozo boys.

Lisa's melodic voice repeated in his mind until he shouted, "Okay, already, I get the point!"

The point was – take smart action. Don't run around in circles doing dumb things.

He reentered the data storage system and brought the video of the intruders back onto the screen. Then he cut a clean, 60-second segment showing their faces. The clip included the quote from Mr. Gold Chain, a.k.a. Buddy, saying they had better shoot Marty because he might have information exposing the Company.

Marty went into his e-mail system and wrote a cover letter mentioning that he had information showing these were FBI operatives who had broken into his office. They were talking about murdering him. He attached the file containing the video and shot the e-mail over to Thomas Fredericks at the Post. He was a columnist Marty knew from working here in the District. Marty kept him updated on the happenings around the Capitol. He knew that Fredericks had a system that could download video e-mail because he had talked the man into getting it. Cutting-edge stuff right now, Marty had said, but in a year or two, everybody will be sending secretly-recorded digital movies of the bizarre things they've witnessed. Previously, Marty had sent Fredericks a few videos. But it was a two-way street, and Fredericks had referred to him a few clients who wanted consultation on security matters.

He took one more look at what was downloading in realtime from the office. The intruders weren't there. He got up with intent to leave when it struck him. Didn't Mr. Gold Chain – the one called Buddy – pull a black box out of his bag before heading for the corner of the office, out of camera range? Marty had thought he was checking for listening devices. But no. Marty bet that Buddy had a box of bugging devices, probably a remote camera. That's why they didn't mess the place up. They intended to catch him on film. It was also why they only did a cursory search, and it explained why they missed discovering the e-cam in Marty's security system. It stared at them from the eye of the wooden wolf which sat in the corner baying at a silver moon. They were too busy putting in their own camera to find his.

Great. But how was he going to get his gun if these thugs were watching the place?

He had a sudden defenseless feeling. If they had his office address, they would have known where he lived. It was only a matter of time before they got here. There was never a moment he needed a gun more than now. The feds intended to kill him. Kill Marty Price, so they wouldn't be late for the Vegas convention. He bet they had a sniper watching his office right now.

No, not in broad daylight.

But if they were watching on their camera, they would come running when he went to his office to get his gun.

He wished he could borrow a weapon so he wouldn't need to go down there. But you didn't lend guns out in the District. With the imminent danger guns posed to politicians, the city government had an ordinance requiring that all firearms be registered. And if you lost your weapon, or it was used in a crime, you were not going to get another permit. He did, however, have a friend, Jonathan, in Virginia who was loose with his weapons. But that would be a couple-hour drive. The man was probably at work anyway.

Grabbing his phone, he dialed the number for Commander Ken Nelson, head of the second district Metro police. When the officer's voice mail said he was on vacation, Marty left a message telling Nelson the feds had broken into his office and were threatening him.

Marty clicked off and thought about calling Metro dispatch and reporting the break-in at his office. But the perpetrators weren't currently there, and the police would take hours before they responded. By that time he might be dead. All because they didn't want to miss Vegas.

He wondered if he could disguise himself and go into his office for his gun looking like somebody else. That might throw them off his trail. Give them a decoy to track, forcing them to split their energy. At the minimum, they couldn't I.D. him with their remote camera, so they wouldn't come to the office with their guns blazing. They might think he was Marty's business partner.

Marty got out his makeup kit and went into the bathroom. He was studying his face, going to stick on a silicone patch to round out his cheeks, when he realized the inevitable. He would have to get more data on these folks. The only way to do it was to go into the Hoover Building and get onto their computer system.

Yes. That was it, despite the danger of getting caught.

Monty Bradshaw had stopped his access to the FBI system via hacking. But if Marty went in and got on the system in a normal fashion, disguised as an FBI agent, as Tucker Johnston, there was nothing Bradshaw could do. And Marty had Johnston's I.D. Now all he had to do was look like him.

He pulled out the badge from his wallet and looked at the picture. Tucker's nose made Marty's look stubby in comparison. Marty would have to build his up, make it more Romanesque. Marty also had angular lines on his jaw and chin compared to Tucker's oval face. He would have to add a little putty here and there to round things out. Then there was Tucker's brown eyes. Lucky for Marty he still had the colored contact lenses from his days in L.A.

But the big problem was the hair. He took a plastic cup, mixed some black dye, then covered his dirty-blond flattop and darkened his eyebrows. After using the blow dryer, he redesigned his facial features with putty, then smoothed the putty over with skin-colored toner. Finally, he put on the contacts and darkened his eyelashes. Looking at himself in the mirror, he compared what he saw to the picture on Tucker's I.D. Good enough for government work, he figured.

He shifted through his black sports bag, found Tucker's brown-leather wallet, and stuffed it into his pocket. Then he unplugged his laptop from the docking bay, inserted the wireless Internet card, stuffed the computer in the black bag, and headed for the street.

Getting in the Mustang, he was struck by a queasy, uneasy feeling. It was too dangerous to break into the Hoover Building, even with an official badge, when he wasn't carrying his gun. It would be about as smart as sticking your face into a hornet's nest to see what was inside. He had to go to his office and get the gun. There was no way around it.

His office sat on the hill above the harbor, next to the Chesapeake and Ohio Canal. Like most everything in Georgetown, it was built of brick. Part of the redevelopment going on above Northwest K Street, the building was five stories tall and was built in a conservative, neo-Federal style. He decided to park out of the way on K street in case the Company thugs were looking for his Mustang. Up the hill, he entered the building. In the hall, he stood before the wood-paneled entryway to his office. Taking a deep breath, he opened the door, then stepped inside. Punching the keypad for the security system, he turned off the alarm. He wondered how in hell the Company boys had bypassed that system without anybody from the other offices stopping them. He consoled himself; they had only made it halfway, having missed detecting his e-cam.

He crossed the waiting room, going past a couple of the deep leather chairs. Entering his office, he went behind the solid maple desk. With baroque inlay and carvings, it was an antique he had gotten at a government auction. Nearby was a closet. He opened the door, went inside, turned on the light, and shut the door behind himself. After moving a few boxes, he pulled up the carpet. Underneath was a floor safe. He dialed the numbers and yanked up the metal plug. Reaching down, he picked up a metal box. Underneath were his .40 caliber Glock semiautomatic and a couple spare clips. He took off his coat, put on his shoulder holster, and stuck in the weapon. Shutting the safe, he put the rug back down and left the closet.

Going for the office door, he stopped and looked in the corner of the room. The wooden wolf was two feet tall and stood on an end table. He patted it on the head as he checked his e-cam. To have been out of range of the camera, a person would have had to stand against the wall next to the picture. He looked at the scene from the wilds of Alaska. Dismissive in attitude, he pulled the picture off the wall. He had to laugh at the gall of these people. One of the Company men had taped a flat plastic panel to the backing of the picture. A wire attached to a tiny, tubular, electronic camera lens which had been jammed through the corner of the frame. After pulling the wire loose, Marty hung the picture back on the wall, then went to the office window and looked outside.

Below, the pale-green waters of the C&O canal met the street out front at a perpendicular angle, then traveled through a tunnel under the road. A group of tourists were on the banks of the waterway taking pictures of the historic buildings. At the outdoor café across the street, a lone couple was laughing. No one else was around.

Believing it was safe to leave, he grabbed his briefcase and left the building. Crossing the street, he went to the outdoor café perched next to the canal. He sat at an ornate, wrought-iron table and called a taxi.

The waiter came and he ordered a cappuccino.

Bozo boys.

In his mind he heard Lisa's warning all over again.

He wondered if he was in danger, or if he should run.

No. His conscience was bugging him. There was no way to explain to Lisa that he'd picked up his gun, instead of going to the Hoover Building to turn himself in.

Turn himself in?

What was he thinking?

That wasn't what Lisa meant when she said to go to the Hoover Building. Two days of paranoia had turned his mind to mush. But maybe she was right. He had gotten his gun instead of going to the FBI headquarters and forcing someone to acknowledge his complaint. After all, he had the wallet and badge of the FBI agent who shot Jack. He could have started at the front counter by displaying the badge and saying this man Johnston had tried to kill him. But instead of doing that, he was preparing to go to the Hoover Building disguised at a federal officer in order to pry loose some information.

Some women passed on the path that ran along the bank of the canal. They joked, talking about taking an early lunch.

He suddenly wished he had co-workers with whom he could joke. In the past, he had scorned routine office work, but suddenly, he envied the women and their staid, calculated world. At least when the boss puffed up and said something grandiose, then contradicted himself, they could joke about it during lunch. All Marty had was a dead ex-partner.

Outnumbered.

He thought about the absurdity of his situation, trying to single-handedly take on the FBI. Or rather, the Company, whoever they were. Hell, even if they were ripping off all the energy devices that competed with the oil and nuclear industries, he'd never have a chance of getting anyone to listen to him. People expected this sort of thing when big government supported big business. How could you fight them? What he needed was somebody on his side. An advocate. A lawyer.

A lawyer?

Marty wondered why he hadn't called Mike Greene, his attorney, the moment Jack was shot. While the waiter came and left his drink, he dialed Mike's number.

Mike's secretary answered, saying he was in court. Did Mr. Price want to leave a message?

Marty asked for Mike's cell number.

No, Mike didn't give out that number.

Marty told her he already had it, but he wasn't in his office.

Begrudgingly, she gave him the number.

Marty called.

Mike didn't answer. Instead, the voice mail came on.

Marty left a message, asking Mike to call him, telling him the story about a group called the Company who worked with the FBI. They killed Jack Watson and covered it up. Hid the body. He had one of the murderers' FBI identification badges. But right now, he was running out of options. They were everywhere. Next they would be at Lisa's, intimidating her to get answers. And he wasn't going to let that happen. No way.

Marty turned to watch a bulky white SUV roar to a stop in the driveway across the street. It whirled back and zipped into a parking space in front of his building. The man wearing the gold chain, Buddy, jumped from the driver's seat. He walked with a cocky swagger, heading for the door of Marty's building.

Marty pulled a newspaper from his briefcase. He held it in front of his face, then peeked around the edge of the page. He considered going in after Buddy and beating some answers out of him, but a bulky Chevy zoomed up the hill from K Street and pulled to the curb in front of the café. Mr. Hawaiian shirt expelled from the front passenger seat. While the driver stayed in the car, Mr. Hawaiian Shirt hastened around the car and across the street towards Marty's building. He turned back when another SUV drove up and stopped in the street. He pointed to the corner, and the second SUV took off. Then he turned and went towards Marty's office.

They were back. The whole damn team. Probably covering every direction out of there.

Marty looked east down the canal in time to see a sturdy hunk-of-a man jump from a bulky sedan on the next street over, then head in Marty's direction.

Marty gasped. He was surrounded with no escape route. Lucky for him the fools hadn't noticed he was sitting at the outdoor patio. Not yet, at least. They were too busy watching his building.

Without out making any quick movements, Marty left the patio, stepped up to the bulky Chevy which was parked at the curb. Drawing his gun, Marty's intent was to take the driver hostage long enough for him to get out of danger.

Suddenly a taxi pulled up and double-parked at the restaurant.

Marty stuck the gun in his shoulder holster. Slowly blowing out his breath, he walked to the cab and got inside.

"Where you go?" said the thin black man who spoke with a thick accent.

"Hoover Building," Marty said.

10

The J. Edgar Hoover Building was a tan concrete-and-glass contemporary architectural monstrosity. Occupying the entire block between 9th and 10th at Pennsylvania Avenue, it sat a few blocks from the White House. With waffle-iron sides, it had command and control offices jutting up on one side of the building. When the taxi approached, tourists were backed up in a line outside, from the public entrance, down the stairs, and along the moat which surrounded three sides of the edifice.

Marty got out of the taxi and headed up the cordoned-off stairway leading to the agent's door. With his briefcase in one hand, he held his cell phone to his ear with the other.

"Honey, no, we'll get a marriage counselor," he exclaimed, pretending he was talking to his wife as he approached the guards. "It'll work. We've got to stay together. Think of the kids."

He stepped to the side of the guards, letting some agents pass. Gripping he phone, he said, "C'mon, babe, we'll spend the weekend together and work this out ... No, I can't come now. I've got to go upstairs and explain a case to the boss. How about a late lunch, or an early dinner?"

He glanced at the guards. They were watching him. One had a sad frown on his face, the other was all smiles, shaking his head. "Okay, dinner at the Watergate. See you at six." He snapped the phone shut, pulled out Tucker Johnston's wallet and flashed the I.D.

"The Watergate ... that'll work," said one of the guards as Marty entered the doorway.

Marty stopped. "You think so?"

"Give it your best shot."

"Thanks."

Marty walked into the monstrous foyer of the building, and momentarily found himself marching behind a group of agents. They were talking about an operation and how they had to cover their butts, not create another Waco. He followed them inside the elevator, and up to the fifth floor. The guy in the lead hit the keypad on the vault-like door to the Strategic Information Operations Center. The door opened. Marty followed them in. The agents headed off to one of the active-operations suites. Marty hung a turn and went into the galley and poured himself a cup of coffee.

Plunging into a stuffed chair, he decided to call Lisa and tell her he'd gone down to the Hoover Building. If he didn't show for dinner, they were holding him. He dialed her number, but under the clear plastic face of the cell were the words *No Network.* That's when he remembered he was inside a sealed vault. No microwave communication emissions could get in or out of there.

He sipped on the coffee, wondering how he could get more information on the Company. When he stepped out in the hall, a group of agents filed past and abruptly stopped in front of the door to one of the operations rooms.

"We've got to blast this jerk, right now," snarled a burley agent, hands on his hips, glaring past Marty. "Not tomorrow, not after we have a hostage situation."

Watching the man, Marty glowered, thinking he was talking about him and his battle with the Company.

As a woman punched in a security code, the barrel-chested male caught Marty's grimace. "Wadaya want? A trial?" he said.

"Huh?" Marty mumbled.

"He's wearing armor," said the big man, "and there's three dead."

Marty looked from face to face. "Damn," he groaned, "we've got to move."

"You got that one," said the big man, who turned and went into the active-operations command room with Marty and the other agents in tow.

The Strategic Information Operations Center had four separate crises headquarters. The rooms were separated by thick, sound-proof windows. Each had secure phone lines to the White House, the CIA, the DEA, and the Pentagon. The carpets were blue, and there were no exterior windows. The room Marty had entered had three wall-screen-sized video monitors each displaying different broadcasts of the crisis situation out in California. The volume was up on one. The moderator reported that it wasn't a lone robber, but three. They had left the bank and were walking down the street in Garden Grove, California, shooting people.

An agent muted the volume, and another screen lit up with a secure broadcast from the FBI headquarters in L.A. The report said that the Bureau had one agent on the scene, but he didn't have armor-piercing bullets.

"What the hell?" said a man who had stopped near Marty to watch the live, large-screen image of the robbers blasting an undercover police car. The car crashed into a storefront window and blew up into flames. The agent looked at Marty, whose eyes were glued onto the TV. "How could we have a man in the field without armor-piercing bullets?"

The man's I.D. said he was Special Agent Bill Moore. "I don't know, Bill," Marty said. "They have assault rifles. I wonder how close a man with a pistol could get going up against them. You know, three of them against one of us. Then there's the stray bullets from the local police. How would you get in there?"

"There's still no excuse for not having a couple clips of real ammo." Bill Moore sat down in front of a computer.

"I agree," Marty said. He watched the video monitors until Moore got up and crossed the room. Realizing this might be the big moment when he cracked the Rose case, he sat down at a computer, found the search engine, then entered the name George Harrington. A list of files came up on the screen.

Moore was suddenly back, sitting at the workstation next to Marty. "We should carry rifle-launched grenades. Blast these bastards to hell."

"At least M-24s."

"Huh?"

"The Remington sniper rifle. It's good up to a 1000 meters. With a teflon-coated full-metal jacket, they wouldn't know what hit them."

Jabbing a finger, Moore said, "We've got to get those."

"Well, yeah. One agent with the correct rifle, and this would be over."

Moore shook his head and grumbled, then went back to keyboarding.

Staying at the computer, Marty traced Harrington to his supervisor. He worked for Commander Krocker, the head of the Behavioral Sciences Unit at the Quantico Training Station. Marty printed the data.

"Ah, no," Moore said when the moderator from Garden Grove reported the agent at the site of the robbery had been hit. He left Marty and went over to a group of men siting around an oval situation table.

Marty couldn't worry about that. For him, the FBI was the perpetrator. And here he was, hooked into their mainframe. Seizing the moment, he searched through the programs, looking for one that tied into the federal data highway. He found one called Interlink. He opened it, and was able to retrieve a system-manager override-program from the memory banks he rented on a Internet server in Maryland. That allowed him to search the high security computers at the Quantico Training Station. That was where this Krocker fellow worked.

He considered Monty Bradshaw downstairs, doing everything he could to stop Marty from entering the secure files. Fortunately, the cybersleuth could only trace Marty's entry no further than the FBI data portal where Marty was sitting. But there was a new problem. The search of the computers at Quantico showed that all information relating to Krocker was top secret.

Fine. Marty would hack into the high-security data bank. That shouldn't take much since he was sitting at a high-security portal. When he found Krocker's file, it had a single two-word statement: *Eyes Only*. That meant that the data on Krocker were so secret only those who absolutely needed to use it could see it.

That upset Marty. All this trouble, and he couldn't get anything on Harrington's boss.

He decided to look for information on himself.

There wasn't anything in the top secret files on Marty Price.

He tried the interagency files.

Nothing.

"His name was Sanchez," Agent Moore said, now back, looking over Marty's shoulder. "He's dead."

"Dead?" Marty said, faking disbelief.

"Yeah, what are you doing?"

"I'm looking up the file on a convict who sold body armor. I believe his stuff got to those guys in Garden Grove."

"Good idea," Moore said, going back to keyboarding. "How did you get on this case?"

"That's my old turf. I volunteered."

"I didn't know you could do that."

"You don't work for Krocker."

"Big Bad John…" Moore said without looking up.

When Marty found a page titled Command Search, he entered his own name in the blank and hit the button. The page faded and a new one opened. He found himself staring at his own picture. He flinched, thinking that Moore would see that it was him. Then he remembered his hair was dyed black and he was wearing a facial make-over.

He hit the print button. Within seconds, the printer spit out his entire file.

He thought for a moment. Here he was on the FBI computer. Couldn't he test Johnston's I.D.? See if it was still valid? After all, he might have to use it again to get out of the building.

He made a search for the Hoover motor pool and found that this workstation allowed him to check out a car. If he could get an FBI car in Johnston's name, he figured, that would prove the I.D. was still good. Abiding by the prompts, he entered Johnston's name and I.D. number. It really shouldn't work, but – bingo. A Lincoln Towncar waited for him in the basement.

He chuckled. Considering the slow pace the government moved, it would be a week or two before the data on Johnston's death would be entered into the computer system.

Too bad it was dangerous sitting here. He'd like to find out what else he could do with Johnston's badge. But no. What he really needed was somewhere out of the way to study the files he'd downloaded and make an action plan.

Marty took the printouts and followed an agent out the door and into the low-level security area. He wandered the halls until he turned into the outdoor courtyard which filled the inner section of the Hoover Building. The sun was shining, and it felt like a refuge from the cold world. Sitting in a plastic chair, he looked at the picture of his own face staring back at him.

Momentarily, he laughed.

Was this really happening?

11

"I don't care if you have to carry the package yourself," Krocker roared into the phone. "I want it here at my office in the morning." When the Fed Ex employee didn't respond, he added, "Thank you for your help," then he clicked off.

He knew he should have waited last week in Azerbaidzhan for the final processing of the new drug, not have it sent in the mail. Hell, the package could get lost. At least he was able to pick up the portable memory eraser.

He felt the warm rush of an epiphany. He could use the Eraser on Harrington and Walters, then no one in the states would know about it. And after he erased the memories that cluttered their minds, they would act like new hires. Dedicated. Put in extra hours. Help him to button down the Company and get it to run efficiently like the army.

At the door, he paused and looked back at the computer. He had so many projects it was hard to keep track of them all. At least the new mind-control drug was on its way. It was far more astounding than the portable Eraser, so astounding he called it the *God Rx.* It had been mailed Thursday from Azerbaidzhan. Did he tell anyone in the U.S. about it? He didn't think so. If he had, they would have to be silenced.

He shut the door. Thinking about the new drug, he smiled and danced a little Two Step as he went down the hall, happy that – *finally!* – the mother of all mind-fucks was coming online.

Forty miles away, Marty took a quick glance at his picture on the front of the FBI file, then turned to the next page where the narrative started. It talked about his background and his detective work in L.A. He scanned though the rest of it. It was old stuff, centering around a brief investigation made on him by the FBI before he was hired by the Commerce Committee. The last page turned to recent material, saying that he had been approved by the Metro Police Department to carry a concealed weapon to all the Inaugural functions. Finally, there was a log note which said the file had been accessed that morning, followed by an absurd statement: *10 Most Wanted.*

"That's ridiculous!" Marty exclaimed. "You can't put 10 Most Wanted in someone's file without some explanation."

"What's that?" said a black woman with soft eyes, oval face, and understanding smile. Middle-aged, she sat on a bench beyond the flower planter next to Marty.

"Look at this," he said. Getting up and trying to maintain his cool, he handed the document to her. "This guy made the 10 Most Wanted List, but there is no mention of a crime being committed."

"Quantico," she said in a quick, self-assured fashion.

"Waddaya mean?" Marty grumbled.

"I can't tell you how often this happens. They think they're so far above the rest of us down there they don't believe they have to follow guidelines. I'd send it back to them."

"And how do I do that?"

"I have my secretary handle it."

Marty's eyes slipped down to her badge. She was Claire B. Wilson, Deputy Director of Information Technology. Marty gulped. If there was anyone who could bust him for falsely portraying himself as a federal officer, it was Claire. Recovering his breezy demeanor, Marty said, "How did you know that's what was happening?"

"The code on the printout. It tells all." She pointed. "C-J-K … Q-V." She laughed. "That fool again."

Brows raised, Marty shrugged. "What fool?"

"Krocker."

"Marty looked at the document. "Huh?"

"Commander John Krocker at Quantico, Virginia."

"Oh, I get it."

She took that last page of the document. "I'll get it fixed."

"Thanks."

Marty wished he had the courage to tell the whole story. The tone of understanding in Claire's voice told him she was a kind woman. She would listen. And if she was brave enough to call John Krocker a fool, surely she'd be courageous enough to get Marty's story a hearing. Why not go with her and tell her everything?

Something on the document caught Claire's eye. Brow raised, she studied Marty. "Are you on this case?"

He didn't know what else to do but nod.

"No respect." Her head shook with anger. "Can you imagine this guy shooting an FBI agent right here in the District?"

"How did you know that?" Marty said.

"The grapevine."

"Really?"

"I heard something came down at the Riverview. This has got to be the man." Claire stood. "He's as good as dead."

"No kidding," Marty agreed.

He watched her leave, thinking it was funny, almost. In a so-called Information Age, all you had to do was switch the data, and reality changed. Look at Claire. She was ready to join Krocker's manhunt to kill Marty, but he hadn't done anything. Just think what it would be like after Krocker's data-doctoring played the six o'clock news. School kids would clamor for Marty's execution. At least he knew what he was up against. Big John had accused him of killing Tucker Johnston. That's what it had to be.

He stood, thinking he would go to the bar up the street, have a drink and consider his next move. His hand was on the glass door of the arboretum when his phone rang. "Marty here," he mumbled, taking the call.

"God damn, it's good to hear your voice!"

When he spoke, Marty's words came out meekly, squeaking like a mouse. "Jack?"

"You're not going to believe this –"

"No, I'm not."

"Good one, Marty! Always the first one to the draw. Listen, I'm at Southeast Community Hospital. I was shot by a robber."

"Not by a fed?" Marty interrupted.

Jack howled at what he took to be a joke. "Hey, chock up two for you. Listen. I was hit so hard I don't remember what I was doing in DC. All I can think of is that I was making a surprise visit to see you. You still with Lisa? I've been praying that it would work out for you two ever since I ... well, it's a long story. My memory's a little off. Where are you? In DC?"

"I'm at FBI headquarters," he said. "I came to turn myself in."

Jack hooted for quite a while on that one. When he finally came back on the line, he explained he was on painkillers and his emotions were amplified, but dammit, he didn't remember Marty's jokes being so funny.

Marty turned towards the plastic chairs and sat down. "How's the business out in L.A. going?"

"Fantastic. I was, ah ... working on a tough case, and I dumped it to get some, er, distance. A vacation. You know, fight the burnout before it takes you down. I hope my memory returns like the doctor said. At least I was able to remember your phone number. What's up with you?"

Something in what Jack had said reminded Marty of his conversation with David Rose. Peeved now, Marty said, "I tried to find out who killed you, but now you're not dead."

Jack was suddenly sober. "I'm not following this."

Marty explained that it was a joke, then switched the conversation to old times. When he said he would head on over to Southeast General that evening, Jack said, "Great."

"I'll be there, you can count on it." Marty thought for a second, then added, "I was going to call you. I heard someone in L.A. had shot you."

"Well, yeah, the people got away. When it happened again here, I talked to God, I'm telling you. That's all that saved me."

To Marty, Jack sounded like he had a selective-memory problem. Like he'd been traumatized and couldn't remember what had happened in DC, but he was clearly lying about LA and about the crook who shot him getting away. Had he been threatened like Rose to keep his mouth shut? It sounded like it. Marty better not push it until he recovered. "I wish you would have called," he said, "when you ran into crap back home."

"I came out to talk instead."

"I'm honored. I'll come by tonight, if that works for you."

Jack laughed. "I'm not going anywhere."

"I have to run right now. But hey, I've got an idea. When you get out we'll go listen to some jazz, maybe go eat at the Riverview. Remember the last time we were there?"

"The place on the river, we ... that was years ago. You hadn't met Lisa, yet. I don't remember what happened."

"It doesn't matter. I'll see you tonight."

"Great."

Marty clicked off and put the phone in his pocket. Things were falling into their own strange place. Jack had lost the parts of his memories that pertained to the case. It was the recent stuff, even the shooting at the Riverview. Almost like he'd had a seizure. It couldn't be a concussion. No, Marty had talked to enough traumatized clients and forensic experts to know how a person reacted to a concussion. They were vague about everything. Not selective in their memory, like Jack. He guessed that the FBI had taken Jack to Quantico, not the injured agent, and they had questioned him, then used an electroshock device to stimulate a seizure and blot out recent memories. And now, they would be threatening him – probably to kill Cheryl – so he wasn't going to acknowledge that they shot him in LA. Surely he remembered that. Nor would he talk about the theft of the patents, either. That would be like signing his death warrant.

The driver hit the gas peddle, and the Ford Excursion command vehicle swung around a diesel rig, then drifted into slow lane, heading north on Highway 395 towards the Capitol. In the back seat, Krocker had Harrington on the phone. "Where in DC would the bastard be hiding?"

"We'll figure it out," Harrington said.

"What about his e-cam?" Krocker asked. "Did you get to his data base?"

"Not yet, but we're using the Carnivore program to trace his e-mail. We'll retrieve everything he sent."

"How much information do you think he has on us?"

"We have to believe he knows everything that Watson knew, and more by now. He's had a day to dig into it."

Krocker glanced east across the Potomac River into Maryland and let his eyes drift along the cut of the tree line. "I don't trust Archer's competence on this; he's too kicked back. Did you check Watson out yourself?"

"I stopped by the hospital and talked to him," Harrington said. "Watson didn't even know why he was in Washington."

"Did you remind him that the girlfriend dies if he talks about the Rose case?"

"Yeah, I did that. I also put Eric and Carl on Price's case. They said they're going to bring his head to you on a platter."

Krocker winced. Eric and Carl were young, but they were dedicated free agents, and they looked up to him. It reminded Krocker that he had a mentor once. That was Lieutenant Colonel Patrick McCool, the burly, red-haired Irishman whose ancestors had been fighters for the last ten generations. McCool had been Krocker's boss at Fort Bragg, and he was the one who forced Krocker to master the use of the computer, saying that war was going high-tech. The two had been called up for the police operation in Panama, with McCool leading the team assigned to track and apprehend the dictator. A major drug lord, the despot was on the lamb, hiding somewhere outside of Panama City when they arrived. Krocker immediately went to the dictator's hometown and forced confessions out of people until he got enough information to round up a group of political insiders. Soon Krocker had a dozen of them at a hacienda. Tied into chairs and gagged, they were about to watch each other be tortured if they didn't tell where the dictator was hiding. After seeing Krocker slice a man's finger off his hand, one man, a banker in a white dress shirt, was willing to tell all. He gave Krocker directions where to go, and he said he would call off the guards, so Krocker could get into the dictator's hideout without a fight. Krocker called McCool, who came in with another translator to listen as the gentleman make the phone call. That's when the whole thing fell apart. In the swiftest move Krocker had ever seen, the banker pulled a gun from his boot and shot McCool between the eyes. An Army private nailed the banker as Krocker went into a rage, shooting the rest of the men.

Over the years, Krocker had obsessively relived that incident again and again until he accepted responsibility for McCool's death. If Krocker had exercised more control over the troops, the banker would have been searched more thoroughly and the gun would have been discovered. Krocker eventually quit the Army, but he always remembered the hard lesson.

Control.

That was at the heart of a good operation, a good organization, a good life.

"You there?" Harrington said, over the line.

"Yeah," Krocker said, coming out of his thoughts. "Get back to me if something turns up."

No respect!

Claire's words shot through Marty's mind like lead from a hot gun. It left him wondering how he could possibly be blamed for killing an agent. He guessed the story would say that Tucker Johnston had gone to the Riverview for dinner, and Marty shot him in cold blood.

But the damn thing was, Marty was there when Jack shot Tucker Johnston. And he didn't have an alibi because Jack didn't remember. On the other hand, Krocker had figured out that Jack had given the lead on the case to Marty; that was why Krocker had set him up. Now they could justify shooting Marty when they caught him, and people like Claire would say, good riddance. And there wasn't anything Marty could do to stop them.

Still in the patio at the Hoover Building, he grabbed the picture of Krocker from the stack of printouts. He was the commander of the Behavioral Sciences Institute at Quantico. What a front. As an officer, he had the people on the cutting edge of police science doing projects for him. Like stealing energy patents so the traditional energy producers could charge higher prices.

Or – wait a minute. Let's suppose Jack's theory was wrong. The government could be stealing high-tech machinery for its own benefit. But why? The feds had their own high-tech firm that bought and sold research data in Silicon Valley. It didn't need to steal anything. The thefts only made sense in the context of the commander's team benefitting from it themselves.

He felt his gun under his coat and considered paying Krocker a visit. Thugs like the commander didn't scare him. Anyone could stare this type of sociopath down if you remembered to keep your self-respect and not to give in to the intimidation.

His thoughts turned to the gangster case he cracked in L.A. He had arrived at the walled, palm-tree-studded estate off Wilshire via the trunk of a sedan. He had been stuffed in there by a gang of men in natty suits who worked for the drug king, Teun Vanderbraak. He was the West Coast boss of European designer drugs, ones like Ecstasy. When they dragged Marty before Vanderbraak and threw him on the concrete deck of the Olympic-sized pool, none of the sunbathers bothered to turn. You didn't watch the king do business, you simply followed orders.

Sitting under a sun shade, the spindly-built Vanderbraak told Marty to stand.

Marty got up.

Vanderbraak lit an oval-shaped cigarette. "You fucked up."

Marty bit his lip.

Vanderbraak said, "How did you get into our computers?"

Marty said, "Just hacking. I found a backdoor."

Vanderbraak blew a smoke ring. "And now what are you going to do?"

Marty shrugged.

Vanderbraak held out his hands palms up. "We could pour hot oil on your face while you think about it."

Marty had heard of a victim profile from the L.A.P.D. Someone was torturing people with hot oil, then leaving the bodies in dumpsters. He knew that's what Teun had planned for him. "I messed up. How can I make it up to you?"

Vanderbraak said, "Tell me who the pimp was who snitched on me."

The sun was suddenly hot; the breeze, cool; the scent of the eucalyptus, sweet. And Marty heard the voice of his martial arts instructor saying: *It's not about odds, it's about seizing the perfect moment.*

Marty stood humbly before Vanderbraak and said, "You'll never guess who it was."

Teun blew a smoke ring. "Surprise me."

Marty smiled, then jump-kicked to the side, whacking the nearest guard in the throat. Dropping to the ground, Marty rolled behind the drug king.

The other guards had a choice of running to grab Marty or risk shooting their boss as they fired past him.

While they charged, Marty grabbed Vanderbraak's head and jerked it so fast the neck cracked. Then he slammed both fists to the side of the drug king's skull, and his eyes popped out of their sockets.

None of them could have imaged that someone so powerful could die so quickly by the hands of someone who appeared so meek. In the frenzy that followed, Marty seized the moment and picked up the downed guard's gun. He shot one gangster and the rest scattered. And while the guests scrambled for their cars and roared off, Marty walked tall under the hot-noon sun, out the gate, and up the boulevard.

After that experience, he never wanted to face pure hell again. And sure, maybe it was good for him, getting him to move and settle in Washington, away from the site of the ordeal where punks would challenge him to test their mettle against the guy who killed the king. Making the move, after all, caused him to meet Lisa. But still, the thought of being humiliated didn't scare him after the experience in L.A. When someone wouldn't get out of your face no matter what, you settled it with the jerk. You didn't go beg the police. No, you fixed it yourself.

12

"I have a car here somewhere," Marty said to the woman behind the counter at motor pool in the Hoover Building.

The bright-eyed attendant said, "What is the name?"

"Tucker Johnston," Marty said.

She glanced at his I.D., then entered some information into the computer and handed him a set of keys. "The car's in space B-5 in back."

Marty took the keys and headed into the waffled-concrete dungeon below the Hoover Building. He discovered the car was a brown Lincoln. He got in and adjusted the deep, comfortable seat. He drove up the concrete ramp and waited for the guard to lower the iron blockade down into the pavement. Out on Pennsylvania Avenue, the first thing he wanted to do was get the putty off his face. He was tried of the itching, and tired of not being Marty Price. But he left the disguise on and headed for his office. He needed to get his things out of his car.

Crossing Rock Creek on M Street, he rolled down the windows and was caressed by the cool breeze. In the park below, trees glistened where the sun met the droplets of freshly-fallen rain. It was a glorious day. Why not go up the freeway ramp, head off into the wilds of Virginia, and keep driving?

Great idea, except for one thing – Krocker.

Underneath the expressway that passed over K Street, he found a parking space near his car. His security system hadn't been tripped, which assured him that the vehicle hadn't been tampered with. He knew it was risky getting his computer and his tool kit from the car, but he needed them to carry out his plan. His idea was to search Harrington's home, and he wanted to break into Krocker's office too. Experience had shown him that security was sloppy in any police agency, and there would be some piece of evidence somewhere that could clear him. Yet he also knew that eventually the government would close ranks around Krocker's story. The fable of Marty being a murderer would be an established fact once it played on TV. Television established its own truth.

But why hadn't Krocker filled in the information about Johnston and released the false case against Marty? Could it be that first he had to have

Marty in captivity in order to be certain he hadn't released any information that supported Jack's theory?

He thought about the contract signed by David Rose and the disk stating Jack's accusations. He would send the stuff to Derek Walker, but there weren't enough supportable accusations to make a case against Krocker. Anyone could write a contract. Besides, Rose would deny the whole thing. Still, the fact that Krocker was unwilling to accuse Marty of an specific crime when he put him on the 10 Most Wanted List suggested that there was significant data out there that could be used against the commander. In fact, it was almost as if Krocker had been in the process of entering Marty's data onto the federal system, accusing him of murdering Johnston, when he was interrupted by news of the video Marty had sent to the Post. Whatever happened, one thing was clear. Marty needed more facts on the case, and Harrington's was the place to start. Fortunately, the printout on Harrington from the FBI computer showed his home address.

But first, he headed around the corner to Starbucks. Once inside, he locked himself in the restroom and scraped the putty off his face. Afterwards he took a handful of liquid soap and washed his hair. He did that a couple more times until the dye was out. Finally, he left the restroom and stopped and celebrated life for a moment with a grande cappuccino.

Agent Harrington lived near the Richmond Mountain Estates in Fredericksburg, 50 miles south of the District. His house sat in a grass field surrounded by a tall, board fence. Marty parked in the drive before the gate with the flourescent-red, keep-out sign. He looked around. The closest neighbors were on the other side of the thicket of hickory and oaks he had passed getting through to Harrington's drive.

The dogs were barking now.

Picking up the sack of burgers he had purchased in town, Marty got out of the Lincoln and looked between the cracks in the fence. The house was a newer two-story middle-class home. Relentlessly symmetrical, it had shuttered windows stacked one above the other. In neo-Grecian revival tradition, a gabbled portico jutted from the roof and was supported by tall, white pilasters. Under that, on the porch, a smaller set of columns supported a transom above the door. There was an attached two-car garage that had a room overhead with a dormer on the roof. No vehicles where visible, but a pack of dogs waited inside the fence.

Going to the trunk, he got out his black sports bag. At the gate, he took out his picks and fiddled with the lock until it came undone. Then he opened it a crack.

"You cute little babies," he said with sugar-coated words as the Rottweilers snarled and fought with the gate, trying to push it open so they could get to him.

"That's no way to treat your Uncle Marty." He reached into the sack for a burger. He didn't know if it was the cheese or the special sauce, but he knew from experience that no dog could resist. In fact, burgers were so reliable in calming canines that he took them to every house he planned to search. If there wasn't a dog, he could eat a burger for lunch.

Taking a cheeseburger out of the sack, he held it up to the opening in the gate. Growls. Dogs spinning in circles. No takers.

He threw the burger over the fence.

While one of the dogs backed off and ate it, the others kept yipping.

Taking out a second burger and tossing it over the fence, he wondered why people starved guard dogs. Couldn't they see that it was a setup? But then again, you'd have to be crazy to walk into a yard with four of them. A guy could fight one, but not that many.

"Shut up!" Marty growled, stuffing another burger though the fence.

The smaller dogs backed up and watched the largest one eat.

Marty pulled out yet another burger and threw it to the dogs. Then opening the gate, he set the last burger in front of the biggest dog.

It glared at him.

He reached down and picked up the burger.

The dog jumped up on him, going for the snack.

Marty stuffed the sandwich into the dog's mouth, then headed for the house.

It was obvious that Harrington was hiding something. Why else would there be a tall fence, dogs, and an infrared security system?

Thanking heaven for the little things, Marty was glad that over the years he had watched Jack disable a dozen of these alarms. You started by disconnecting the phone line, so a signal couldn't be sent to the security company. Then you searched for an alarm speaker poking out from under an eve, and you cut the wires.

When he finally got inside, he made a quick search of the house, looking through the office, the upstairs bedrooms, the family room, the kitchen, and the garage for obvious clues that Harrington knew something about stealing patients. But there were no strange devices, no piles of computer disks, no papers, nothing. In fact, there wasn't anything which indicated that a larger treasure was hidden nearby. About all he learned was that Harrington lived alone.

He could have cursed, but instead, he retraced his steps, looking for clues. The carpet on the floor approaching the closet in the master bedroom was worn. Marty went inside and rapped on the walls, looking for hidden compartments. Not finding anything, he searched some more, looking behind pictures for wall safes, and pulling back rugs to see if there were trap doors. In the living room, a massive coffee table sat between a sofa and love seat. The sides of the table were completely covered with wood. He rapped on them. One end sounded like a drum when he hit it. He fiddled about until the end lifted straight up. Inside was a hollow shell with a floor. A grey metal safe sat there. It looked to weigh well over a hundred pounds. Marty realized he could spend the rest of the afternoon cracking it, or tear the rest of the house apart.

He noticed a tubular roll of paper on the bottom of the cabinet next to the safe. It was obviously too long to fit inside without bending it. He figured it had been tossed there until Harrington could find a better place for it.

Marty unrolled the paper across the top of the table and discovered blueprints for retrofitting a two-story building. He smiled when he noticed that the basement of the building was labeled *Heaven*. That was when he caught an address. The building was located in Widewater Beach, VA. That was maybe a twenty-minute drive from Harrington's home. This could be his big lead. He had to go for it. Otherwise, he could spend the rest of the day bucking the tide, trying to crack the safe, taking the chance Harrington would drive up – when he probably had already discovered gold.

Widewater Beach sat on a verdant peninsula of land. On one side, the Potomac rolled past. The other side formed the northeast shore of Aquia Bay. Fort McLean sat proudly across the waters on the far southern side of the inlet. The address from the blueprints revealed a gravel drive leading into a thick, deciduous forest. The road was marked *Private*, which was typical for this area.

Gun on the car seat, Marty drove up the drive. He had gone a quarter mile when he came to a cyclone fence with barbed wire on top. He couldn't help notice the similarity of this fence to the one at the U.S. government's Midway Research Station, which he had passed five miles back along the highway. That facility had signs indicating its name. The Widewater facility had none. It didn't surprise him. He had called the county assessor on the way over. A clerk had told him this was not a federal facility, but rather, the property was owned by a company named American Chemical with an address in Baku, Azerbaidzhan. Marty's first thought was that this was a front-organization to do the FBI's bidding, maybe its research. But he wouldn't know for sure until he got inside.

He stopped the car at the heavy iron gate. Past the fence, the road curved into the trees. He thought about climbing over the barrier and scouting around, but he would be setting himself up if he left the car here. To hide it, he would have to go back a mile or two to the train tracks and put the car in the bushes.

He put the car in reverse, but stopped and stared at the card-lock outside the driver's window. On a hunch, he pulled up close and took out Johnston's wallet. There were several cards inside. One had caught Marty's attention. It was made of red plastic, but there wasn't any writing on it. He guessed it had a programmable computer chip embedded in the plastic and was used for a private facility, maybe to open a security gate on a condominium. Or maybe this gate.

He hit the button for the window and slid the plastic card through the card-reader.

A light flashed green and the gate cranked back out of the way.

Got it!

He put the car in gear and headed up the drive. He nearly choked when he saw a man passing through the bushes. Burly built, he carried a black assault rifle in one hand, and held back a pair of tracking hounds by a leash in the other. Inspecting the parameter of the fence, he didn't turn to look at Marty. Or if he had, he had already looked, and Marty hadn't seen him do it.

With the gate closing behind him, Marty slowly blew out his breath, calming himself. If the guard wasn't concerned, then Marty must have passed inspection with his ability to get through the gate. Now he needed to appear as one of them. Whoever they were.

He drove until there was a break in the forest. Across the open field stood a two-story unpainted concrete building. It had the look of a small factory. There was an entrance at one end, next to a gravel parking lot. He parked, stuffed his gun under his coat, and got out. Heading for the entrance, he carried his black bag containing his laptop computer and his breaking-and-entering tools.

A man with a scowl suddenly pushed through the door of the building. He had bushy eyebrows and a thick mustache. Behind him was a man with a beard and an untamed crop of gray hair. The man in the rear seemed to be pleading with the other man. But Marty couldn't tell what was happening because they were speaking a foreign language.

Before the men said anything to him, Marty asked, "Harrington here yet?"

"No," said the man with the gray hair. He continued to follow the other man, and together they got into sedan.

Marty kept walking. Next to the gray metal door, there was another card-lock on the wall. He inserted Johnston's plastic security card and heard a faint click, then headed into the door.

Inside, the industrial-concrete façade ended. The foyer was covered with polished pink-and-white marble. A grandiose chandelier hung overhead. Marty went for the elevator. When the door opened, he entered and hit the second floor button, intending to find the boss's office. That was always on the top floor.

The elevator doors sprung back, and Marty stepped out onto the thick red carpet. He walked past a nook with a sofa and house plants, and went on up the hall. At the far end, he listened for sounds, but didn't hear anything.

There were card slots on every door, similar to those that took plastic hotel keys. He inserted Johnston's plastic card in the last door. Nothing happened. He went to the next door. When he tried the same thing, it opened. He looked inside. A man dressed in a white lab coat sat at a computer workstation entering data on the keyboard. On the desk was a gold-plated model of a Bentley along with a stack of technical books.

The man looked over the top of his reading glasses. "Can I help you?" he said.

"Harrington said to meet him here," Marty said. "Have you seen him?"

The man pointed at the left wall. "Up the hall," he said, going back to work.

Marty shut the door.

Feeling lucky, he went to the next office. The door opened, and no one was inside. He went to the computer. He tried to access it, hoping to find something to use to nail the FBI and get back out of here before Harrington and Krocker caught up with him.

When the computer didn't respond, Marty realized he could spend precious time hacking into it, or he could keep moving. Deciding to keep going, he pulled open a closet door. Inside was a coat, tie, and pair of jogging shoes. A gym bag contained toiletries. Marty figured they had a shower in the building.

He opened the other closet door. There was a legal briefcase with wheels on the bottom and pop-up pull-handle. He picked it up. It was heavy, seemingly fully loaded. Setting it on the workstation, he opened it and startled at seeing bundles of hundred-dollar bills.

He picked out a packet of money and thumbed through it. The cash was real.

He turned around, looking things over. What was the FBI doing with cash? It had to be an underground operation.

His eyes scanned the bookshelf. Something was wrong. He grabbed a book. It was written in Russian. That explained the two men out front of the building. It was obvious from the cut of their coats that they were part of the staff, not the janitors. In fact, they were probably nuclear scientists from the old Soviet Union, hired to do Krocker's bidding. The possibilities had Marty's thoughts swirling. If anyone knew what to do with the plans for the Hydrogen Accelerator, it would be them. But why would they leave a couple-hundred grand sitting in the closet? Did they feel this was a safe place to keep their money? Or maybe there were more Russians, and this was the payroll?

He knew the answers to his questions were hidden in the building, along with information that would explain what the Company did. But whatever it was, it was big time, and they would not go down without a fight.

Leaving the room, he grabbed the Russian's cell phone off the desk. He figured he could use it for a few hours without being worried about Krocker and the Company intercepting the calls. Surely they were tapped into his own cell by now.

When he entered the next office, an orange CD case caught his attention. It sat on a workstation next to a computer. He picked it up and looked inside.

Nothing.

The computer had a CD burner. Marty pressed the button for the disk-writer and a CD popped out. He put it in the case and put the case into his bag.

Reaching over on the desk, he picked up what he took to be a black camera bag with an attached carrying strap. He pulled back the velcro top and discovered batteries and a charger cord, along with a silver case. The case clipped shut on the side and opened like a book. He unlatched it. There was a keyboard on one side; on the other was a small computer screen. When it was clipped shut, the surface area of the case was a somewhat larger than the size of a palmtop computer, and about twice as thick. Interestingly, the keyboard folded open and out on either side, and when extended, it was nearly the size of one found on a notebook computer. He figured the device was a new rendition of the personal digital assistant so popular on the market. But it looked foreign-made, something that belonged to the Russians. When he saw that one end had Universal Service Bus plugs, and the other a wireless modem and a connection for a satellite downlink, he realized it was a high-tech PDA, something in the experimental stage. There wasn't anything like it available on the market.

Marty glanced around. A sleek, gold-gilded statue of a naked woman sat in the corner. An impressionistic painting hung on the wall. There was a certain elegance about the room. It had to be where the boss worked. Maybe he downloaded files onto the palmtop? Realizing that the handheld could unlock the key to the Company puzzle, he put it in his bag.

Marty pulled open the desk drawers looking for something to identify the person who used the room. There wasn't anything with a name on it. But in the bottom drawer there was a strap-on pistol. He figured it attached to the wrist so it could be hidden under a coat. It fired by hitting the side of pistol with the palm of the opposed hand. Made of non-metallic material, it was a weapon that could get though metal-detection machines at an airport. He cocked it, then snapped the trigger. Interestingly, an auxiliary barrel – passing over and around the regular barrel – extended forward when it fired. That would get it past the end of the coat sleeve so it wouldn't get hung up when it fired. A very deadly weapon, he realized, and put it in his bag.

Hand on the doorknob, he considered his options. He knew he had pressed his luck a long way and had to hurry and get off the premises. But perhaps this was his day to die. If that was so, he wanted to go to the basement and see Heaven. That's what it had said on the plans for the building. Heaven was in the basement.

Hoping there would be a shoot-out, Mack Johnson tooled the bulky Ford Excursion command vehicle on a holding pattern around the golf course at Tidal Basin, listening to a country music station. Buddy Young sat beside him, fiddling with a pistol. In the back seat, Commander Krocker watched the computer screen on his operations consol. The phone rang and the commander reached for the receiver.

"Krocker here."

The voice was sarcastic. "You've got a dead man driving an Agency car ... just so you know it."

Recognizing Harrington's voice, Krocker said, "What the hell are you talking about?"

"Tucker. He's out driving around. Is that spooky, or what?"

"How?"

Harrington said over the line, "Somebody checked out a car from the Hoover pool in Tucker's name, and he is out in the field."

Krocker mumbled, "I didn't order it. Where's the car?"

"Near the annex."

Krocker hit a button on the computer attached to the command consol. Federal security vehicles had transmitters in their trunks which allowed them to be located by a global positioning system. The monitor immediately displayed a multi-colored map of DC. Blinking blue dots showed the locations of the Bureau's on-duty cars. There were two vehicles assigned to Krocker stationed in Northwest Washington. One at Price's office; one at his house. A half-dozen cars doing regular FBI business were spread across the city. He clicked on the zoom-out symbol, and the map became more condensed, taking in a larger view of the Metro area. There was a blinking light in Widewater, below Quantico. "Do you think it's one of us, or some kind of a computer glitch?"

"My take on it is that it's live, not a data figment," Harrington said.

Krocker stared off into the broad blue waters of the confluence of the Potomac and the Anacostia Rivers. There were a dozen pleasure boats heading in and out of the harbor. "Where are you?"

"You sent me back to Quantico, remember?"

"Track it down and see who is using Johnston's I.D. Be careful. It may be another agency trying to rough us up."

"And if that's the case?"

"Find out what they have on us," he said, "then make them forget they met you."

"All right. You think it has something do to with Senator Stanton taking an interest in our adventure at the Riverview?"

"That's why we have to talk to whomever is in the car in order to rule Stanton out."

"What if they're really on to us? Know everything about the Company?"

"It's spring. Heart attacks are in season." Krocker knew Harrington would take that to mean he should hit the guy on the neck with the END device. Set at the right pulse and wattage, the END device would interrupt the brain's electrical transmissions as they passed through the brain stem on the back of the neck. When the brain stem faltered, so would the autonomous nervous system, including the heart and the lungs. It made for a perfect imitation of a heart attack.

Harrington chuckled. "I thought that was your job."

"See who it is," Krocker said, "then get back to me."

"Got it."

Getting out of the elevator in the basement, Marty faced a single metal door. Slipping the plastic card into the lock, he opened it. Inside was a small white room with a glass see-through wall. Beyond the glass were stacks of integrated computer components which reached all the way to the ceiling.

He went to the counter top where a standard ergonomic keyboard sat before a couple of over-sized monitors. He wasn't intimidated. Working data-fraud cases had put him in the driver seat of a dozen big corporate frames. He pressed some keys. Nothing happened.

He felt around, searching for computer jacks, someplace to tie into the mainframe. He found a metal strip on the back edge of the counter top that could be folded up. Inside was a hollow space with a half-dozen different types of jacks for data devices.

He opened his black bag and pulled out the laptop computer that he had brought from home. He connected it into the system though a USB jack. He fiddled for a few minutes, but the mainframe wouldn't respond.

Deciding to hurry things up, he unplugged the laptop and headed inside the door where the mainframe components were stacked. He pulled off panels, searching for a jack to plug straight into the heart of the computer's wiring. Disconnecting a wire, he plugged the laptop into its place. He tested the connection and discovered he had an output port. He tried a few more.

No luck.

He changed programs and tried again to enter the mainframe's data highway.

Nothing.

He tried another program.

Same response.

Finally, he got lucky plugging into a bus which allowed him to enter and receive data. Free to move as he pleased, he roamed the system. Getting into the directory, he discovered that there were a number of networks tied into this computer. The Crays in the basement of the Pentagon. The FBI machines in the Hoover Building. Army Intelligence. A dozen more.

It made no sense. This computer should be a subunit of the FBI network, not the FBI master operations unit.

Then he had an epiphany. This computer, called Heaven, was poaching on several of the U.S. computer networks. He bet no one outside Harrington's group of employees knew about it. That meant that Harrington and his Company were acting outside the oversight of the U.S. government. If that was true, then Jack was wrong. It wasn't the FBI stealing high-tech devices, but Harrington and Krocker. They were doing it to build machines like this.

He found the computer log and requested that the mainframe show him the current operations in progress.

Heaven responded. There were two workstations running electronic design programs. He figured those people were here in the building. He noticed that the Interlink program was being used in the field to access the FBI network. Another unit, vehicle 513, was receiving information through Heaven from the federal GPS locating system.

Still connected to Heaven via his laptop computer, Marty delved deeper and connected into the federal geographic positioning system. A map of Metropolitan Washington came on screen. Circular blue, white, and orange lights blinked, indicating where various federal security patrols were located.

He moved the locator closer to Widewater. A car was about fifteen miles out from the facility. He clicked on it. It was number 513. He went to options and found the tie-in to the FBI motor pool. Car 513 was checked out to Harrington. Hell, the bastard would be there any minute.

He clicked on car 478. It was already at Widewater Beach. He tied into the FBI machines and found that Johnston had that car.

Great. Marty was posing as Johnston and using the car checked out in his name. And Harrington was coming because he had traced it to this location.

Time to leave.

But first –

He glanced about at the mainframe. How could he make access to Heaven when he had left the building?

On a hunch, he pulled out the high-tech palmtop computer which he had stolen from the office upstairs. Folding out its keyboard, he turned it on, thinking it could have a wireless link to Heaven.

He searched the mainframe for active links. There were six. He figured he and Harrington were two of them. He guessed the other person tied into Heaven with the Interlink program was Krocker. There were two people doing science work in the building. That made five connections. The last link might be the personal digital assistant. With his own laptop, he sent an instant message to the unknown sixth connection. The high-tech palmtop responded, showing the message he had sent.

Wow!

Now working on the palmtop, he explored its functions. It couldn't do much of anything on its own. But it could broadcast and receive data over a wireless modem, and that link tied directly into Heaven. That meant the palmtop was really a remote control station for the mainframe.

Pay dirt.

He could take the personal digital assistant with him and stay in touch with Heaven. Then he could connect to her when he needed more information about the government. Believing that the palmtop's commands could override the programmer's commands from the keyboard at the workstation out front, he gave the mainframe the command to shut down all the other links to the mainframe.

In response, the screen on his own personal laptop computer when blank.

He walked out front and found that the workstation monitor had shut down too.

Back on the Company's palmtop, he told Heaven to restore the links.

The screen on the workstation lit up with information from the mainframe. That showed him that the palmtop was indeed controlling Heaven, and that he had suddenly become the final arbiter on who would use her because he possessed the PDA. Making sure he wouldn't lose that control, he set up a new programmer's entry code – *Stargazer* – then packed up and headed towards the door.

13

Leading with his pistol, Marty stepped out of the stairwell and into the foyer.

No Harrington. Nothing but glitter.

He crept to the window and looked across the Widewater facility.

No one outside. No new cars in the lot.

He gripped his pistol hard, then opened the door and hustled to the Towncar. He got in, started it up, and headed down the long drive. After breaking through the trees, he reached the gate and slid Tucker's plastic key into the card-lock.

The gate slid back.

"Don't move!" someone yelled, enforcing what they said with a sudden blast of a gun at close range.

The rear side-windows of the Towncar shattered.

Marty's body jolted like it had been hit with a power line.

Catching his breath, Marty turned to look. Harrington had stepped out of the bushes and was advancing. He pointed a stubby automatic rifle towards Marty's head.

"I said, don't move," Harrington bellowed. Weapon trained on Marty, he approached the car. "Give me the gun. Slow, no fast moves, or you're dead."

Marty tossed his gun out the window.

Harrington picked up the pistol and stuck it in his belt. His automatic trained on Marty, he crossed the front of the car, as if he were intent on going around and getting into the passenger seat.

The breeze blew through the window, boasting the sweet scent of spring.

Marty cringed at the irony: The birth of life wafting so close to impending death.

You don't have nine lives.

His thoughts racing on fast-forward, Marty focused on something he'd heard years ago, back when he started out as a P.I. It was his weapon's instructor, telling him that you don't get a second chance if you miss the perpetrator on the first shot. It's not like the movies. You've got one take. Then it's his turn to nail you.

Marty slammed his foot onto the gas pedal, and at the same instant, he forced his upper body down onto the passenger seat.

The Lincoln shot forward as Harrington fired the automatic, blasting out the windshield and shredding the seat next to Marty's head.

Marty flexed all his muscles, bracing himself, holding his foot on the accelerator.

Bullets ripped though the back of the car.

Marty sat up. The car was off the road on the grass. He had knocked Harrington down, but he was lying on the ground, firing.

Marty took control of the wheel and spun out onto the driveway and raced away.

On the main thoroughfare, when he came to a fork in the road, he chose to drive parallel to the train tracks. He stopped at a crossing. It was blocked by a chain locked between two metal posts. There was a sign saying only authorized vehicles had permission to cross the tracks at this location. He rammed though the chain, snapping it. Then he crossed the tracks and drove up the gravel road. Where the trees thinned out, and there was only bush, he drove off the road into the thick cover.

Opening his bag, he took out the palmtop. He used it to tie into Heaven at the Company building. With the Interlink program, he got in the federal global position system and located Harrington's car. It was leaving the Company property, turning onto the main road, following Marty.

Now in the guts of the GPS program, he entered hypothetical information, so that on the federal locator system his car would appear to be moving up the road, heading towards Jefferson Davis Highway, despite the fact it was stuck in the bushes. Then he reprogrammed the GPS locating system to show that the Lincoln was continuing west for the next hour. Now when Krocker and Harrington looked for it, it would seem that Marty was taking a trip to Manassas, even though the car wasn't moving.

He relaxed back into the leather seat and decided to search for more information on Commander Krocker. Cruising through Heaven's files, he located a few which related to the commander. Surprisingly, none where labeled in such a way to lead Marty to believe there was a direct data-link between Heaven and Krocker's office at Quantico. That was odd. Or was it? If Krocker was in charge of the Company, he would have a secure computer, so secure even Heaven couldn't get into it without his permission.

Scanning the GPS program, he found that Krocker's command vehicle was leaving the District and heading south. He suspected that Harrington had contacted Krocker, and the two where attempting a pincer movement, going to trap Marty's vehicle as it moved west, not knowing they weren't following a real car, but a GPS data-ghost.

Looking at his own location, Marty saw that he was two miles from the nearest intersection. He got the name of the street, then pulled the Russian's cell phone out of his pocket and called information. The operator gave him the number of a local taxi company. He called and ordered a cab to pick him up at the intersection in thirty minutes.

With the breeze at his back, and the trees arching overhead, he walked along the highway and planned his next move. Now was the best time to get into Krocker's office. Only problem was Tucker Johnston's I.D. badge wouldn't get him in the gate at Quantico. Not after Harrington had caught up with him. He was still mulling over possibilities when he got to the intersection. After a few minutes, the taxi pulled up. He got in back.

"Where's the closest department store?" he asked.

"That would probably be Fredericksburg," said the driver, a slow-speaking, portly, middle-aged man.

"Any place nearby where I could buy tennis shoes? You know, so I can go jogging."

"There's a store in Dale City that'd probably have it."

Marty was hurried but hesitant. Dale City was close to Quantico, but was no more than a pit-stop for hungry tourists. He chose instead to backtrack to Fredericksburg.

On the trip over, Marty took the CD disk he had stolen from the Company and plugged it into his laptop. The first few files showed advanced computer components. Marty figured that these were data-devices that the covert organization had ripped off from the patent bureau. The next file showed a diagram of a mechanism that looked similar to an ink pen. But it wasn't for writing. Rather, press the button on the end, and it would send a laser beam that was intense enough to blind a person.

What was the mission of the Company? Killing people? He didn't think it had anything to do with taking energy devices off the market to prop up the traditional energy companies. No. These people where stealing high-technology and using it to further their own reign of terror.

He opened another file. Inside was a diagram of a tubular device, similar to a small flashlight. It generated a pulsating electrical charge. Called an electro neuron disruptor, or END device, it interrupted the electrical transmissions in the brain. Placed to the forehead, it would destroy short term memory. Set higher and pressed against the temple, it would stimulate a seizure. Set higher, it could cause blood vessels to rupture. If held to the back of a person's neck, it would cause a cardiopulmonary collapse similar to a heart attack.

What an insane device. But it explained a lot of things. Professor Rose had been hit with the END turned up to a high setting. His son was hit with a low setting. Same for Jack.

Fredericksburg sat on a vast cutaway in the broadleaf forest, fifty-five miles north of Richmond, Virginia. Home for many Marine families, it embodied the best of the South. People here knew they didn't need more government regulation, and they voted that way. But that didn't limit them. They had their own Broadway-style theater, a Montessori School, the beginnings of a computer-tech alley, and of course, the Virginia Running Shop. That was where Marty purchased a pair of Air Ride shoes and a jogging outfit.

Back in the taxi, Marty told the driver to head to Quantico Marine Base. On the way back to Interstate 95, he had a mini-aha experience, and had the driver stop at a department store. Inside, he bought a new cell phone. What better way to beat the wiretap Krocker had on his old number?

Back in the car, he programmed his old cell to forward calls to his new number. That way he could receive calls from the old number, read the caller I.D., hang up, then hit the missed call redial button on the new cell. Doing that, he would bypass the bug on the old phone and not lose any messages.

Would that work? he wondered. Not knowing, he decided to play it safe. Opening the palmtop computer, he tied into the program connecting the FBI to the local phone system. Finding that there was indeed a tap on his cell number, he disengaged it by rewriting the bugging program. From now on, the program could not accept Marty's old number, nor his new one, nor Lisa's.

Now he was ready to go to the FBI training station except for one thing. On the palmtop he brought up the Web page showing the 10 Most Wanted mug shots. His picture wasn't there. Great. That meant Krocker's case against Marty had stalled as it went through the proper channels. It also meant that Marty still had a few precious moments to built a case against Krocker.

Passing through the Marine Corp Outer Area west of the Jefferson Davis Highway, Marty asked to be dropped off at the Lunca Recreational Facility. It was a public outdoors center with a sky-blue lake, canoes, barbeque pits, and showers. Everything one needed to spend a refreshing afternoon in the midday sun forgetting about being too tough and too proud.

Marty paid the driver, then went into the dressing room and changed into his new jogging outfit. He didn't think about what he was doing. He had been to Quantico before. Had accompanied a marine to a demonstration on the small arms range. He had been inside the FBI Academy, too. It was just up the road. What he noted on those adventures was that wherever you went there were joggers. Now stepping out of the dressing room wearing his Air Ride shoes, he stuffed the palmtop computer in his pocket and suddenly became one of the team.

14

The FBI Training Station was shrouded behind a thick, green, broadleaf forest. A security shack sat on the medium of the roadway at the entrance. Cars were backed up, waiting behind a metal guard-arm. A woman was on duty. She wore a white, uniform-style shirt and black pants. A badge was clipped to her pocket, and a radio was strapped on her side. She was talking to the driver of the lead car.

Coming up the other side of the street, passing the cars, Marty jogged behind some women. He eyed the guard. She was ramrod straight, and she appeared to be handling security according to a formal procedure.

Pain … Agony … Hurt … Love-It …

The FBI motivation slogan played in Marty's thoughts. It was on a totem pole. He'd seen it last time he was here. Now, he concentrated on it to calm his mind, like one might chant a mantra:

Pain … (the women joggers turned up the heat and sprinted away from him)

Agony … (the guard turned to watch)

Hurt … ("let'smoveitslacker!" roared the guard, making fun of him)

Love it … (Marty waved as he ran though the gate)

Now fully into the role of a special agent, Marty caught up with the joggers and ran with them until finally taking a left and heading north. He stopped next to a towering, newly-constructed, tan building which sat on the red soil surrounded by freshly-planted shrubs. Hands on his knees, he bent over, catching his breath.

Wow!

The jogging scam worked.

He headed towards the information center, where he asked for the lost-and-found.

The woman smiled gracefully. "What did you lose?" she asked.

"A black bag," he replied, lying. "You know, the type with a strap."

"Like a gym bag?"

"Yes. Had it in the taxi, set it down somewhere."

She went in the back office and came out with a hefty nylon bag.

"All right," he said, seeing the bag. It wasn't his, but maybe it contained some clothes.

The woman handed it to him.

He left the building and entered the next one, a multi-floored, tan-and-white structure that could have been a corporate office or sat on a college campus. Inside, he found the men's room and went into a stall. He whipped out the contents of the bag and found a pair of pants. They where too long, but a light blue cotton shirt with button-down collar was his size.

He pulled off his T-shirt and went to the sink and washed off the sweat from the jog. He toweled down. Back in the stall, he put on some cologne, followed by the shirt.

He studied the pair of faded blue jeans. If he put the guy's walking shorts on underneath, and if he tucked the pant legs up, he might get away with wearing them.

He tried it and it worked.

Outside of the building, he found a map of the training station posted on a bulletin board. He studied it and found the Behavioral Sciences Building. It was located two-hundred yards south of where he was standing. He headed that direction and, thinking about hypothetical constructs, he stopped, sat on a bench, and got out the Company's palmtop computer. He connected to Heaven, then patched into the program that linked into the computers on the first floor of the Hoover Building. Creating a hypothetical profile for himself, he would now be called Hal Carpenter, on special assignment to the director of the FBI. He copied his picture from his regular file to the Carpenter file. Then he erased everything in the FBI files on Martin Price.

Entering the Behavioral Sciences Building, he went to the elevator, and hit the button for the basement. Stepping out, he faced tall white walls and a locked metal door.

Back on the palmtop, he breached the base security file and found a list of door-lock codes. When he located the code for the basement door to the Behavioral Sciences unit, he punched it into the keypad of the security system. Opening the door, he went inside.

The hallway was painted beige. Moving down it, he passed a series of white metal doors on either side of the hall. He read the name plates, looking for Krocker's. He found it at the end of the hall.

There was an eye-scanner on the door, controlling who could unlock the security system on Krocker's office. He knew he couldn't get his irises to pass for Krocker's, but there had to be a way around it.

Using the palm top computer, he searched the base's security system, but he didn't find anything that gave a hint as to who had an override program for the lock on Krocker's door.

Trying another tactic, he used Heaven's Interlink program to enter the FBI computers downtown. Running a search, he found some files with the key words *Krocker* and *Franklin*. The pathway for one file led into Director Franklin's computer.

Inside the director's data system, Marty found the object of his search: A digital copy of Krocker's irises. The director evidently kept the photo as a backup for getting into Krocker's office in case something happened to the commander.

Bringing the picture of Krocker's irises up on the screen of the palmtop, he held it in front of the scanner. The scanner blinked red, then the message screen read: *Access Denied.*

Facing grave disappointment, Marty wanted to know what went wrong. If the scanner denied access, then it had read the iris scan off of the palmtop and rejected it. So the palmtop did convey the image of a pair of irises to the scanner, but they were the wrong irises. Marty wondered about it. What if Krocker didn't want Franklin getting into his office? He would have altered the iris scans that were given to Franklin.

Marty redirected his search back into Franklin's computer. He reasoned that most of the director's files would be new or recent because he had only been appointed to his position a few months beforehand. That meant Franklin had asked Krocker for the iris scans recently.

Did Krocker give him false iris scans? Or did Krocker get into Franklin's computer and alter the scans that he had given him, thus rendering them useless?

More than likely, Franklin found out about Krocker's security system, then ordered Krocker to have his eyes scanned at the FBI Headquarters. That would mean the original scan was a good one, but Krocker had gained access to Franklin's computer and had altered the primary scan.

Marty dug into erased files on Franklin's computer. He found the original iris scan and ordered it restored. Then he downloaded it onto the palmtop, got the picture of the irises on the screen, then held the PDA up in front of the scanner on Krocker's door. A green light flashed. That was followed by a click at the door.

He grabbed the doorknob and went inside.

Krocker's office was painted sterile white, and had a peach-colored sofa and chair, and a state-of-the-art computer workstation. There was a polished set of brass numb chucks sitting on the desk.

Marty went to the computer. It was housed in a double-wide standup metal box. The screen saver didn't change when he moved the mouse. Nor did it change when he pressed the buttons on the keyboard. Marty looked at the back of the metal case. There were a dozen Universal Service Bus connections. He pulled a USB cord from Krocker's computer and plugged it into the palmtop computer from the Widewater facility. Then he ran a line out of the palmtop and back into the commander's computer. Next he asked Heaven to analyze the data passing through the palmtop as it went from the remote source, passed though the PDA, and entered Krocker's destop computer.

Heaven told him that he had intercepted the data train from Krocker's command vehicle.

When the command vehicle tried to reconnect, he copied the pass-word information coming from the field command consol. He cut the command vehicle off once again, then sent the copied pass-word data into Krocker's desk computer. Engaging the office computer, he immediately enabled the keyboard and monitor.

Now working from Krocker's office keyboard, he moved the mouse, and a page came on the screen which contained a couple dozen icons. He checked to see what programs were running. His main concern was that Krocker experienced the disruption of data at the consol of the command vehicle and suspected that someone had tapped into the data flow. Marty analyzed operations of the command vehicle computer, but it was standing idle. Krocker wasn't using it. After a few moments, the Interlink program booted up inside the command vehicle. Marty waited and watched. He used Heaven to analyze what Krocker was doing. The mainframe told him that Krocker was downloading data from the FBI files at the Hoover Building.

Believing it was safe to continue, Marty tied into the data-bank server that he rented in Maryland. After downloading a program from his own files, he set it up to erase the history of his intrusion into Krocker's computer. Now the commander couldn't tell he'd been there, and in an hour, the erasure program itself would self-destruct.

Clicking on the main page icons, he found the master search function. He entered the name Buddy. There were a dozen references. One to a Buddy Young. Marty figured this was the thug that he had caught on his e-cam raiding his office. He looked in the file and found that the guy was a retired communications operator for the Army's 82nd Airborne Division. He clicked on the photo and got a good look at the man's picture. He was definitely one of the men who broke into Marty's office.

He scanned the computer in the Hoover Building but didn't find anything on Buddy Young. That's what Marty had figured. Young wasn't in the FBI computer because he wasn't an agent. Rather, he was private muscle contracting with Harrington and Krocker's covert operation.

He tried to look up Tucker Johnston. There was a reference linking Johnston's death to Jack Watson. Further searching led to notes on Jack's case, how he had tracked down the patent theft in L.A. Marty e-mailed that file to Thomas Fredericks at the Post.

He clicked through the files listing operatives and immediately recognized a picture of Mack Jones, a.k.a. Mr. Hawaiian Shirt. He'd been an FBI contractor, but he'd quit a few years ago. That must have been when he went to work for Krocker.

Marty searched some more and discovered a file about Jack written by the people who'd questioned him, Doctors Archer and Burns. He scanned it. Jack had told them the same story he had reported to Marty. There was also something telling. When they had finished the interrogation, they had given him the standard electroshock with the END device.

There it was.

Marty wondered why Krocker would risk keeping notes on this kind of illegal operation. Sure, his office was virtually impenetrable, but still, he must have known the files could be used against him. There was only one explanation. Krocker had the type of narcissistic personality where he thought he was invincible. Fate couldn't run against him. So it didn't matter how much incriminating evidence he kept. It only supported his belief in his own glory. Yet it seemed there was something else going on here. He guessed that Krocker had so many illegal operations that he couldn't possibly keep track of all of them with simple mental note-taking.

Marty opened a file called *Election*. The contents told how Harrington had introduced himself at an OPEC oil-producers meeting in Paris. Saying he was an emissary from Gregory Bond, the presidential candidate, he showed a fake letter of introduction. Then he displayed a DVD computer-rendering of candidate Bond asking OPEC for help in winning the election.

Huh?

Was this Oilgate? Evidence of electioneering fraud like Watergate?

Marty read the writeup. Apparently Harrington asked the OPEC ministers to cut world oil production so that the price of oil would rise in the months before the election.

Okay. That fit with what had happened during the last election, but why use a fake letter of introduction if Harrington had a digital video of the presidential candidate wherein he asked for help? Probably because the video was a fake, too, just like the letter.

Why not? It was possible to take an image of a person and plug it into a video editing program and substitute someone's likeness for the image of someone else.

Marty could imagine Harrington taking a Middle East oil minister aside and showing him the DVD of candidate Bond. It would show the candidate saying that he would support OPEC with a quid pro quo payback after the election if they would cut oil production now.

His thoughts swirled. The election had been a close call. High oil prices had caused a drop in the stock market. When the market fell, the economy slowed. People were upset and voted for a new administration. Sure, that was only one of many interpretations of what had happened during the complex election process. A more general view was that Bond's opponent simply didn't speak the voters' language. Another issue was trust. And on and on. But maybe the Company's subterfuge had set the economic slump into motion. Maybe it hadn't. That wasn't the important issue at this point. The real issue was that the electioneering scam was a criminal act, a subterfuge far bigger than the dirty tricks pulled by Nixon's little band of Watergate plumbers.

Marty copied the election file and sent it as an attachment to the editor at Global, the multi-media, telecommunications giant. In the accompanying letter, he noted that he had found the election file in the office of FBI Commander John Krocker. Marty said he wanted to discuss it in an interview. He left his cell number. He also sent a copy of the file to Derek Walker, Senator Stanton's head assistant.

Marty sat back and relished the moment. But his glory was short lived. He suddenly realized that if Global showed the Oilgate file on the air, the public would never believe that Krocker did this on his own. No. They would call for impeachment of President Bond.

Damn!

This was all messed up. Marty liked Bond, and had voted for him, because the guy was simply too cool. Now Marty had sent a broadside in Bond's direction without really meaning to do it.

Glum-faced, Marty kept searching Krocker's computer. He discovered that the commander called his secret organization the Company, which was what Marty figured. It was initially funded by the U.S. black budget, the top secret subsidy for high security operations, equipment, and intelligence. The Company's job was to track down militant groups and to destroy their organizations before the situation turned into another standoff like Waco. But the Company ran into trouble with oversight. Krocker had gone too far, killing people to silence their organizations. The leaders of the Senate-House Joint Intelligence Committee cancelled the program. But it didn't stop there. Krocker found ways to make the Company's budget self-sustaining outside the purview of the Congress. He was also able to transfer the ownership of the Widewater building to a fake company. Then there was the laboratory in Azerbaidzhan.

Azerbaidzhan?

Incredible. The Company had worldwide contacts.

Struck by the enormity of Krocker's power, Marty studied more files. They seemed to say that Krocker was setting himself up to take over the FBI. From that position he would impact the government. That made sense, Marty realized. Krocker could operate a reign of terror over Washington from the Hoover Building and not be subject to losing everything during an election. It reminded him that J. Edgar Hoover had set up a dynasty at FBI, but it was nothing compared to this. Hoover merely planted false evidence on liberal leaders and kept sex files on an errant Congress.

Marty knew it was no time to worry about Krocker's goals. The commander could walk in and simply shoot him, say he was an intruder. Problem was, Marty had become awestruck by the endless profiles in terror. The screen before him detailed a project to build a memory eraser. The machine wouldn't damage cells, but would make people forget whatever they were thinking when the machine was activated. Marty was incredulous. This was how Krocker was going work his way to the top. He could do anything to anyone, and they'd forget it. He sent an e-mail copy of the Eraser file to Lisa, hoping to show her the magnitude of Krocker's incredibly evil nature. Maybe now she would understand how important it was for Marty to keep on this case.

Knowing he had lingered too long in a dangerous situation, Marty got up from the workstation. He was at the door when he realized that he forgot to check the inner security system guarding Krocker's office. He sat back down at the workstation and checked the security file. Krocker had an e-camera recording the activities inside his office. Marty erased the memory of his entry, then reset the system for the e-cam to come back online twenty minutes after he had left the room. With that, he headed out the door.

15

Marty shut the door to Krocker's office and turned to see a woman glaring at him from the second doorway down the hall. He smiled. "How's your day going?" he said.

The woman inspected him with grave hesitancy. "Fine. How's yours?"

"Another interesting day," he replied, slowly inhaling, trying to calm himself.

The woman wore tight-fitting, navy-blue jeans and a maroon-colored, corduroy shirt. A long, braided pony tail hung around her shoulder and down across her beast. "Business with the commander?" she asked.

"Yes."

"But he's not here."

"I know." Marty approached and held out his hand. "I'm Hal Carpenter.

"I'm Tanya Burns," she said.

He watched her bite her lower lip. "You work for Krocker?" he asked.

"No, Rolland Archer," she said.

Marty smiled. "Must be interesting work," he said, realizing that this was the Burns who had interrogated Jack.

"Why do you say that?"

"Just a guess … what with Rolland doing experiments and all."

"Hal, look," Tanya said, "let's cut the small talk. If you're here checking up on us, why not step into my office and sit down?"

"Fine," Marty said, following Tanya through her door.

She held out a hand towards the sofa. "Want some coffee?"

"Yes, please." He glanced around. There were a dozen plants, giving the room an air of fullness. Now if he could only bluff his way out of this one.

"What sort of investigation are you doing on Krocker?"

Marty chuckled. "Me study John?"

Tanya handed him the cup of coffee, and she looked into his eyes, lingering momentarily until she moved to sit down. "Come on, who could get into Krocker's office? No one around here. You represent the Inspector General's office, or someone higher."

"You could look it up on the computer, couldn't you?"

Sitting on the edge of her chair, she nodded.

"But you don't need to tell Krocker I was here, do you?" When she shook her head, he relaxed back into the soft sofa. "The director thinks John is breaking the law. What do you think?"

Tanya got up and moved to her workstation. She entered some information into her computer. After she had read the screen, she said. "You work for Franklin, don't you?"

"I'm a troubleshooter." He studied her big-eyed face with its Roman nose and soft skin. "Is Krocker breaking the law?"

"I thought the director knew what we were doing here."

"Electroshock treatments. Stealing patents. Come on."

She blinked a few times.

Marty leaned forward on the sofa and glared at her. "I know Jack Watson. He helps me investigate FBI matters. He can't remember shit. It's time for somebody to sing and take government-witness immunity, don't you think? Or does everybody in this outfit want to take the fall with Krocker?"

Tanya slumped down into a chair. "I knew we shouldn't be doing it. But my options were joining the interrogation team or quitting. I had no other choice."

"So what do we have here?" Marty said.

Tanya told the story of her and Rolland discovering that Krocker was stealing patents.

Marty got up and got more coffee for both of them. "When I present this to the director, Krocker is going to go ballistic. And until Krocker is corralled, you better get out of Dodge. Take a vacation, but give me a number where I can reach you. You have a cell phone, don't you?"

She nodded and gave him the number.

"If you get into trouble, call me. Especially if you get any threats." He gave her his new cell phone number, and got up and headed for the door. Standing in the archway, he said, "This will blow over."

Her sad-eyed faced drooped and she looked morose.

"It will," he said.

Upstairs, he pushed his way thought the glass door and headed for the street. He felt good about what he'd accomplished. He had been in the throes of desperation, and a crooked commander had built a case against him. But he'd turned the problem back on Krocker, sending reports to the media. Now it was Krocker who would be investigated, he who would get some hard time in jail.

"Excuse me, sir," came a voice from behind him.

He turned. Clean-cut and ramrod straight, two uniformed FBI security agents stood before him. The brawny man had his gun drawn, pointed down at the ground. "What is it?" Marty said.

The no-nonsense woman said, "What was your business in the building?"

Marty calculated the odds. He had released some data, enough to nail Krocker. Could it have been intercepted? Did Marty have to make a run for it? Could he get the gun from the muscleman? He realized he needed more information. "I have an appointment with Commander Krocker, but he is not here yet."

"Can I see your identification?" said the woman.

"It's in my car," Marty said. The man with the gun smiled, then forced it back down. Marty continued. "What's this all about?"

"Stay where you are at for a moment, please." The woman stepped back, and keeping a watchful eye on Marty, she talked over her security phone.

"We have to check your security clearance," said the male trooper. "Probably go to headquarters."

"No, I don't think so," Marty said. "You're connected into the entire FBI network. My name is Hal Carpenter. I work for the director. Look me up."

Another sentry ran up. "I'm going to have to search you for weapons, sir," he said.

"No way," Marty snapped. He faced the woman using the intercom. "I'm Hal Carpenter! Look me up!"

The woman on the two-way radio ignored Marty, saying, "Get a car over here."

A fourth agent charged up to the group and grabbed Marty's arm and jerked it up behind his back.

"Stop it!" Marty exclaimed, stomping on the guy's foot, pulling his arm loose, shoving the man away, then yelling, "Get back!"

"Don't move!" yelled the agent with the gun

Marty pointed at the woman on the phone. "Give them my description. That's a direct order. I'm Hal Carpenter, Special Operations. I work for the director. Move it, or lose it!"

The guards held their distance, looking at the woman on the intercom.

Glowering, she studied Marty. "Right, he is blond," she said into the radio. "Yes, they're blue." She stepped toward Marty and asked him, "What is the code word in your file?"

Marty had made a joke when he put together his Hal Carpenter file. Now it didn't seem so funny. "I don't have a code word, dammit," he said.

While the guy with the gun smirked, the woman said, "He says he doesn't have a code ... Well, yeah, sure. The direct quote was: *I don't have a code word, dammit.*" Suddenly, her expression twisted into a child's funny-face, like she was imitating a monster. "That's the code? Whoa..."

The woman approached the troopers. "At ease!" she ordered. "Put the weapons away." While the men moved back, she said, "Sorry, Sergeant, we were ordered to check everybody going in and out of the Behavioral Sciences Building. You didn't have your identification. We had to follow orders."

"Good work," Marty said. "You can't be too careful with all the wackos trying to blame the FBI for everything." He hesitated, studying the woman. Squint-eyed, he asked, "What is the problem at Behavioral Sciences?"

"Some sort of security breach. You would have to go to headquarters to get the details."

Marty nodded. "Carry on."

Walking with a bounce in his stride, Marty headed for the gate.

What triggered the search? he wondered. Was it Krocker's door being opened without the commander being on base? Did Tanya call security? Or did they trace his illegal entry onto the federal data highway back to Krocker's office?

None of it made sense.

Or did it?

He had sent the file on the election rigging to the editor at Global. That could have been traced to Krocker's office, to the computer which sent it.

But wasn't it supposed to be the other way around? Shouldn't the multimedia giant be calling Marty for an interview? Not the FBI tracking the leak of the file through Global.

Mulling it over, he headed towards the entrance to the base.

Funny. Moments ago he had been angry enough to lay down his life as he fought for his right not to be searched. Now he finally understood those who swore they wouldn't be taken alive. They were protesting the loss of their fundamental dignity.

At the gate, the sentries had changed. Now, a sinewy male decked out in back and white stood in front of the guardhouse watching Marty approach.

"Have a good walk," the guard said.

"Thanks," Marty replied.

Back at the Lunca Recreation Center, he called a taxi and changed back into his own clothing. Watching the evening come on, he sat on a picnic table and waited. His thoughts turned to Heaven, the mainframe at Widewater. The government would be shutting her down along with the rest of Krocker's projects. Marty wondered if he could download the computer's files and use them afterwards.

He laughed. Here he was thinking about saving a computer from the junk-heap when he had nearly ended up in the brig. Lisa was right. If a guy could sleep with a computer, he would be the first. A technophiliac, she had called him.

He took the taxi back to his office in Georgetown. Down the hill, where K Street ran under the freeway, the streetlights cast a pink aura over his car. He grumbled at seeing the parking tickets stuffed under the wiper blade. He tossed the tickets on the passenger seat, got behind the wheel, then headed east to the Rock Creek Expressway, intending to go to Lisa's house.

His cell rang. It was Global, the media giant. The spokeswoman wanted him immediately at their downtown office for an interview to discuss the election. He said he wasn't dressed for it. She said they had an entire wardrobe, just come over, the cameras were ready to roll. He said that he had been jogging and he would have to go home and take a shower, but he would be there in an hour. She said come now. They needed him before their lawyer went home so he could sign the contract for the show. It paid well.

He asked how much.

She said it would be a hundred grand for the first interview, and fifty more for the followup.

When he hesitated, she said that in a few hours he would be the talk of Washington. Why not let folks get the correct version of the story before the Star Review spun it off into the gutter? Besides, Global was willing to pay whatever it took to be the first with the scoop on the rigged election. Then she asked if this was a stall for more money.

He said to make it a hundred and fifty for the first interview and he'd be right over.

She said yes. Jessica Long would be waiting to do the interview.

He said okay. He knew it made more sense to go to his home and change clothes rather than do it at Global. But what was he thinking? He couldn't go home. If the Company had occupied his office, they surely were holed up at his house, too. He'd better go to Global and talk about everything he saw on Krocker's computer.

Plummeting through the dark, Marty headed the car towards silver-crescent moon hanging over the Capitol. Ending up on H Street, he talked to Lisa on the cell. He told her about sending the report on Krocker's electioneering scam to Global, and having arranged an on-the-air interview with their newswoman, Jessica Long. Lisa said she would watch the show, and he clicked off.

Global's white concrete headquarters jutted up ten stories from a small complex of buildings eight blocks north of the Capitol dome on First Street. Waiting at a stop light at North Capitol, Marty felt a sudden queasiness, like something was deadly wrong. Thinking about it, he realized that the Washington offices of the major networks were compact, subtle, and they blended in, like NBC on M Street. You could walk by it and not notice it. People did everyday. That was because the media in Washington didn't have the office towers and the mega-lots like in New York and L.A. They were set up for interviews, not for productions. So he couldn't imagine that Global's office was so extravagant that it had a wardrobe that could fit anyone who walked in the door. Nor could he imagine they had showers for guests.

He picked up the handheld computer. Pulling up the GPS screen, he saw a couple-dozen flashing markers stationed around the Capitol. Most of them surrounded Global.

Marty tossed the palmtop on the seat, crossed a lane of traffic, and spun the car around the corner onto North Capitol Street. Pulling over near the Phoenix Park Hotel, he parked and delved deeper into the computer files to find out what the blinking lights meant. He knew that the blue lights represented FBI cruisers, so he went into the FBI system, trying to hook into the computer traffic between the vehicles parked near Global and the downtown office. He intercepted information on the suspect in Operation Strike. Glancing at the report, the first words that caught his attention were *black Mustang* and *Martin Price.*

Crap!

He took off, slowly at first, getting back into the traffic. Turning on E Street, he floored it, making an evasive right, followed by a left onto K Street, where most of Washington's deals were hammered out.

Heading west, he slowed down and looked back.

How did Global get involved in setting him up?

And why?

He made a jog, got onto Massachusetts Avenue, and roared through the tunnel. At Du Pont Circle, he slowed, knowing that the District cops always sat there, across from the Hilton, waiting for speeders going around the loop. And sure enough, the mid-sized white Chevy was there tonight.

Now on Embassy Row, where ornate mansions with spotlighted flags lined the road, he glanced in his rearview mirror and saw the red and blue lights of two government security vehicles as they slid one-after-the-other around a corner and give chase up the two-lane road.

He let them gain on him. When the lead car was nearly touching his bumper, he hit the brakes hard, cramming his foot all the way to the floor.

The lead cruiser crashed into the back of the Mustang, then spun into a parked car and rolled on its side.

Cramming his foot to the floor, Marty took off.

But there came the whining sound of a 5-liter engine eating up his tail pipes, and when he looked to his left, he saw the shadow-covered face of the other agent, racing his car neck-to-neck with the Mustang.

With a grinding crash, Marty banged his car into the front of the federal police vehicle.

The federal cop held tight and smashed his car into the side of the Mustang.

Marty hit the brakes.

The federal car shot around Sheridan Traffic Circle and slid to a stop, blocking Massachusetts Avenue. As the driver rolled out the passenger door and held an assault rifle over the hood, Marty banged the Mustang into the curb at the center of the traffic loop. And bouncing across the grass, he spun around the dark bronze statue of General Sheridan seated on a tall horse.

While another federal car entered the chase, circling the loop behind him, Marty hit a hundred miles an hour on the side street. Ratcheting around the next corner, he flipped off his headlights and raced into night. Sliding this way and that through a few more corners, he listened to the sirens fading. He continued zig-zagging until he was on Water Street. At the Rock Creek Expressway, he headed south along the Potomac River. On Independence Avenue, he turned east, doubling back across town, figuring the pursuers would get hung up looking for him on the West End, and he'd get away.

He crossed the black waters of the Tidal Basin between the two well-lit white giants: The towering Washington Monument and the domed Jefferson Memorial. Wanting justice, he didn't know if he would get it before he ran out of time. Soon Washington would close ranks, and the truth would be buried. Then it wouldn't make any difference if he released more information or not. The wonks, the pols, the media giants would simply say he was crazy, and then they would dump his story about the election scam. A reporter he knew said that had happened to him. Now Marty was sorry he had scoffed at the idea.

Approaching the eastside of town, he picked up the computer and looked at the screen. It showed several Metro police units coming in his direction about six blocks away, circling around R.F.K Stadium. It was the troops stationed across the Anacostia River coming to join the manhunt.

He turned a hard right, went down a few blocks, then parked in the shadows behind a dirty car with a flat tire. Sitting out front of a gaudy, bright-red row house with a weed-covered lawn, he considered his options:

Go back out on the street and have a show-down.

Wait here until the feds tracked him down and shot him.

Play cat-and-mouse until Krocker's bullet got him in the back.

Hell! These options sucked.

But wait. If he used Heaven, he had a chance to take command of the manhunt.

That was an imposing idea.

He grabbed the personal data assistant and tore though the files. He discovered that FBI headquarters was reporting that his Mustang was last spotted on Independence Avenue. He pinpointed the computer which made the report and overrode that data connection to the federal system. Then he released a hypothetical data-ghost. It showed that the Mustang was in the tunnel that crossed under the Capitol Mall.

He leaned back into the bucket seat, wondering if he could set up another theoretical construct, where the manhunt went after Harrington or Krocker. Track them down instead of Marty. He had a strange uneasy feeling that he might be able to do it.

Back on the PAD, he wrote a draft of a statement which he attributed to the FBI director, Franklin. It said there was a massive manhunt for Harrington. He had killed an agent in Washington and had blamed it on Martin Price. The troops had to immediately stop tracking Price and go after Harrington. Marty released the report to all federal security agencies.

He opened the 10 Most Wanted List on the FBI Web page and bridled at seeing himself.

Going into the data-entry section, he switched Harrington's photo and statistics for his own. Then he erased the overwrite function and exited that program.

Next he located the computer program which operated the switchboard for the phones at the FBI headquarters. He closed that down. The radio dispatch too.

He looked up Harrington's car. It was at Widewater. He wrote an all-points-bulletin, saying the number one man on the most wanted list, Harrington, had been spotted at the research facility at Widewater. Marty released that memo and sent a copy to all the major media outlets. Then he cut the FBI computers off of the national data highway.

Out of curiosity, he plugged the name of Global's editor into the palmtop and searched the files of the Company computer at Widewater Beach. Hell. The editor, Donald Jenkins worked for them. That explained everything, especially why the FBI had someone looking for an intruder in the Behavioral Science Building. Jenkins got the file Marty had sent and called Krocker.

How much of DC did Krocker control?

Who knew?

He folded up the palmtop, started the car, and headed out. Crossing the Anacostia River on Pennsylvania Avenue, he turned southeast on Southern. Jack's hospital was a few miles down the road. Marty bet he could go in and see Jack unhindered.

16

Greater Southeast Community Hospital sat in a neighborhood of old rundown townhouses on the District's southern edge facing Maryland. On its backside was a large federal park. It couldn't be any more remote, which kind of made bureaucratic sense. After all, this was the welfare joint.

The parking lot was lit with soft white lights. Marty went to the emergency room door and parked. Flashing Johnston's FBI badge, he learned that Jack was on the fifth floor. Up there, he stuck his head out the door to the stairwell and didn't see any cops. So he walked over to the nurse's station and held out his arms and made a shrug. "Where's my partners?" he said.

The young black nurse in the white lab coat with cornrow spires in her hair said, "They ran down the hall and jumped in the elevator." She pointed. "Just a minute ago."

"I'd better make sure Watson is secure," Marty said. "Where is he?"

She pointed. "Take the first left. Room 515."

Marty walked down the polished linoleum hallway and found Jack's room. The door was shut. He knocked.

"Come on in," said the voice from the other side.

Marty stepped in and shut the door. The room was painted light blue. The second bed was empty. Jack had the TV on.

"Marty, baby, you made it!" Jack roared. Flat on his back with the top of the bed tilted up, Jack had white gauze wrapped around his head. His torso was completely bandaged.

"What's a partner for?" Marty said.

"Partner?" Jack's eyes opened wide and he hit the mute on the TV. "Are we working a case together?"

"No, not really. Are you going to be okay? I feel kind of responsible since you were hurt coming to see me."

"Don't worry about it."

Jack grimaced. "Lisa called. She's worried about you."

"You remembered it."

Jack scratched the top of his head, mussing up his black, already-mussed-up hair. "Yeah, she's scared shitless, but she wouldn't give me the facts.

What's going on?"

"It's a federal case," Marty said. "Mistaken identity. Had me on the 10 Most Wanted List when it was another guy, Harrington, who was the culprit. He had switched my data for his on the FBI computer, and almost got away with it."

"What a story. How did you get out of it?

"Hacked into the federal system and switched the data back the way it was supposed to be."

Jack laughed. "Now they're going to arrest you for computer fraud?"

Marty laughed. Thinking it was time to recharge the batteries, he set the personal data assistant on the luggage rack, took out the electric cord, and plugged it in. "Been to the deli on La Cienega lately?"

"Sure have."

"Some things never change." When Jack nodded, Marty said, "What's happening with Cheryl?"

Jack's eyes lit up. "I called and told her about the shooting, and she thought maybe I was dying. She said she was getting on the next flight. I was shocked. I didn't think she cared." A tear dripped from Jack's eye. "She must have never given up. I was a jerk. I told her so. I said she didn't have to come now. It could wait until I got back. We talked for … who knows. Half the night. She's going to be here when I get out."

"Fantastic."

"You and Lisa … we'll double date?"

"You got it, buddy."

"You didn't tell me it made the news!" Jack exclaimed, grabbing the remote and hitting the volume.

A picture of Marty's face covered the TV screen. The reporter was giving a rundown.

"Well, yeah, the feds thought" – Marty pointed at the picture of Harrington on the TV screen "I was him. They chased me all over, saying I killed an agent at the Riverview Restaurant."

"Look at that," Jack roared. It was the Director of the FBI saying that Marty was the man of the hour. "I'll be seeing you with Jessica Long this time tomorrow."

Marty shook his head. "Not Global. They don't like me."

"Yeah, right." Jack flipped though the stations until he got Global's news station.

It showed anchor Mitchell Stone turning to the studio's wall-screen video monitor which displayed the picture of a reporter in the field: "*Jessica, what do you hear from the Capitol? Any word on how they bungled this?*"

– (Jessica Long in red suit in front of White House) "*Reliable sources say that the FBI confused Marty Price with Agent Harrington. Price was having dinner at the Riverview Restaurant at Georgetown Harbor. He walked out to the plaza and witnessed Harrington kill Special Agent Johnston. Harrington saw Price, took a few shots, but Price escaped. That's when Harrington got on his radio and said Price was the shooter.*"

– (Stone) "*And that's when the manhunt started.*"

– (Long) "*Yes, that's it, Mitch, and he's been running every since.*"

– (Stone) "*Hopefully Marty Price will be able to sleep in his own bed tonight. Thanks, Jessica.*"

– (Long) "*I'll keep you updated.*"

– (Camera cut to Stone; his face tightened) "*The latest word is that Harrington's been located. He's holed up in a federal building at Widewater, Virginia. He says he won't be taken alive. The government has brought in some big guns. Ted Williams is down there. Ted –*"

"Heaven's in danger!" Marty wailed.

Jack lowered the volume. "What are you talking about?"

Marty opened the palmtop and punched in some data. "A computer. It saved my life, let me get into the federal system. It's almost human."

"Yeah?"

When Heaven responded to his prompt, Marty ordered the computer to download a copy of all of its memory banks. Split them up. Send pieces to all the major computers in the federal network then link them together and consign the executive-command file to the palmtop. The computer took the order. He figured it would take five or ten minutes for the Heaven to perform the operation.

"Once a geek, always a geek," Jack said.

"Yeah."

Marty's phone rang. He fumbled in his pocket and answered it. "Marty, here."

"I thought you were going to protect me."

"Tanya?"

"Yeah. Krocker called. He ordered me to Quantico."

"Don't go."

"I'm not."

"Let me help."

"You can't help; you're not even in the FBI."

"I'm sorry."

"What were you doing in Krocker's office? I don't understand. Who sent you?"

"I'm a friend of Jack Watson's. I had to find out what happened to him. Where are you? I'll check the computer and see if they're closing in on you."

"National."

"Hang on a second." Marty brought up the screen showing the location of federal security vehicles in Southwest Washington and Northern Virginia. "I'm sorry about all this. I gave the media information exposing Krocker, but they closed ranks, trying to protect him. He's got connections everywhere."

"That doesn't help me," Tanya said.

"I'm plugged into the federal GPS. A FBI vehicle is headed towards the airport."

"Dammit, my guns are in the car."

"I'll help you. I'll be there in ten minutes."

"They're crazy. They'll shoot you on sight. They killed Chris Walters."

"Who?" Marty asked.

"Walters. The lead scientist on the Eraser Project. Krocker's killing everyone who can take him to court."

"Hell."

"I'll get back to you."

"Tanya..." Marty listened to the dial tone. Tanya had hung up.

"What the hell is going on?" Jack said.

"They're killing everyone who knows about the secret project Harrington has at Widewater." Marty headed for the door. "I've got to go."

"But Harrington's trapped."

"I've got to help Tanya. She's an agent who knows about everything. They're going to silence her."

"You're a hero. Let someone else help her."

"She'll be dead before the feds understand what's happening."

Jack sat up straight in the bed. "Yeah, and you'll be dead too."

"That's the chance I have to take." He opened the door.

"Hang on. What did you mean telling her that you were a friend of mine?"

"Tanya was with the Feebies who helped you at Quantico. You were lucky."

"Tanya saved my life?"

"Yes. And she helped me too. The least I can do is be there for her."

Jack swallowed hard. "Go for it, buddy."

17

Marty ran out of the hospital, scrambled into his car, and roared though the dark streets heading for the expressway. He didn't know how he could help Tanya, or even find her, but he felt an intense need to go to the airport. After all, she was being punished for helping him.

Crossing the Anacostia River, he watched the computer screen go blank.

"Fucking sonofabitch!" he cursed, pounding his fist on the steering wheel. Heaven had been cut off from the handheld. It had to mean she was destroyed. He was still fuming about it when he turned off the Washington Expressway and went through the loop for the passenger drop-off at National airport.

Pulling over, he scanned the crowd under the lights.

No Tanya.

He circled the loop again and entered the multi-deck, short-term parking lot. He drove through all the levels, looking this way and that. The lot was well lit, but nothing stood out. No security vehicles, no cops, no embassy cars with special plates.

He pulled in an empty space. Reaching in the back seat he found a baseball cap and put it on along with a pair of sunglasses. Not much of a disguise, but it invariably worked. People remembered stereotypes – a guy in a ball cap. Regretting he didn't stop at his friend Jonathan's and borrow a gun, he got out of the car, cursing Harrington for taking his weapon earlier in the day.

He took the stairs to the next parking level, then poked around the cars that were parked illegally next to the skybridge door. That's where Krocker's people would be if they were anywhere. Not finding anything suspicions, he crossed to the terminal. He was partway over the bridge when two men marched into the corridor from the terminal side of the archway and headed towards him. The one in the Hawaiian shirt, Mack Jones, held Tanya by the arm. The other one, Buddy Young, wore a trench coat. It looked like he had a gun in his pocket trained on Tanya. She was staring at the ground, puffed up with a sad, defeated face.

Marty couldn't be more pleased. Now he would finally get a chance to meet the boys on his own terms, except there were two men behind them, walking close up. It had to be a backup crew.

He knew the odds had turned against him, but if he suddenly pivoted and headed back, his movement would be noticed. So he kept coming, breathing deep, clearing his mind. When they were about to pass side-to-side, he knuckled his fist and slammed his full weight into Buddy's stomach, throwing the man into the two backup brutes.

Buddy's gun fired, shattering a full twenty-foot-long widow.

"Jesus!" wailed a woman, as people dove to the floor or scattered like pigeons.

Marty spun off of Buddy, hit the one backup thug in the groin. Then he executed a spinning kick, and hit the other guy in the throat.

Tanya wrestled with Mack Jones.

When Buddy drew his weapon from his jacket, Marty punched him in the ribs, elbowed him in the throat, then grabbed the gun out of his hand and ran after Tanya and Mack, who were racing towards the other end of the skybridge, Tanya in the lead.

Unwilling to take the risk of hitting Tanya, Marty fired into the wall not far from Mack.

Mack let Tanya go, stopped, and turned to face Marty.

Marty glanced back. The thugs had pulled their weapons. In rapid secession, he fired a bullet into the jerk who was the closest, leaving a hole where his heart had been. Then he shot the other one in the head, and dove to the ground as Mack fired.

"Hold it!" Buddy screamed when fragments from Mack's bullets ricocheted off the piling next to him.

Facing Mack, Marty knelt on one knee and aimed with both hands.

Mack turned and ran.

Marty chased.

Sticking the gun in his belt, Mack rounded the corner and came to an abrupt stop. Turning back, he pointed at Marty and yelled, "He's got a gun!"

A troop of armed guards raced around the corner and charged into the skybridge.

Marty made a quick stop, turned, and ran towards the terminal.

The sentries gave chase.

When Marty raced into the terminal, the crowd pushed back.

Amid the screams, he glanced about.

No Buddy. But there was a couple of guards coming from the direction of the southern-most boarding gate.

Sticking the gun in the back of his belt, Marty went the other direction, outpacing the slower people in the frantic crowd. When a man broke through an emergency exit and the alarm sounded, Marty followed, pulling off his hat and stuffing it into his pocket. Going through a labyrinthine passageway stuffed full with employees, he followed a group of women who knew how to use to the underground tunnel to get to the parking structure.

In the rush, someone dropped a fluorescent-orange vest, one used by the workers when they were out on the tarmac. Marty put it on and ran.

Going down a flight of stairs, racing along a corridor, then coming up in the parking structure, Marty made his way back to his car. He figured he couldn't stay at the airport and search for Tanya. Too many people had seen him.

He left and got on the freeway and headed south towards Quantico. Turning on the radio, he heard the news that the standoff at Widewater Beach had ended. Vowing not to be taken alive, the rogue agent had blown up the building. Fire crews were now arriving on the scene.

Marty was aghast. Why would Harrington get himself killed? He had evidence which he could have used to hang Krocker. He didn't have to take the fall; he could have plea bargained.

No, that wasn't it. Krocker had detonated an explosion which destroyed the Widewater laboratory. That's what it had to be. A failsafe device. A remote-controlled bomb. Krocker had blown the building to cover up any evidence that might lead back to him.

Marty watched the oncoming headlights and moved to the slow lane. If Krocker was desperate enough to pull the plug on his research facility, he was desperate enough to spend his last bullet killing Marty.

Picking up Buddy's H&K .45 Special Forces automatic, Marty smiled. Maybe it was time to go one-on-one with Krocker.

18

Night hung over Quantico like doom's dark shadow.

Waiting in a patch of forest, Marty cocked the weapon and sighted across the road. His plan was to wait until he saw the command vehicle heading for the FBI Training Station, then step out and blast Krocker.

His phone rang and he answered it. "Marty here."

"Martin Price?"

"Yes."

A man with a whiskey-smooth drawl said, "This is certainly a pleasure. I'm James Franklin, Director of the FBI. Can you talk for a minute, or are you out solving some more big ones?"

Marty held back his anger. Maybe there was another side to this story. "No, I wasn't busy. Sorry about what happened to Harrington."

"Let's not worry about it – except for the reward."

"Reward?"

"Yes, we need to talk about it. How about my office? Let's say, tomorrow. Then we'll go on up Pennsylvania Avenue. The President wants to meet y'all. I think he has a good job for you."

Marty was perplexed. No mention of the Krocker or the Company. Just come on down and meet the President. When he realized that the director was discreetly making a deal to cover up Krocker's misdeeds, he laughed.

"What?" Franklin said.

"You sure you're done chasing me?"

Franklin's cordiality grew tart. "I suspect that depends on whether you're done chasing us, now doesn't it?"

Marty's heart told him to tell the man to go to hell. But he was so fraught with mixed emotions, thinking he might have to kill Franklin too, that he didn't dare speak.

Franklin said, "Look, Martin, you are a good man. We were meant to be on the same team."

"If that's the case, how does the president fit into this?"

"You never let up, do you?"

"Please, I meant no disrespect."

"Okay, think apology," Franklin said. "Think president with a big heart. And think opportunity."

"The president wants to apologize to me?"

"Yes, he takes it personally. He was shocked that we had a manhunt going in his backyard and an innocent party was almost killed."

"Almost killed?"

"Harrington painted you as a psycho-killer. We had snipers on the buildings, your office and home surrounded. It wasn't going to be pretty. So what about coming in from the cold and having a little chat? Tomorrow night, my office at six. Then we'll head on over to see the president. In the meantime, you cool your jets, and I'll cool mine."

"Right. You, me, and the FBI. We'll laugh off Krocker's election scam and smirk at the Ten Most Wanted List."

"Young man, I'll pretend I didn't hear that. You have one last chance. Want to meet the president? Or do you want to go to hell? Don't answer that in anger. I'm a reasonable person. However, I've been pushed to the limit by too many shenanigans, such that I'm over the line. And it's my butt if I don't get things settled down. Want to call it quits, take your dough, leave the stage, be a hero? Or do you want to think about it and call me back?"

Marty stuffed down his heart and tried to remember everything his grandmother had learned about good graces. "When you put it that way, sir, I well … yes. I'd like to meet the president. I'm one of his fans."

"Then it's a go."

"Yes, sir."

"See you tomorrow at the Hoover Building. No guns, no theatrics. Bring the lady if you want. We'll all go over and meet the prez."

"I'll be there."

Franklin clicked off.

Rolland Archer lived in an elegant Paladian villa on a lazy country road south of Arlington, Virginia. It was built of white brick, had a grey-tile hipped roof, and stood three stories tall. An enormous portico lorded over the massive front porch.

Tanya Burns got out of the taxi, crossed the cobblestone drive, went to the door, and rang the bell. She had never been here before and didn't know what to expect.

"This is a surprise," Rolland said, answering the door.

"There's something we need to talk about." Tanya stepped into the entry hall, then glanced past the triumphal arch into the interior of the home.

"It's okay, we're alone," Rolland said, moving into the large, open salon, where dual-staircases led up to the balcony

Hands on her hips, she walked beside him. "Krocker sent his muscle boys to shut me up."

"What?"

"He called me and wanted me to meet him at Quantico. I went to the airport instead, figuring it was a set up. But he sent Buddy and Mack. They found me before my flight took off."

Lines of worry cut across Rolland's brow. "What did they say?"

"Some sort of malarkey about Krocker giving me a direct order to be at Quantico … that I was considered AWOL because I went to the airport."

"He never got out of the military, not in his mind. How did you get away?"

"They were dragging me out when Marty Price jumped out of nowhere, knocking the four of them on their butts."

"Four of them?"

"Yeah. They were armed and he only had his bare fists. Who is this guy, anyway?"

"The media says he studied martial arts … L.A. Self Defense Academy." Standing face-to-face, Rolland studied her. "Are you sure you're okay?"

"I'm getting used to living hell, thank you."

Rolland's lips pulled back into a sympathetic smile. "This explains everything. Krocker killed Harrington. Now he wants us out of the way so no one knows about the Eraser … the patents."

"Except Price."

Rolland's face was inexpressive as he turned and headed into the spotless kitchen. With dual stainless-steel ovens and cookware hanging on hooks, the room was equipped to turn out a feast. "How did Price know about you?"

"I caught him coming out of Krocker's office."

"What a day to pick to go fishing." Rolland shook his head at the irony. "How did he get in there?"

"Fake identity saying he worked for the director."

"Unbelievable." Rolland raised a cup, saying, "Coffee?" She nodded, and he took another mug out of the cupboard. "I wish someone would explain to me … Price becoming a hero…"

"He data slammed the Bureau, displacing Krocker's reports with a conflicting story, that Harrington was the perpetrator who killed Tucker Johnston. After that story went national, Krocker and the director had to go along with it. Now they'll kill him, and us, and their strategy will go forward."

"What's their strategy?"

"Taking over the government, if they haven't already." She walked over to Rolland and looked into his soft eyes. "Been nice knowing you."

His eyes on hers, Rolland said, "Don't give up so quickly."

Tanya made a perky-faced smile, swivelled her hips, and spoke with a drawl. "Some good games on tonight. How about a brewsky and a big-screen TV?"

Rolland laughed. "I was thinking more along the lines of killing the sonofabitch."

Tanya's eyes opened wide. "You wouldn't?"

Rolland grabbed his cup and headed out of the kitchen. "Wanna bet?"

Square-jawed with a handsome face, FBI Director James Franklin could have passed for an aging actor. Glaring at Krocker, he said, "How did y'all lose control, John?"

Krocker frowned with disbelief. He had been running the operation to silence Harrington when the director called him to his office to inform him that he had learned that the editor at Global had intercepted a report on the election fraud. "I didn't lose control," Krocker said. "Price is a perverted genius, killing Tucker and blaming it on Harrington."

"This is not about Tucker, or Price, or Harrington," Franklin said. "It's about you losing control of your organization *and* about your trying to rig an election. Do you understand the review I'm going to have to personally endure over this fiasco?"

Krocker was flabbergasted. Didn't this blow-head know that he had stopped an eco-terrorism group from sabotaging a nuclear plant? That he had disarmed a survivalist group who had access to a shoulder-launched missile? Had won medals as a Marine? Where was the respect? Krocker wanted to lecture the fool, but knew enough about his supervisor to realize it was time to act humbled before him. "I apologize, Jim. I am truly sorry."

Dressed in a pin-stripped, worsted-wool suit, Franklin made a few short yeah-right nods with his head. Finally, he said, "I called Price and I settled it. Why can't you learn to be civil and negotiate with people, before they run off the deep end?"

"You settled what with Price?"

"Everything. He'll meet me and we'll go over and talk to the president. Maybe he'll get a job offer, who knows? In the meantime, he keeps his mouth shut about the election scam."

Krocker was incredulous. Here was a perpetrator who had taken control of the most advanced computer network in the world, and Krocker had to destroy the machine to keep him out of it. If there was ever an enemy, Price was it. "Not blow him away?"

"He's a hero. We can't shoot him." Hands on his hips, Franklin stared at the ceiling. "What were you thinking … keeping records of your petty little fraud? That you're goddamned invincible?"

"I couldn't have imagined you or I getting rolled over, not when we're so close to the president. Not when we are right, and our cause just."

"You're not close to the president. He doesn't know about your operation, and doesn't want to know about it. And don't put my name in the same sentence at yours when you talk about rigging the election. I wasn't here yet."

"But I got the president elected," Krocker howled.

"Oh, please," Franklin huffed. "There were a dozen incidents of fraud supporting both candidates. That's the way it is with every election. The only way you are special is that you got caught. Now, this Price fellow, he's a hero, not because he exposed your election gambit, but because he stopped Harrington, the bad cop. People will mourn his loss. We can't kill him, he knows that. It doesn't matter if the story is a hoax. Everybody bought it."

"But I can fix it. We don't have to buy his bullshit."

"It's over, dammit. The president himself is planning to meet Price and thank him for his good work." Franklin tapped his knuckles to his flattened palm. "Death won't work here."

Eyes simmering, Franklin turned to gaze out the window of his eleventh-floor office. On the west end of the Capitol Mall, where the darkness of night had cast a shadow, the spot-lighted Washington monument rose from the vast green lawn like a sharp phallus penetrating the cold grey sky.

Krocker glared at Franklin. For his efforts to get the president elected, Krocker didn't get promoted as promised. Instead, he received a politically-appointed sycophant for a boss, one who told him that he couldn't ever get credit for anything. At least Franklin didn't know the details on the Company operations, at least not yet.

Krocker threw up his arms. "You're saying you bought this guy out."

Franklin didn't turn to look. "That's right."

Krocker's lips twisted into an exaggerated frown. "I thought he was a justice freak."

Franklin watched a limo with a motorcycle escort drive up. It was the vice president. "The man's here. I hope I can convince him that we've got this settled." He turned and stood toe-to-toe with Krocker. "Because if Price figures he's got the Administration in a corner, and reneges on our agreement to work together ... hell, I don't know."

The director turned away, and facing his plush, mahogany desk, he tidied up a stack of papers and put them into the out-box.

Krocker felt a sudden lust to come from behind him and hit Franklin over the head. Bust his skull. Crush him. The urge didn't surprise or shock him. It was simply the way he reacted to people who oppressed him, starting way back when he was ten. That was when his mother had abandoned the family, leaving Krocker to live with his alcoholic father. His dad was as huge as he was obsessive. He would come home from a business trip and put on a white glove and run his hand over the counter tops. If the glove came up white, Krocker could go to the movies. If there was dirt on the glove, the kid had to start cleaning. It didn't seem fair. As a teenager it made him so mad he shattered his father's nose with a baseball bat. After that, he was shipped off to a Virginia military academy where he discovered he didn't need a family. No. He had a uniform and a future.

Now, watching the director's wide shoulders, Krocker focused on the situation in front of him. Two men in a lush, honey-colored Ceylon satinwood-paneled room discussing his fate. He had to worm his way out of this misunderstanding. Or else he had to pull the electro neuron disruptor out of his pocket and hit the director with it. Hit him with it right now. That would end Franklin's threat to fire him.

Oh, sure, Krocker had allies on the Hill who would lead the fight for him to retain his job. They would stymie an investigation of his covert activities if it came to that. But if he was fired, they couldn't get his job back. That was an executive branch decision. He would lose everything.

Krocker eased the END device out of his pocket and turned it on. He had learned that if you touched it to the skin just ever so lightly, the tool wouldn't leave a mark.

His back to Krocker, the director said, "I hope this place is presentable."

"We're doing fine," Krocker said, reaching for the scruff of Franklin's coat and pulling him backward. Before the director could protest, Krocker pressed the electric prod lightly to the back of the man's neck.

Director Franklin's body jerked up straight, and with paralyzed lungs, heart, and larynx, he stood before his desk and mouthed a scream that was never heard.

Krocker followed Franklin's moves as the director stretched up on his toes and involuntarily pranced across the rug like he had been hung from a noose and his feet barely touched the floor.

Knowing the END device disrupted all of the brain stem functions, including the sleep-awake, arousal system, Krocker said, "Easy, Jim, it's only a dream."

Franklin gagged on his tongue, sounding like an infant who was stuck in the middle of saying *ga-gaaaaaa.*

"Let me help you," Krocker said, lowering Franklin by his belt face down onto the floor while keeping the END device placed on his neck.

Franklin's lungs wheezed as if they were sucking up tight, expelling the last of their air.

"The vice president's going to get us out of this mess," Krocker teased.

Giant muscle tremors shook Franklin's body until he suddenly lay rigid on the floor.

A knock came at the door.

Krocker didn't as much as blink.

Franklin's eyes rolled back in his head and his face turned from red to blue. Then his body relaxed.

Krocker clicked off the END device and yelled, "Help!"

19

"We were talking, and his eyes rolled back, then he fell," Krocker said.

"That's awful," said the vice president.

They were standing over the dead FBI director, watching one of the vice president's security crew examine the body.

"Maybe we can revive him," Krocker said.

"Rick … Bob," the vice president said, "handle this. I'll be in the next room." He looked at Krocker and pointed to the attached office where the director's secretary worked during business hours. "Let's talk," he said.

At fifty-nine, Vice President Russell Clark moved with a halting gait, like an overweight athlete who had been stuck into a natty, charcoal-black Hugo Boss suit. When they passed though the doorway, Clark shut it behind them. "Sit down," he said.

Krocker sat in the computer chair and looked to the V.P. for the next move.

Clark said, "How are you handling this?"

Krocker said, "I'm fine. We had a working relationship, but we hadn't had time to become friends."

"It could happen to any of us. Couldn't it?"

"I suppose."

Clark was suddenly angry-eyed. "I shouldn't have had to come down here. You and Jim could have handled this deal with Price by yourselves. Why didn't you?"

"I'm not going to defame a dead man. But I will say that Franklin tried to deal with Price without consulting me."

The V.P. looked like he was going to snicker. Instead, he said, "If it was your call, what would you do to settle with Price?"

Krocker's lips pressed tight together, he nodded, then said, "Is this a heads-up conversation just between the two of us?"

The hard lines on the V.P.'s face faded. "Yes, it works better that way."

Blank-eyed, Krocker stared at Clark. "Price got into this for the money, searching government computers to find something he could use to blackmail the Administration. When he hit the jackpot, he came to Harrington asking for ten million to keep quiet. I didn't like it, and I figured I needed to take charge personally. I dealt with these kind of punks in the army. You tell them to shut up. And if it doesn't work, you make them shut up. But no, Jim wanted to pay Price. I didn't see how that would get us anywhere. He'd be back when the money ran out."

Clark flashed a disarming smile, then sat on the corner of the desk. "How often do they search these offices for listening devices?"

"Daily."

Clark squinted. "Franklin didn't work for my team. He squeezed through the vetting process with the backing of our religious supporters. But now his job is open, right?"

Krocker looked to be unaffected by the idea. "That's correct, Mr. Vice President."

"Call me Russ." The V.P. raised a brow. "I don't know how you got into this mess with Price, and I don't care how you get out of it. On our team, you eat your own mistakes." He faked a grin. "Literally, if you have to."

"Fair enough."

"I want a guarantee that this is the last we'll hear about the OPEC report."

"I can do that."

"Winners don't whine. If this falls through, you'll take the blame for it, okay?"

The deal stank. But Krocker realized that if he could hang in there, he would eventually have discrete information on most of the power-brokers in Washington. Holding that over their heads, he would get whatever he wanted. "I'll handle it," he said. "Don't even think twice about it."

"Okay. Remember, the president doesn't know anything about the election scam, and he is fascinated with Price's story … his evading federal security. He is planning to meet with Price Thursday evening. This has to be settled before then. Can you work something out with Price by that time?"

"I thought it was Wednesday."

"With Franklin dying, we'll be able to get it pushed back a day."

Krocker nodded. He would rather have the vice president commit to a terminal solution. But he could see that Clark wasn't going to obligate himself to anything that could come back on him. Rather, it appeared that he wanted Krocker to take the heat whichever way it went. But more so, it looked like Krocker was getting matched off against Price. The vice president would deal with whoever came out of the ring alive. That meant that Krocker had to kill Price on his own, and take the heat if it fell through. Betraying no emotion, Krocker said, "I'll have it settled by the meeting on Thursday."

"Good." Clark's phone rang, he answered it, talked for a moment, then said to Krocker, "Hang on a second." He left the secretary's office and shut the door behind himself.

Krocker leaned back into the chair. He was in the same position as Price. In a pinch, Krocker could threaten to release the election story to the press, and the Administration would have to give him whatever he wanted to keep quiet. He hadn't considered doing that until now, but it had been an option ever since day one when Joe Cooper agreed to help him on the deal.

Back then, Joe Cooper was presidential-candidate Gregory Bond's campaign strategist. He and Krocker met at the punch bowl during a fund raiser. Krocker had joined the festivities because he believed in Bond, a conservative Southern Senator with a bent for law and order. In the course of the evening's pageantry, Cooper, the policy wonk, was talking with an economist, Professor Bernstein. The man had joined the campaign to explain Bond's economic strategy. Krocker baited the two of them when he asked Bernstein what it would take to win the election from an economic angle. Bernstein said the economy would have to bottom out in order to get the other party out of office. Cooper interrupted, saying, not necessarily; Bond could win simply on personality, regardless of whether the economy grew or shrank. When the economist shook his head, disagreeing with Cooper, Krocker asked what sort of event could sink the economy before election day. Bernstein said one possibility was a stock market crash; that would slow the economy and frustrate the middle-class voters. Both men watched Krocker scratch his head. Finally, Krocker asked what sort of thing could make the stock market crash. The men batted that around until they agreed that the fastest way to torpedo the stock market would be a rise in oil prices. But that would not happen, Bernstein lamented, because the Organization of Oil Exporting Countries wouldn't cut production in order to tighten the market. No. They had agreements to keep oil production stable, so the world economy wouldn't collapse. Krocker laughed, saying that sounded like a flimsy deal. Bernstein said, no, it was rock solid. Krocker acted naive, wondering out loud if anybody from the campaign had taken the time to ask OPEC to change the arrangement – and to cut oil production – until after the election. Wouldn't that sink the economy? Krocker asked. That would be election fraud, Bernstein said, walking away, leaving the two men to themselves.

Cooper and Krocker stared at each other until the commander asked Cooper if he could give him information on the OPEC board of directors. Cooper nodded, asking what Krocker had in mind. Krocker said he could manipulate the data. Cooper wanted to know what that meant. Krocker laughed, saying that sounded naive for a political consultant. "Okay, I'm naive," Cooper had said, but he still wanted to know what Krocker had meant. Krocker asked if Cooper had seen the movie where the president's staff manufactured a fake war in a Hollywood studio, then sold it to the American public by playing it on the network news. Cooper had. Krocker said he had a group of operatives who could create a video. It would look like candidate Bond was making an appeal for OPEC to cut oil production. Bond wouldn't have to know anything about it; Krocker could lift Bond's facial impression off a campaign commercial and build a digital video around it. Then one of Krocker's spies would catch the oil barons in their hotel rooms at their next convention. Show them the DVD in private. Cooper was fascinated and worked with Krocker on the project until Harrington took it over. The last time Krocker talked to Cooper about the project was that very evening, right after Harrington was killed. That was when Cooper asked Krocker to take full responsibility for the election scam in order to isolate the Administration from it. Krocker didn't see where he had much choice on the deal, so he agreed. After all, Joe Cooper was now the president's chief of staff.

Ten minutes had passed when the vice president came back and picked up where he left off, saying, "Let's say you fix this OPEC thing –" Clark crossed his arms and glared blank-eyed past Krocker. "What can you do for us if we let you on our team?"

A hint of a smile rose on Krocker's lips. "My speciality is covering up government mistakes. But I can manage spin. Keep an organization in line. Keep my lips sealed."

"Great." Clark leaned forward and his mouth twisted into a sympathetic smile. "I'm sorry you can't get a medal of valor for helping on the election, but it's too much like Watergate to even talk about it. You understand?"

Krocker smiled. He knew that it was anyone's guess whether the election scam worked or not. The directorate of the Organization of Oil Exporting Countries operated in secret. Despite their recent communications with the Administration, no one on the outside knew for sure if they agreed to Harrington's proposal and ordered a cut in production. It seemed like they did, because oil production fell. But even if the directorate had ordered the cut, OPEC was so big and its production so vast, the people in charge could never know for certain whether the member countries were adhering to OPEC production guidelines. All anyone could tell for certain was that production dropped six months before the election. Then world oil prices rose. That was followed by the crash of the New York and Nasdac stock markets. Again, no one could prove the crash was related to the increase in oil prices. That ambiguity left the wonks with only one established fact when they debated the election. Lots of Americans voted for Bond because he said he'd fix the nation's energy problems. The economic problems, too.

Krocker said, "You really think this is as big as Watergate?"

"Big enough to lose our jobs if it leaks out."

"But it worked, huh?"

Clarks's mouth pressed into a tight frown. "I don't know what to think. I just learned about it." He studied Krocker until he said, "What did you promise those sheiks we would offer in return?"

Krocker knew that Cooper handled the Administration's communications with OPEC once Bond was elected. Seeing Clark act dumb about the whole thing made him want to laugh. But then, maybe Joe Cooper had kept his word and hadn't told anyone in the Administration what was going on. Instead, maybe he simply molded presidential policy to accommodate OPEC. "You know the U.S. agreement – we enforce the peace, OPEC maintains production stability?"

Clark nodded. "Uh-huh."

"I asked OPEC to cut production and risk a world economic collapse. In return, the U.S. would accept higher oil prices. We would temper the American outrage by calling for more production at home. We would also deal with OPEC's home-grown revolutions. Stop them from overthrowing any more of the governments."

The vice president laughed. "Sounds like you promised them the world." Expressionless, Krocker stared at Clark, and the vice president changed demeanor, sounding more supportive. "Where did you get the idea?"

"I talked to an economist."

"Who was that?"

"I can't tell you."

Clark nodded. "Anything else I need to know?"

Krocker shook his head.

"Good. Do something about your computer. Erasing the hard drive isn't enough."

Krocker didn't have to be told that tonight he needed to fix the computer and get rid of Price. "I'll get right on it," he said.

Clark studied him a long moment. Finally, he said, "Do you think you could run the FBI?"

Krocker nodded with certainty and enthusiasm. "You bet."

"It would only be temporarily."

"That's okay. It would be a good experience."

Clark pulled a cell phone out of his coat pocket. He spoke to Krocker as he dialed. "Did you find all the copies of that report Price sent to Global?"

"We have a screening device covering all electronic mail going in and out of Quantico. That's why I can tell you that Price sent four messages. I recovered one that was sent to a Senate aid before it was delivered. Someone is picking up the other ones."

Clark nodded, then spoke into the phone, saying, "We're going through with it. We'll meet to discuss options, tomorrow. Okay?" He listened for a moment, then chuckled. "See you later."

The vice president clicked off and turned to Krocker. "You are temporary acting director of the FBI. In that capacity, you will answer to me. Not to the attorney general. Me. Do you understand what I'm saying?"

Krocker swelled deep with pride. He'd done it. He'd pulled it off. "The full legal implications, Russ."

Clark held out his hand to shake. "Welcome on board. I'll see about getting the job confirmed in the morning. Tonight, I want you to keep a lid on the Bureau. Buckle it down. Anybody wants to leak information, shut their damn mouths."

20

Standing in line at a convenience store in Chevy Case, Maryland, Marty saw a rack of flowers, fresh bunches in plastic wrap sitting in buckets of water. He walked over and picked out a colorful bouquet and gave them a sniff.

Springtime.

I suspect that depends on whether you're done chasing us.

Marty heard Franklin's voice in his mind. It was quite clear. The director was willing to bribe him to shut up. What did Franklin offer him anyway? A job? Marty was too tired to remember much about the conversation, except that the chase was over and that he let himself be bought out. That was a good thing. Now he might live.

Marty paid the cashier for the flowers and ice cream. Outside, an airy fog rolled over the parking lot, and night clouds reflected the city lights downward into a brown haze. He pointed the car into the mists and headed towards Rock Creek Park.

In the jaws of the dusky canyon near Lisa's home, he realized he should have sent Krocker's note on the election to all the media outlets. It would have had the markings of an FBI document, coming off Krocker's computer the way it did. How could they not believe him? But again, you would think that the Post would have responded. They knew his office had been searched by the FBI and that he had been threatened. No, instead the Post had joined Global and the rest of Washington in closing ranks against him.

Feeling chilled despite the heater being on, he told himself that Jack was right. He had to let it go.

"They taught you to shoot, didn't they?" Rolland said.

"Sure did," Tanya replied.

They were heading down the stairs to Archer's basement. At the landing, he pulled out his keys and opened a metal door. The room inside was packed with military equipment.

Tanya looked at the huge stash of gear. "What were you preparing for, the revolution?"

"I ruined a perfect wine cellar preparing for this day. I hoped it wasn't coming, that I could retire and forget about all the things I've seen. But it looks like you don't retire until Krocker pulls your plug." When she didn't respond, he said, "Now, you're thinking, how could I have hired you when I'd been anticipating this day for years? Well, I'll tell you. I expected to take over the operations at Quantico, because Krocker had become so preoccupied with other matters. And I expected to name my own replacement."

"Other matters?"

"The FBI took on a bigger role in world affairs as part of the prosecution of international terrorists. It meant more government mistakes for Krocker to cover up. More time out of town."

She watched him pick up a gear box and plop it on the work bench.

"But what I couldn't conceive was that he would go through with knocking everyone off related to the Eraser Project; then use it for himself. Somehow I couldn't accept the truth about him and what we had become. We're a racketeering organization, and he's insane. We weren't protecting the United States. We were breaking the very laws we swore to uphold. If I could have admitted that sooner, I would have never brought you into this. I'm sorry."

He went to a metal case, dialed some numbers on the lock, and opened it. He pulled out a machine pistol and handed it to Tanya. "Can you handle a MP-5? It's a full automatic."

She pulled back the action and looked into the chamber, seeing whether it was loaded or not. "No problem."

He walked to a closet and flung back the sliding door. Inside where a half-dozen black jump suits. "See if one of these fits," he said, grabbing a suit and putting it on over his clothes.

Tanya set down the pistol on a workbench and pulled out one of the pairs of body-hugging coveralls. Holding it up in front of her to test the size, she said, "What are we going to do?"

"Track down Krocker, sedate him, then go from there. Maybe electroshock treatment and a seizure. Whatever it takes to put him out of business."

"If he resists?"

"We'll do to him what he was going to do to us ... Listen, this is easy to talk about, but hard to do. Like, say, Krocker tries to knock the weapon out of your hand. Do you have the will to shoot him so that doesn't happen?"

"He's taking the bullet, not the gun."

"Got it."

Tanya put on the jumpsuit. "You might lose your retirement over this."

Rolland turned and caught her eye. "I got you into this, I'm getting you out of it."

She pursed her lips hard. "I take it you didn't hear about Chris Walters, or you would have said something."

Hands on his hips, Rolland took a deep breath, then stood motionless. "What?"

"He's dead."

"Dammit. Krocker couldn't leave it alone. He had to do it. We're next, no doubt about it whatsoever."

Tanya stopped and stared past Rolland.

"What are you thinking?" he said.

"The Eraser is the tip of the iceberg. Krocker surely has projects none of us know about, especially if he has resources spread across the globe."

"That could very well be. My guess is that the director doesn't know what he's doing, either."

"Could we call him?"

"I would expect that Krocker has already implicated us with Harrington. We would only show our hand if we called the director." He opened a locked fireproof file cabinet and pulled out a laptop computer. He put it on the workbench and booted it up. "We'll get an idea in a minute."

"Huh?"

"This is one of Harrington's earlier experiments. It's tied into our system via satellite."

"How did you get it?"

"I made a switch when I heard it was on it's way to the scrap heap." He keyboarded for a few moments, then said, "Crap. Listen to this: *Burns will need to be questioned regarding her activities with Harrington, seeing how she participated in murdering Johnston.*"

"He's set it up to look like Harrington really did kill Johnston," Tanya exclaimed. She sighed, then said, "Where do we go from here?"

"Marty's house, or his girlfriend's.

"Why?"

"Price is next on Krocker's list."

21

Lisa's home was built of smooth-cut brownstone and embodied a neo-Swiss Colonial design. Efficient, yet overtly comfortable, it had long cedar balconies stretching across the entire front and back walls of the second floor. Aluminum chimneys poked through the middle and ends of the gabled roof.

Out front, Marty looped around the drive and parked under the spotlight near the stand of dogwood trees. He grabbed the ice cream and the flowers and headed up the steps to the cedar-board porch. He pounded on the security door until something leaped out of nowhere and grabbed him by the leg.

The packages scattered, but he laughed. It was Nikki, the fluffy white cat. She had clawed her way up his pant leg all the way to his pocket. Despite the pain of her claws, it was good to see her. "Miss me, did ya?" he said, taking hold the animal.

Lisa opened the door. She wore a Japanese crepe kimono with satin trim and high, shirred waist line. "I didn't keep dinner warm," she joked. "I figured you'd grab a burger between shootouts."

Flashing a fool's grin, Marty dropped the cat, clutched Lisa, and squeezed. They embraced long and hard. He finally pulled back and sighed, "You don't know how good it is to see you."

She pressed herself against him. "Yes, I do."

They embraced again.

He finally let her go, picked up the packages, then handed her the flowers, saying, "Got something for you."

"Thank you," she said, sniffing them.

"I got your favorite ice cream."

"You did?"

"I don't think I want any, but if you have some hot chocolate, I'll watch you have a scoop."

"You're on," she said.

A few minutes later, they were seated on high-backed stools in the dining-room, facing the gold-flake counter top that extended through the opening in the wall into the kitchen.

"I didn't realize you broke into Quantico," Lisa said. "How did you do it?"

Marty set down the white porcelain mug. "I joined a group of joggers and ran through the gate."

"No way."

"Yup. Then I used Heaven ... she's a computer ... and I cracked the security system at Krocker's office."

"I knew there was another woman," Lisa said.

"Not to be jealous. Heaven's as big as a basement."

Lisa studied his expression. "She was almost human, wasn't she?"

He nodded. "She's off-line now."

"The techno jerk in you probably fell for her right away."

He grinned. "Love at first byte."

She laughed, then thought-lines creased her brow. "With Heaven getting some down-time, we'll be able to try the couple thing for a few days until she gets booted back up. Right?"

Marty threw back his head and roared. He knew that Lisa always saw the good with the bad, and that it was almost uncanny the way she had him figured out, almost to the point of predicting his actions.

Lisa set her spoon in the bowl. "What did you find out about the patent thefts?"

"Krocker had a group of ex-Russian scientist at the Widewater lab. They used the stolen technology to build killing machines."

"I didn't see anything about it on the news."

"It won't be reported."

"Don't tell me they're going to cover it up."

He took her smooth white hand and felt its warm touch. Looking into her concerned eyes, he said, "Rather than kill me, the director of the FBI called and set up an interview for tomorrow. He wanted to know if I was done chasing his people. I had to say, yeah, I was. Otherwise, it looked like he was going to let Krocker kill me. When we meet, we'll go from his office to see the president. The prez empathizes with me. You know, a solitary man getting tossed around by the forces of big government."

"The president?"

"You and me, baby, and, well ... they'll probably double the Secret Service detail, but we're going to the White House. Beats dying."

"Martin Price, if this is one of your jokes, I'll never forgive you."

"Not a joke. The prez thinks I'm a hero."

"You are a hero."

"I guess. But I'll have to let the rest go because, well ... they're letting me off, not killing me."

"They still want to kill you?"

"The Company does."

"What's that?"

"I'm not talking about it. If I get started, I'll want to go on another crusade." He took the empty mug to the kitchen sink, saying, "The FBI anticipated that I'd had enough. They called the truce. I don't want to think about what I saw."

"David Rose, Jack, the memory eraser, a secret facility, patent thefts, and you're going to simply forget it?"

He stared hollow-eyed across the dining room. The round hickory table with pie-cut-inlay design sat near an antique bird's-eye-maple cabinet filled with chinaware. A triangular William and Mary walnut-framed mirror hung on the wall. The room was wrapped in white ash paneling. Beyond the archway in the far wall was the white-carpeted livingroom. A plum-colored, flair-arm love seat and sofa were surrounded by red, African sapele-wood tables. "I have to forget it," he said, knowing she would lose all this if he didn't keep his mouth shut about the Company. "If I don't, I'm dead."

He walked into the livingroom and let his gaze slip out the window. A misty drizzle had gathered on the dogwood trees, where it dripped onto the ground. He wondered how he could let it all go when Krocker was still out there. Were they even safe now? A quirky chill shot through his shoulders.

Lisa said, "Jack doesn't know a thing about the Riverview shooting. Nothing on why he's in DC. And he's blabbering on about what an angel Cheryl is. Wasn't it she who dragged his face through the mud?"

"You don't want to know the details, honey."

"Yes, I do," she said, joining him before the window.

"They hit Jack an electro neuron disruptor. What he has forgotten depends on how high the device was turned up."

"I've never heard of such a thing."

"It's like the old electroconvulsive therapy, but you don't have to go into a convulsion. Not unless they want you too."

"You simply go into a daze?"

"Yeah, like Jack. He can't remember the last day or two."

"But what about the rest of the story? He must remember what happened in L.A."

"They probably threatened to hurt Cheryl if he talks about what happened. And if I don't shut up, they'll give me the same offer about you. That's why I gave into Franklin and quit the investigation. If I stayed on it, or said something about the election fraud, they would hurt you." He glanced around, putting his hand to his mouth like he was calling somebody in the distance. "Krocker, baby. If you're listening, I'll never talk about the Eraser Project, the election scam, nothing. Okay? Now leave me alone."

Lisa's expression turned sour. "They can't be listening."

"They have the technology to do anything they want. That's why I gave up. It would take an army to beat them."

She studied his dark, baggy eyes. "Could they use the Carnivore program and figure out that you sent me the email?"

He shook his head. "I don't think the government cares. If they're listening, it's only to make sure I've given up. That's pretty obvious."

"You mean they expect us to go to bed and forget it? Simply go to sleep?"

"Relax and let it go." Yawning, Marty stretched towards the ceiling.

She rolled her eyes. "Pretend we saw nothing –"

"No cash, no crooks, no bullets –" he said.

"– no Jack –" she added.

"– no computer –"

"– no chase –"

"– no sex," he joked.

"Sex?" she exclaimed.

"Oh, it was nothing," he said, grinning.

"You tell me you want to stop dating and live together, but you come home and tell me casual sex with these FBI floozies is nothing." She pointed to the doorway. "Go!"

He laughed so hard, he nearly fell over. Then he grabbed her from behind. She resisted his pass, but he forced himself closer. Feeling her hair tingling against his face, he whispered in her ear. "I don't want the FBI to hear this. They'll use it to control me. But I lusted for their computer. I raced across her keyboard. It was digital technophilia. My fingers pulsing, her keys humming, until … until …"

His phone rang. "What now?" he said.

"Let it go," she said.

"I can't. Our lives might depend on it." He answered the call.

"Marty – wow! You're a hero!" It was Mike Greene, his lawyer.

"I guess."

"I'm sorry it took so long to get back to you," Mike said. "I knew you wanted results, not promises, and I didn't get out of court until five. Did you see the clip on TV … what they did to Harrington?"

"Yeah."

"You sound glum. You're okay, aren't you?"

Marty looked into Lisa droopy face. He was stupid in coming here and putting her at risk. "No, Mike, I'm not. The head of the Company, John Krocker, he is still loose. And he knows I've got the information that could hang him."

"The patent theft?"

"That's nothing. He tried to rig the last presidential election."

"No way."

"Yes, it's true. He went to OPEC saying Bond wanted a cut in oil production. In exchange, he said Bond would do something for OPEC when he got elected."

"I don't understand."

"If OPEC cuts oil production, the price of gas goes up, which is what happened before the election. The economy slipped, too. Don't you remember the pre-election stock crash?"

"As a result of a cut in oil production?"

"It's possible that's what set the chain of events into motion. But whether it did or not doesn't matter. It was a conspiracy to rig the election. Oilgate. It's right next to Watergate in the world of dirty tricks."

"You're saying you know this really happened?"

"Yes. I took an account of it off Krocker's computer and sent it to Global News. But they called the FBI. When I showed up for the TV interview to discuss it, I discovered the place surrounded by cops. That's when the chase started."

"Ah, geez. All evening I was negotiating with the president's staff and no one told me. Can you believe that?"

"Well, yeah, who is going to talk about an attempt to rig the election? It would set off a scandal. Maybe an impeachment."

"They'll simply deny it."

"Right. How far did that get Nixon?"

Mike was silent until he said, "Is there anything else I need to know?"

"It depends. Are you willing to fight these people and get them off my back?"

"I'm one-hundred percent behind you."

"Okay, listen. I used a bait-and-switch tactic, shifting the murder accusation from myself to Harrington. Neither he nor I killed Tucker Johnston. It was Jack Watson, my ex-partner. Johnston attempted to kill Jack in order to stop his investigation of the Company. Now Krocker is using the switch I made on the data, blaming Harrington for Johnston's murder in order to cover his own butt."

"Huh?"

"Krocker murdered Harrington at Widewater because he knew too much about Krocker's operation."

"Insane. Nothing is what is seems."

"Yes, and silly of me, but I thought they would stop trying to kill me after Director Franklin called and asked if I wanted to call a truce. He said he wants to talk tomorrow, then go up the avenue and see the president. The problem is that Krocker will try and kill me before then. He will do it to stop me from ruining his career."

"People don't kill people in the District. Not even over this. We negotiate."

"Harrington is dead."

"That's the exception that proves the rule. I'll talk to Krocker's overseers and get him off your back. It will probably take until morning, since it's getting late, but I'll do it – guaranteed."

"That all sounds cool, but listen. Harrington emptied a fifty-round clip trying to kill me today. Now it's Krocker's turn."

"My fucking god," Mike exclaimed, "I didn't know we came that close to losing you."

"It's not over. Krocker's gunning for me."

"Where are you?"

"My girlfriend's house near the Rock Creek Golf Course."

"What are you doing to handle security?"

Marty gave a wry laugh. "I was thinking about borrowing a full automatic and tracking the bastard down."

"Okay, Martin, I understand you're numb from the chase, but we've got to slow down and try to follow legal procedures. How can I help to stabilize the situation?"

"Make it safe, dammit. Get Krocker off my back. I want to get married. Not go the grave."

"I'll send a couple armed guards out there. They're professional. They handle the slack the District Police can't pickup. I can get them to your place within the hour. I do it all the time for people. They'll park their car in your driveway, then walk the property. How's that sound?"

"They have to be connected by radio, and there has to be at least four of them. And make sure they understand that Krocker has toys that can blind a person at a half-mile's distance, give you a heart attack, stimulate a seizure. He will kill them with as little thought as swatting a fly. They need to know this."

"Give you a heart attack?"

"I saw the plans on his computer. I'll show them too you."

"Okay, send them over. Tonight, we'll post the guards around Lisa's house. Stay up until they arrive. Do you have a weapon?"

Marty had the .45 he took off Buddy Young at the airport. "Yeah."

"Hang onto it until the guards get there. I'm going to call my friend. He has the connection to the president's chief of staff. We went over this today. They believe your allegations that the Company is trying to kill you, and they're very upset. So don't give up; they're on our side. They'll get Krocker off your back."

"Fine, but I don't know if an bunch of rent-a-cops can protect us."

"I'll see if I can get Secret Service on this, too. And look. After we fix things, let me get you an interview on Dean Jones Live. They're hurting for something important. By the looks of the news, you're it."

"Does it pay?"

"They're talking six figures. It's that, or we'll move onto the next show."

"You're on," Marty said.

Totally-ass predictable!

Krocker watched the guard take the backup security van and head to the street. He was going after coffee. What else would he be doing? That left three guards and one car.

Wearing a ski mask, he moved out of the foggy mists at the edge of Rock Creek Park, over the wire-mesh fence, and into the trees in the back of Lisa's yard. If the guards followed the same pattern they had been going through for the last hour, two of them would sit in the car and yack while the third would circle the house. The fourth had been walking the property line. Fortunately, he left. He was the only one smart enough to carry his pistol in his hand, ready to fire.

Cautious not to make a sound, Krocker glided across the wet soil until he stood behind a bush that was beyond the reach of the spotlights shining on the back lawn. Momentarily, he studied the house. A light was on inside a first floor window. He guessed that was the kitchen. In front of the back door, a cedar deck held a barbeque and a wrought-iron table. A wood shed sat to the side of the deck.

Krocker watched and waited. When a guard circled around the house, Krocker threw a rock over his head. It make a cracking sound when it landed in the forest behind Lisa's house.

The guard stopped and stared into the darkness surrounding the giant-sized oaks.

Krocker stepped out of the shadows and grabbed him about the neck. Holding a rag flushed full of ether to the sentry's face, he watched the man slowly give up his struggle and pass out.

Krocker eased the guard down onto the ground and propped him against a tree in a sitting position. Pulling out the END device, he turned it on. Then he pressed one end of the tubular device to the area above the man's ear and gave his head a short blast of electricity. That would stop the man's hippocampus from translating his experience of being choked and drugged into long term memory. When he woke up from the ether, he would never remember what happened.

With the first guard dispatched, Krocker headed around the house. Coming up behind the car in a parking area off of the circular drive, he got on his hands and knees and crawled. At the passenger-side back door, he listened to the men talk. The one bragged about how he fought in Desert Storm. Krocker could have laughed. Those who fought – *really fought!* – didn't talk about it.

"Got the coffee," Krocker said, jerking open the back door.

The man in the passenger seat kept on talking, while the driver turned to look at Krocker's automatic with the silencer staring him in the eyes.

Krocker grabbed the man in the passenger seat from behind and held the rag with the ether to his face. After the man passed out, Krocker held out the rag to the terrified man in the driver's seat and said, "Make it easy on yourself. Sniff this."

The big-eyed man with the bloated face said, "I got kids … pleeeeze…"

"I won't hurt you," Krocker said with a steady, reassuring voice. He held the rag under the man's nose until he went to sleep.

In the dark, Marty sat up in bed. "Honey, did you hear that?" he whispered.

Lisa tossed in her sleep.

"Listen," he said.

She twisted, turned.

He hit the light on the night stand. "Honey?"

Eyes closed, she kept tossing.

Not understanding, he pulled her close. "Wake up."

When she flayed the air, he believed she was having a seizure. He pulled the case off the pillow, bunched it up, and stuck the end of it between her teeth to keep her from biting herself. Holding her down, his thoughts whirled. Turn the END device on low, they toss and turn; turn it up higher, induce a seizure. Thinking the worst, he glanced about the room.

"You bastard!" he exclaimed, seeing a man in a ski mask. Wearing gloves, the intruder pointed a pistol at Marty. "You just can't let it go.

You've got to control everything!"

Marty turned his attention to Lisa. She had stopped tossing. He pulled the pillow case out of her mouth. He held her blank face in his hands. Her eyes didn't open. "Baby, I'm sorry, I really am. I'll get rid of this asshole. I'll kill him if I have to."

The intruder chuckled.

Marty glared at the man. He wore black and the mask hid his identity, but he knew it was Krocker. "The FBI has the place bugged, so you can't speak, can you, Krocker? Or Franklin will know you're here."

The intruder stepped forward and stuck the gun with the silencer into Marty's face. Then he waved it towards the door, indicating he wanted Marty to go in that direction.

"Only if you leave Lisa alone."

The masked man nodded.

Nikki the cat jumped on the bed and rushed up to Marty, then slid off on the side, away from the intruder's view.

Marty reached down to pet the cat. "Mommy's going to be okay. You stay here and protect her."

When the intruder coughed to get his attention, Marty picked up his pants off the floor and stood. He dressed himself, knowing he had to get the gunman out of the house. That was his final mission. Get the jackass out. That was the only way to save Lisa, spare her life from the killer.

The intruder waved the gun toward the hall, and Marty led the way out of the bedroom.

When the intruder pointed in the direction of the study, Marty was surprised, but did what he was ordered.

The intruder pointed to the computer. "Erase the e-mail."

Marty entered Lisa's mail server, but he didn't find anything. Someone had already erased the mail, including the incriminating message Marty had sent Lisa from Krocker's office. "There's nothing here," he said.

The intruder pointed towards back of the computer. "Disconnect it and bring it."

Marty unplugged the cords from the gray metal case and tucked the computer in his arms.

They went downstairs and crossed the entry room. In the foyer, Marty went for the closet. "Coat," he said.

The intruded pressed the weapon into Marty's back as he reached inside to get his jacket.

Marty put on the coat, and carrying the computer, he headed out the door.

The intruder pointed at Marty's Mustang. "You drive," he said. "When you fuck up, I'll put a bullet in your head. If you don't fuck up, you might see the light of day. Want to see another sunrise?"

22

"I hope we're not too late," Rolland said, night vision telescope to his eyes, studying Lisa's house from behind some bushes in Rock Creek Park.

Tanya looked at the tall man in the black cap. "I don't want to criticize, but people aren't this predictable, are they?"

Rolland kept watching the building. With the exception of the outdoor floodlights in front and back, most of the estate was pitch black. That didn't really matter. The infrared scope would let him see anything that was warm-blooded. "Krocker is predictable, so are the guards. They're sleeping. Can you believe that?"

"No, I can't. Price would have told them something about the danger of their mission. At least if he wanted to get some sleep himself."

"I say we go in. When Krocker gets here, we'll surprise him."

"The guards don't matter?"

"They will be dead so fast when Krocker gets here it'll be ridiculous. But it will work like a buffer and lets us know when he's coming into the house."

"He's that big a killer, huh?"

"Hitler had nothing on him."

"Suppose we go in and he doesn't show. Marty and Lisa will get up and invite us to breakfast. Right?"

He chuckled. But suddenly, he blurted out, "Where's Marty's car? It's not here."

"The garage?"

"No, Lisa's car is in there. His would be outside if he were here."

"Maybe he went to his house."

"No, it was after midnight when we drove by there. He would have to be with Lisa by now, thinking he was going to protect her."

"He ordered the guards."

"Yeah, but –" He studied the security vehicle. "The guards are dead."

Rolland rolled over the top of the vine-covered wire fence and took off running towards the house. Breaking through the hedge surrounding the garden, he raced up to the guards. He opened the car door and slapped the slumbering sentry on the face. The guard didn't wake up.

Rolland glanced at Tanya, saying, "The bastard's been here."

They raced to the house. On the porch, they looked through the glass panel.

Rolland whispered, "Krocker could still be here. But I think he packed them both into Marty's car … taking them somewhere … going to kill them. You know, have an accident."

"Let's go in." He glanced at Tanya. "You'll have to identify the target before you shoot. Lisa may still be here, and she may have a gun."

"This is nuts," Tanya said.

He nodded and said, "We're going to use a primary attack model. That means we charge inside. You will race through the lower level and fire at anything that moves. I'll take upstairs. You ready for this?"

She forced a smile.

He shoved open the heavy wood door, then charged past the mirrored foyer and into the entry room. To his left, through the arch, he could see into the white carpeted living room. In front of him, across the salon, the steps rose to the second floor. Beyond that was the kitchen.

Rolland raced up the stairs. At the landing, he glanced around, then took a flying leap into the spacious master bedroom. He hit the floor, rolled, and came up standing, his weapon pointed at Lisa.

The night stand light was on. She was asleep.

"Wake up, honey," he said, shaking her shoulder.

She breathed hard, but didn't budge.

"Where's your boyfriend?" Rolland said. "Where's Marty?"

One droopy eye hung open, but it didn't focus.

"Lisa, what happened?"

Her lips moved a little, but she didn't speak. When she fell back to sleep, he opened the night stand drawer and shuffled things about. Then he headed into the attached bath and looked through the medicine cabinet.

"You're crazy, Rolland," Tanya said. "Barging in on her like this."

Black machine pistol in hand, ready to shoot, he glanced at Tanya. "No, Krocker's been here. He's done something to Lisa so she can't wake up."

"Did you think of sleeping pills?"

"Yes, I'm looking for a prescription, but I'm betting he used the END device on these people."

"But Krocker's car is at Quantico."

"He left it as a decoy. He had to hit Lisa tonight before the long-term memory takes effect. After that, he'd have no way of erasing her recollections of what Marty has told her. That's what happened. Then he took Marty's car. Look." He pointed at the coins on the carpet. There was seven of them. They made the outline of a *K*.

"That bastard," Tanya said.

Rolland picked the slim-line phone off the night stand, dialed 911, and set the receiver on the table without hanging it up. Then he raced into the hall. "Let's search this place for clues."

They hustled though the house, looking everywhere. Finally, Rolland headed for the back door. "Let's get out of here.

Tanya caught up with him on the back stairs. "Why not call downtown and put out an alert for Marty's car?"

Rolland raced across the yard and leaped over some low-lying bushes. With Tanya racing beside him, he said, "No, Krocker will have a spy there who will alert him to what we're doing."

"But if your hypothesis is correct, Marty is going to die. We'll never find Krocker in time to stop him."

Grim-faced, Rolland said, "Our number one priority is to kill Krocker before he kills us."

23

His heart pounding like a drum, Marty fumbled to make conversation. "How did you rig the election?" he said. "I mean, it almost looks like your plan worked. OPEC did lower production."

Krocker had taken off the ski mask and seemed relaxed. "I manipulated the data."

Driving south along Rock Creek Expressway, they passed the turn-off to the Memorial Bridge, which linked the District to Arlington Cemetery on the other side of the Potomac River. A drizzle spotted the windshield. Turning on the wipers, Marty stared straight into the yellow headlights of the single oncoming car. He thought about crashing into it and forcing an accident. But he knew Krocker was too smart for that. He kept the cold gun barrel pressed into Marty's neck. Any misstep and Krocker would pull the trigger. There had to be a dozen ways he could cover it up. Trying to stall for time, and praying for inspiration, Marty said, "Ghosting the data. That's it?"

Krocker said, "Imagine a digitalized video of Bond sitting for a TV advertisement. Imagine manipulating the background, the voice … everything … and coming out with a short heart-to-heart plea to OPEC. I think you can take it from there."

"That's absolutely amazing."

"I thought so."

Marty considered his situation for a long grim moment. Finally, he said, "Do you know where I got the file on the election fraud?"

"My office."

Marty laughed. "I downloaded your hard drive onto the Crays at the Pentagon."

Krocker pointed. "Go straight."

They were at the intersection with Independence Avenue. Krocker wanted to continue traveling south along the river and head into the entrance of West Potomac Park.

Marty drove in that direction. The National Park Police Headquarters was to the left. Ironically, the lights were off to save energy, and no one seemed to be around. The only thing that stood out was the white-stone facing of the

Washington Monument which towered in the background a half-mile away. Beyond that was the Hoover building. Marty figured that Krocker expected to walk there after killing him and go back to work as if nothing had happened.

When they approached Ohio Street and the baseball diamonds near the FDR Monument, Krocker said, "Slow down." He pointed towards the curb on the passenger side of the vehicle. "The cutaway. Drive through it."

Marty took the car up across the sidewalk, then down on the grass that ran along the river.

"This way." Krocker pointed. He wanted Marty to double back and go parallel to the water.

Marty turned. There was nothing between the car and the water's edge except a few small stones where the grass met the river.

Krocker pulled a vial from his pocket and took off the lid. With the gun pointed at Marty's head, he said, "Approach the water. When you get to the edge, keep going. You're going to drive into the water. You stop, I shoot. You keep going, I don't shoot."

Marty felt the cold press of the gun barrel at his temple. He realized Krocker meant to drown him. If he floored the gas pedal and jerked the car forward, he'd take a bullet, but maybe by sheer luck, Krocker would get stuck in the car and go down under the water with him.

"What's that?" Marty said, smelling something turgid wafting up from the vial Krocker was holding under his nose.

"You tell me. Take a whiff."

Marty inhaled, coughed, and turned his head towards the window. His sudden sense of stupor told him that the inhaler contained ether and was meant to knock him out. He would drive into the water asleep and drown.

The barrel of the gun dug into Marty's neck and Krocker yelled. "Don't stop the car, and don't turn your head. Take another whiff, or you're going to eat lead!"

Marty stared straight ahead. They were angling towards the water. Krocker had the door open, ready to jump out. If Marty inhaled, he'd pass out and drown when the car sank under the water. If he stopped the car, Krocker would shoot him.

Bozo boys…

Marty listened to Lisa's sweet voice waft through his mind. It was the voice of grace. The voice that brought him to great heights, kept him in Washington, gave him reasons to work, to live. A family voice. The voice that –

"Inhale!" Krocker ordered.

You don't have to die for me...

Heading for the water, and out of breath, and ready to inhale, Marty calmly said, "The Crays are going to send a copy of your hard drive onto every government computer in the United States."

"Nice try. Inhale deeply, or take a bullet. Which do you want?"

For Marty with his mind racing, the car seemed to be barely moving. He had time to think of alternatives. What did Harrington have on Krocker that forced him to kill him? It wasn't really the election scam. No, it was something else. It was –

"The federal computers will say you finished the Eraser Project, and that's why you killed Harrington," Marty said.

"Stop!" Krocker ordered.

Marty slammed on the brakes and the car skidded, the front wheels stopping in the water.

"How could you make the government computers say that?"

For Marty time was moving frame by frame. He saw a picture in his mind of all the federal computers joined together in various subunits, linking them into larger units.

"I put a timed program onto the Crays. They'll send the copy of your drive out in the morning if I don't stop it. Same thing with tomorrow if I don't show up at the president's office." Marty turned his head and looked into Krocker's eyes. "I had to stop you somehow."

Krocker didn't blink.

Marty looked across the black waters. Crystal City, Virginia, was a glitter of light reaching for the sky on the far shore of the Potomac. If he got out of this alive, he and Lisa where going there to party. "You can stop it from happening if you give me twenty-million dollars and let me leave the country. Otherwise, ten-thousand people will see it on their computers. They'll call it the Krocker Chronicles."

"Back up," Krocker ordered.

Marty put the car into reverse and headed towards the sidewalk. "Where we going?"

"We're going to talk –"

Marty could see himself being beat into submission.

"– and if you behave –"

Marty saw himself being cut into small pieces, Krocker's hand on a sharp scalpel.

"– I won't torture you –"

Marty saw his body parts being hauled to the garbage disposal at Quantico.

"– I will put you on the memory eraser, and you'll forget this whole thing … after you turn off the failsafe. Will you do that, turn it off?" Krocker glared at him, waiting for an answer.

They were circling backwards, away from the river and onto the sidewalk when Marty smashed his foot onto the brake pedal, jolting the car to a sudden stop.

Krocker slammed back into his seat, and the force of the momentum flung his gun hand back, away from Marty's head.

The gun roared, shooting out the side window of the Mustang.

The car rolled back towards the water.

Marty punched Krocker in the eye.

"Mother fucking –!" Krocker yelled.

Marty swung his fist again and felt the blood gush from Kocker's nostrils.

Krocker aimed the gun at Marty's head.

Marty swung a fist, hitting the gun backwards.

The gun roared, again, firing behind Marty's head.

Marty hit the angry man in the throat.

Choking, Krocker swung at Marty with his free hand.

Marty blocked the punch, then turned to see Krocker's gun hand moving towards his head. He grabbed Krocker's wrist, holding back the weapon.

"You're dead!" Krocker roared, muscling the gun towards Marty's face.

Marty struggled with the gun.

The car banged against a tree, stopping short of the river.

Krocker threw himself onto Marty.

With Krocker's warm blood dripping onto his face, Marty thrashed at Krocker's eyes.

Krocker let out a ghoulish laugh. "I'll fuck your bitch with a knife!"

Marty's mind took a leap into his past. He was standing in a gym. It was a self-defense class. The students were circled around an instructor who stood in the middle of the mats. The instructor said: "When you're down, let go. You've got to free your hands so you can fight."

The petite redhead, who had rolled Marty over her shoulder Jujitsu-style and had slammed him onto the mat earlier in the evening, said, "But what if the intruder has a knife?"

The instructor was adamant: "I don't care what he has … a knife, a gun, a cock. Let go and pop his ears."

Marty let go of Krocker's gun hand. With cupped palms, he popped both of the big man's ears.

Krocker screamed, reflexively lurching up straight in the seat, firing blindly.

Marty hit the door latch and rolled out onto the ground.
Krocker fired at him.
Marty rolled away from the car.
Krocker bailed out and fired again.
Marty ran.
Krocker raced after him, firing the weapon.
Marty tripped.
Krocker ran up close and pointed the weapon. "Fucking asshole!"
Marty rolled.
Krocker pulled the trigger, but the firing-pin only clicked.
Marty charged Krocker, quick and low, as if he was going to tackle him.
Krocker dropped the gun and took a step forward into a fighting stance and screamed, "Key-eye!"
Marty took a flying leap and kicked.
Ducking, Krocker whacked Marty on the foot, blocking the blow.
Marty rolled off Krocker's back and onto the muddy ground.
Krocker dove at him, the END device in his hand, ready to electrify Marty's brain.
On his back, Marty struck at the hand with the aluminum tube, knocking it aside.
But Krocker came down hard on Marty, knocking the wind out of him, and pressing the END device against his throat.
Marty gagged and, seeing stars, he poked a finger into Krocker's Adam's apple and shoved full force.
A croaking sound expelled from Krocker's mouth, and he fell back.
Marty twisted out from underneath Krocker and rolled up to his feet.
Krocker jumped up and charged, holding the END in front of him.
Marty swung with a mad passion, knocking the END out of Krocker's hand. And blocking Krocker's swings, he made quick jabs, hitting Krocker in the face.
Krocker rebounded, charging like a wild bull.
Marty made a flying kick to Krocker's head. It jolted back like a punching bag.
Krocker roared a mouthful of obscenities as he fell into the mud.
Marty charged and kicked him again.
Krocker fell on his side.
Marty kicked his back, hitting the kidneys.
Retching in pain, Krocker pulled a small gun from his boot.
Marty kicked wildly.
Krocker fired blindly.

Marty fell back, stumbling. He'd been hit in the side.

Krocker stood, tripped, and fell flat on his face.

Marty staggered to the car, opened the door, tumbled in, jammed it in gear, and took off.

24

Night's endless shadow gripped the road.

In the passenger seat of the car, Tanya had the computer on her lap. It showed a map of the rolling hills surrounding Krocker's mini-ranch outside of Ashland, Virginia, twenty-five northwest of Richmond.

"He's going to Ashland," she said. "He wouldn't try to get Price into his condo."

"He's not taking Price anywhere; he'll dispose of him." Entering the Northern Virginia traffic grid on North Glebe Road, Rolland approached the traffic signal and hit the brakes. "Let's go to his condo."

"No. Pull over."

The light turned green and he pulled through the intersection and stopped at the curb.

"How do I search the FBI network for new messages relating to Krocker?" she asked.

"Hit *function 7*, then look at search options. Find *scan*. Click on it, and enter his name. On the next screen, click *interrupt*. That will send you a message when there is any mention of Krocker's name on the network."

Keyboarding, she said, "You're betting he'll kill Marty and then go back to his condo. Wash his hands. Drink a beer. Flip on the Sports Channel."

"Krocker's done it before ... kill someone, then come home and get in the hot tub. The ranch is for the weekends. That's how he thinks."

"But he has to silence us. We know everything."

"He's always got tomorrow. Besides, he knows no one is going to believe us. The network says we helped Harrington kill Tucker Johnston."

Staring at the computer, Tanya said, "He killed Franklin."

"What?"

"It's here, Franklin died of a heart attack. It had to be Krocker."

"Crap."

The storm dumped a gray sheet of water onto the Potomac.

Krocker cursed as he stepped out of the mud and made his way under a tree. He had used his last bullet on Price. That left him feeling naked, vertiginous, like when his father came home when he was a kid.

With the rain to his back, he pressed the button for the light on his watch. When it lit, he felt oriented once more. The watch doubled as a pager and phone. He pressed a button that patched him into the FBI operations switchboard at Quantico.

"FBI, how may I direct your call?" said the voice on the line.

"This is Commander … I mean, Acting Director Krocker. I want you to page Mack Jones. Give him my number. It's on your caller I.D. This is a direct order. It must be done immediately."

"Yes, sir, just a moment, please." The operator clicked on hold. When she came back on, she said, "The answer to the question is *Jackson*. What's the question?"

Jackson was Krocker's secret code. He immediately verified that he was actually himself by saying, "Who is the best president ever?"

The fear overrode the pain.

Holding one hand to his side, compressing his jacket against the bitter wound, Marty raced the car under the mammoth concrete arch where Rock Creek passed under the William Taft Bridge. Praying for Lisa, he hoped she hadn't smothered, hadn't had a stroke. When he hit the corner of her lazy, winding street, the car slid sideways and goose-tailed, the rear-end swinging back and forth until he righted it by slamming his foot on the gas.

The car bounced up the drive. Approaching the house, he slammed on the brakes. The car was still skidding when Marty threw open the door and raced up the stairs.

"Lisa!" he screamed, throwing open the front door.

He took the stairs three steps at a time, raced down the hall, then came to a jolting stop. Bug-eyed, he stared: The bed was empty.

He raced into the bathroom. The cabinets were open.

"Lisa!" he screamed, not understanding what had happened.

He ran to the spare bedroom, then went downstairs. Passing through the kitchen, he jerked open the door to the attached garage. He flipped on the light. She wasn't there, but her car was.

He ran back inside, wondering where the guards had gone.

Grabbing the phone off its base on the kitchen counter, he stood motionless, wondering what he was doing. He finally realized that he wanted to hit the redial button. That would get him in contact with the last person Lisa called.

He hit the button and the 911 operator came on the line. "What is the emergency?" she said.

"I don't know," Marty howled. "I got home, my girlfriend is gone, and I dialed last number called. That's how I got you. Her name is Lisa Page. Do you know what happened to her?"

"What is your name?"

"Marty Price."

"How are you related to Lisa Page?"

"Fiancé."

"We had a call earlier from that number. Lisa Page was taken to the emergency room at Sibley Memorial."

"Thanks," he said, slamming down the phone, knowing the operator wouldn't give him any information on Lisa's condition. That's when he saw the blood on the floor.

He gasped, thinking Lisa might be dead.

Only when he noticed he was holding his side, that he was in deep pain, that in his rush to save Lisa, he'd forgotten his own wounds – that was when he realized that it was his blood on the floor.

25

The thirty-three-room vice-presidential mansion sat on Observatory Hill on the west end of Embassy Row next to the British mission. Built of brick in a Queen Anne style, and painted white, it was three stories tall with a turret and a wrap-around veranda. Tied to the veranda at the middle-front of the house, a long portico sat on white columns and extended shelter all the way to the street.

Inside the den on the second floor of the mansion, Russell Clark was seated in an apricot-colored, camel-back chair with round, tilted arms. The room was decorated with an American-independence motif, and at the top of the ash-colored walls, a gold-gilded frieze trimmed the arched ceiling. President Bond's chief of staff, Joe Cooper, a thin, hollow-cheeked man of forty, sat across from Clark in a beechwood bergère chair with yellow-gold upholstery. A New England candlestand held a tray of pastries and a thermos of coffee. It was late Tuesday night.

"I don't think this will go public," Cooper said. "Not with Krocker and Price going at each other's throats."

Clark's face mushed up into a rubbery frown. "You keep saying that, but I'm still worried about what we did tonight."

"Foisting Krocker's appointment onto the boss?"

Clark's jaw ground tight. He had called Cooper from the FBI director's office seeking advice while Krocker waited in the other room. Now he was stuck with the decisions the two of them had made. "No, pitting Krocker against Price. One of them is going to kill the other, and then I have to work with a murderer for the next few years."

"C'mon, Russ, I gave you that idea. Look at the positive side. We finally spotted Krocker for a kook, and we've moved him up to Pennsylvania Avenue so we can keep a close eye on him."

"Yes. But he's going to want to try and rig the next election ... and on and on. And who knows when the stupid jerk might talk. He really believes he won the election for us." The big man rolled forward in his chair and stood, then he approached the mantle above the tiled fireplace.

Cooper stood too, moving next to the vice president. This was the biggest spin management project he'd ever been on. He wished he could level with Clark that it was he and Krocker who had tried to rig the election, and that Krocker wasn't going to blabber. No. The commander wanted power and was willing to kill for it. Kill Marty Price.

Clark pointed to the ancient map of Washington, D.C., sketched by the original District planner, L'Enfant. "We're not even on this thing."

Cooper spoke with concern. "Does that have something to do with what is bothering you?"

One side of Clark's face twisted up as a brow twisted down. "In a way, yeah," he said. "I've exceeded the limits of my constitutional authority."

The political consultant grinned. "No way. There's precedent for a strong V.P."

Clark caught Cooper's eye. "Yeah?"

"Sure. Think about Aaron Burr. He not only shot the secretary of the treasurey, Hamilton, but tried to steal the Louisiana Purchase and set himself up as king. Then there's Theodore Roosevelt who tried to run the military. And L.B.J., who owned Congress. And George Bush, who had his foot in foreign policy right under Reagan's nose."

"But Krocker and Price ... it's fine if they kill each other?"

"Think like a general. You're leading the troops. Some have to die so the rest can live."

Clark walked to window and looked across the way at the monumental office of the Naval Observatory. Rivulets of rain laced across the lawn and into the gutters lining the street. "Okay, let's say I'm the general. How do I present this to the Inner Circle tomorrow?"

"With complete innocence. Krocker was standing in the director's office and looked like he could take command. You questioned him, and he knew the details of the job better than Franklin ever did."

"Anyone on the Hill knows the job better than Franklin did."

"We all know that, but no one is going to say anything."

Clark was silent for a moment. "Tell me what happens if Price survives his battle with Krocker. He'll see he has the power to get us impeached. How do we handle that?"

"If Price is alive tomorrow, his lawyer will make sure he keeps quiet."

26

The phone on Krocker's wrist vibrated.

He hit the button. "Krocker here."

"What's going on?" said Mack Jones on the other end of the line.

"I'm tracking Price."

"Was he at the house?"

"Yeah, but he got away."

Mack laughed over the line. "Going to waltz in and pick him up. I told you not to go in there alone. Look what he did at the airport."

"Okay, I made a mistake sending you after Burns when we should have been focusing on Price. Can you pick me up?"

"Yeah, but what happened with the jerk?"

"I got him in the car, and had a P-7 stuck in his neck. But he knocked my arm back, and I shot out the back window."

"This guy watches too much TV."

"Help me out. I've got until Thursday evening to shut him up. Then he goes to see the president. They'll buy him out. After that, it'll be my ass if I touch him."

"But he knows about the Company," Mack said over the line.

"Right, so he'll be back on our ass when the hero thing wears out."

"Where are you at?"

"Tidal Basin. Drive out to the park. I'm at the first baseball field."

"I can be there in twenty-five minutes. What should I expect?"

"Nothing. But take precautions. Burns is somewhere in the District."

"God damn her."

"We'll get her next."

"Are you injured?"

"I think I've got a broken eardrum. Bring some painkillers."

"Will do," Mack said. "I'm with Buddy."

"Can you bring him?"

"Hang on."

Krocker listened to muffled voices over the line. He hoped to get Buddy Young back onto the manhunt. He was the best tracker Krocker knew. Mack, on the other hand, had brains, and he questioned things. That made him insubordinate all too often for Krocker's taste.

Mack came back on the line. "Buddy's going to stay here and finish off the bottle we started."

Krocker stared across the dark waters of the Potomac. "You're drunk?"

"No, Buddy is."

"Fine, come by yourself. I want to stop by the condo to clean up, then see about getting my head put back together."

"Right, but you gave me the wrong password."

The two men had a system to tell if the other was in immediate danger. Krocker gave the all-clear answer: "Tough shit."

"How about that," Mack said, clicking off.

In the dark of night, nothing moved.

Rolland drove slowly, scanning the surroundings. They were on a road running parallel to the street where Krocker had a condo. Shade trees cast black shadows. There wasn't any traffic. He eased the car into a driveway that circled around an apartment complex. Pulling into a parking slot in the back of a building, he said, "I'll go through here and climb the back wall. Then I'll break into Krocker's place and kill him."

"I'm going with you," Tanya said.

"No, leave me here; take the car, get out of Washington."

"It's his territory. You'll need a backup."

He turned to look at her. "One person has a better chance than two of making it inside undetected. Take the car to Canada. Call me in a few days."

"Rolland..."

He had the door open. When he turned, she looked into his stark, hollow eyes and said, "You're going to kill him even if you get killed in the process. I don't want you dead. It would be better if we ran. Anything but dying."

Tightening the noise suppressor on his pistol, Rolland looked away. "I got you into this, I'm getting you out of it. Career unmarred, body uninjured."

"That's wonderful, Rolland," she said. "Then I can go to work on Monday as if nothing happened."

Blank-eyed, he digested her sarcasm. Finally, he said, "I went though one of these power struggles at the beginning of my career. Harold Wilkins. Look him up. He was my boss. It was about integrity, and he was willing to take the fall to preserve it. That's where we're at. I blew it. I knew I should have turned Krocker in years ago, but I took each little lie and shoved it down, stomached it, said it didn't matter. I believed the government needed the research done to keep up with other countries … dictatorships where torture wasn't a problem."

Tanya had come around the car and was facing him. Watching him fiddle with the clip to his automatic, she said, "You're confusing FBI work with a male grudge match. Krocker knows you're coming. He has always known it would come to this. It always does. He downsizes every couple of years, kills off everyone who knows anything about how he got what he's got. That's why he's the commander and you're director of research."

When Rolland turned to walk away, she grabbed the scruff of his bullet-proof vest and jerked. "Dammit, can't you hear what I'm saying?"

He spun around. "Yes, I know what you're saying. I feel the same way."

"Then it's the time to learn to live. Not die."

He stared at her but didn't speak.

"Let's leave," she said, a tear in her eye.

He scanned the apartment complex, looking for anyone watching. "I've got to go in there and get him."

She stepped up, wrapped her arms around him, and gave him a bear hug. "Monday, lunch?" she said.

He pulled the night vision goggles over his eyes. "Monday, lunch."

Pointing a machine pistol out the window of the grey Mercedes, Mack scanned the cars parked along the street. Something Buddy had said earlier in the evening spun in his mind: "I thought we were a foursome … you, me, Krocker, and Harrington. Shouldn't we have been consulted if Harrington was going down?"

"You think the news was a spin?" Mack had replied.

"The news is always a spin. What I'm saying is that you'd think Krocker would have given us some explanation by now, wouldn't you? Unless it was a setup, and he killed Harrington on purpose. Then we're next."

Regurgitating the conversation, Mack pulled over and parked the car. Grabbing his stubby automatic, he got out and glanced about the wide-open grass field. Krocker either had to be hurt more than he let onto and wasn't thinking clear – asking Mack to drive into the park and make a clear target out of himself – or Krocker was dumb enough to set Mack up in an obvious, jackass way, and was stupid enough to think he could get away with it.

Crouching low, Mack pulled his cell phone from his pocket and dialed Krocker. When Krocker answered, he said, "I'm here, where you at?"

"At the ballpark," Krocker said over the line. "Was that you parking upstream?"

"Yeah," Mack said.

"I'll be there in a second."

Mack clicked off. When he saw Krocker marching up the middle of the road whistling Dixie, he realized he hardly knew the man at all.

Rolland took a running leap and literally ran up the side of the ten-foot-high brick wall surrounding the condominium complex. On top, he looked around. Brown aluminum-sided four-story condos huddled in three separate complexes, providing privacy for people who worked in the Washington intelligence community. A neatly-trimmed lawn ran between the fence and the buildings. Outdoor spotlights covered the yard with a yellow haze.

He had been here before when Krocker had everybody over for a barbeque. So he knew there was a laser-trip alarm surrounding the premises, in the places people weren't supposed to be after dark.

Jumping down, he knelt in the rock garden. On the lawn, he crawled on his stomach, going under the invisible laser beam shooting above the grass at knee's height. On the other side of the grass, he stood and raced towards the shadows behind the arborvitae bushes next to the four-story building.

The Mercedes crossed the river on the Memorial Bridge. Under the streetlights, Mack glanced at Krocker's blood-stained face. "I don't understand how Harrington got killed."

"Huh?"

"Why was lethal force used when everybody knew he didn't kill Tucker?"

"They didn't. Price switched the information, released an all-points bulletin, then cut the FBI off the federal network. Without being able to contact us, everybody figured they'd better go after Harrington. When he found out about what was going on, he thought I was behind it and went into a rage, saying he was going to fight to the end."

"Why did he think you did it?"

"I didn't talk to him, but it was so overwhelming of a data-switch, he had to think I was the only one who could do it. But it was Price. He broke into my office, got onto my computer, and issued a government-wide security memo saying Harrington was the top man on the 10 Most Wanted List … that he killed an agent … Tucker … outside the Riverview. Well, hey. The agents felt betrayed by the idea that Harrington killed one of our own, and they were not taking it to court. He must have realized that."

Mack scoffed like the story stank. "Price not only outfought you, he got the whole department to believe that cocksucking story. That's what you're saying?"

"Price is whacko. Mad. Money hungry. But he acts like such a twerpy-ass dick that you don't think he could do this shit."

Mack laughed.

"What?"

"Better not ask him to drive next time."

Rolland came out of the elevator on the top floor of the complex and crept down the carpeted hallway towards Krocker's door, praying the guard wouldn't be doing rounds at this hour of the night.

He tapped hard on the gray metal door. When no one answered, he rapped louder.

Still nothing.

He pulled out the automated key-pick, a device shaped like a gun. It could open almost any tumbler lock. He held the barrel to the keyhole on the dead bolt, then pressed the button. Wires emerged from the front of the plastic pistol and wiggled into the hole. Momentarily, a blue light came on and he twisted the device, opening the deadlock.

Rolland repeated that procedure on the doorknob lock. Then, taking a deep breath, he swung the door open. With a light-weight, silenced automatic in his hand, he dove into the apartment and rolled across the carpet.

When no one responded, he got up and raced to the security keypad. He knew Krocker was too self-assured to worry about anyone cracking codes. That's why he bet nothing had changed since the barbeque last summer when Rolland watched over Krocker's shoulder as he punched the code into the security system. Now, when he entered the password, the green light came on.

"I'm not taking any chances," Mack said, parking the car outside of Krocker's gated community. "Let's walk in."

"Good idea," Krocker said.

Mack twisted a silencer onto a pistol and got out of the car.

Krocker had enough drugs in his system to look perky. "I need a weapon," he said.

Mack opened the trunk and reached into a black bag. He pulled out a Beretta service issue 9 mm semiautomatic and stuck it in Krocker's hand. Then he put on a bullet-proof vest. "Go in," he said. "I'll follow you."

Krocker headed for the condo complex. He punched in the security code and entered the pedestrian entrance with Mack following right behind him. Once inside, he went up the winding walkway towards the glass-walled foyer of Krocker's building.

Gun in hand, Krocker crossed the tiled floor under the chandelier. He went into the elevator while Mack headed up the stairs. Krocker was getting out when Mack emerged from the stairwell giving an A-OK sign with his fingers.

Silently, Krocker went to condo and unlocked it.

Suddenly, without warning, Mack flung open the door and walked into the apartment like he was protected from danger like a super-hero. He searched slow and methodical until he was in the master bedroom. He had his back to the wall near the door of the attached bath when Krocker caught up with him and turned on the light.

Without warning, Mack spun around and sent a blast of silent bullets ripping through the wall of the bathroom.

From behind the bathroom door someone screamed.

Mack fired a few more times then kicked in the door. Leading with his weapon, he stepped inside.

The shower stall lay on the floor in shards. Blood was splattered everywhere. A body was crumpled up in the tub.

"That's him ... Archer," Krocker said, stepping inside and pulling on a pair of gloves. "How did you know he was here?"

"I knew it's the only place in the house where the infrared alarm doesn't show movement. Then I smelled cologne. You don't wear cologne. Someone had to be here."

"You never can be too careful," Krocker said, picking up Rolland's gun. Before the other man could move, he fired Rolland's weapon at Mack.

Mack's head burst open like a crushed melon.

Krocker stooped and put the weapon into Rolland's hand, then walked out of the house and off the property like nothing had happened.

27

Enduring an endless night, Tanya hadn't moved.

She knew Rolland well enough to predict he would go in, get Krocker, and come out the same way he had entered, emerging though the apartment building behind Krocker's complex. Her heart sank when the sound of sirens blared, coming from all directions. She wanted to stay at the complex and wait one last minute with the hope that Rolland would emerge, but she knew in her heart he never would. Her mentor was dead. Dead before he could become her lover. She prayed he didn't die in vain, that Krocker was killed in the battle.

Sighing, she started the car and drove out of the apartment complex. She was a couple blocks away when the first of the police cars whizzed past. Then came the emergency vehicles.

She drove aimlessly until she parked in the lot of an all-night restaurant. When she booted up the computer, the message icon flashed. She clicked on it, and discovered that there were ten new references on the government network to the name Krocker.

She clicked on the first entry: *Gun fight at Commander Krocker's condo…*

She clicked the second: *Investigation team sent…*

The third: *Two bodies discovered…*

Her heart sank when she clicked on one which identified Rolland Archer as a dead agent at the scene. After several minutes had passed and she had composed herself, she clicked on the rest:

Second body identified…

Searching for perpetrators…

Commander not involved in condo incident…

"Shit!" Tanya cursed.

Search for accomplice…

Burns is considered armed and dangerous…

"Fuck!"

Details of operation K Condo now classified…

"He did it, the bastard did it," Tanya exclaimed, believing that Krocker had taken over the investigation and had set it up to look like she and Rolland tried to kill him.

Then a new communication flashed onto the screen, and her blood boiled cold:

Acting Director Krocker…

28

Sunshine in the window

Flowers.

The scent of spring.

Pastel-hued walls.

A colorful painting of a Mediterranean village.

Sterile chrome.

An I.V.

"Huh?" Marty jerked up in the hospital bed, not making sense of it all until he remembered he had been shot. He sat there for a moment wondering where the hell Krocker might be. Then –

"Lisa!" he wailed, up and dragging the I.V. pole out the door.

Hurrying down the polished linoleum hallway, he rounded the corner and came to the nurse's station where he yelped, "I've got to find Lisa Page. Do you know where she's at?"

While the staff members encircled him, the titanic black nurse looked over her glasses and stared at him for a full moment before saying, "She sent you flowers. Wadaya want?"

He glanced at the scolding looks on people's faces and realized he'd been sedated, wasn't thinking clear. He lowered his voice, saying, "Can you help me?"

Giving him a prudish, bully-pulpit look, the head nurse said, "Did you think of using the phone?"

"The phone? Yeah, that's it. Is she here in the hospital?"

"Yes." The nurse looked at the computer monitor, made a few clicks with the mouse, then wrote down a phone number. "Are you going back to your room, now, so that we can check your vitals?"

"Yes, of course."

Krocker woke with a startle and glanced around the lush, honey-colored, Ceylon satinwood-paneled room. Realizing he was in his new office downtown, stretched out on the leather sofa, he smiled. He'd made it, he'd actually made it to the top of the FBI. So much for the stupid reoccurring dream. Now maybe it would go away, and he wouldn't have to see himself up for promotion in the Army, ready to become a colonel, but instead getting hit with a court martial.

Bounding to his feet, he headed to the snack room where he twisted the cap off a bottle of apple juice. Thinking about yesterday, he envisioned Mack falling to the floor, his head bursting like a melon. He was sorry about what he'd done, killing off a good man. But Mack would understand. Krocker had killed him so that it would look like Mack and Rolland had a fight. That gave Krocker plenty of room to prove he wasn't even at his condo, let alone involved in snuffing out his subordinate.

Then there was the good news. His ears were going to heal. They had told him that when he had gone to the emergency room at George Washington University. The story he gave about his injuries was that some thugs came out of the dark and tried to take his wallet. They fought, and Krocker had taken some serious blows.

Crossing the office, he went in the attached bath, looked into the mirror, and studied his face. The patch on his broken nose didn't look all that bad. He combed his hair, washed his face, and began shaving.

Believing in the possible, he momentarily envisioned the future. Although he was acting director, he couldn't imagine getting confirmed as director. That usually went to a lawyer. But if he could nail down the second-in-command position, he could have a controlling hand in the director's office while staying out of the heat of Washington politics. He could also influence Congress, as he would have secret files on all the important politicians. Yes. There would be deprecating material planted in homes, on computers, in cars. Pictures of politicians naked, doing pornographic acts. None of them would know how he'd done it because he would use the Eraser on them.

He chuckled. The Company was going to be the strongest organization in Washington.

At the window, he gazed down on the lines of tourists below. This building was his now. But where the hell did he get the idea that he had to go after Price by himself? Hell. Why not use the God Rx? Use the drug to teach a chosen few new recruits that they owed their loyalties to the Company

The God Rx was Krocker's pet name for a drug the lab in Baku, Azerbaidzhan, had engineered. It could evoke a person into a state of the total suggestibility, making them ripe for brainwashing. Sure, it had never been tried outside the laboratory, but why not now? He could order an agent in here, or use one of his operatives. He would give him the drug, and the guy would go into a state of suggestible bliss. Then Krocker would give the you-can-know-justice-today sermon he had been practicing. If the recruit had the God Rx drug in his system, he would be hypnotized by Krocker's little sermon. When Krocker blamed all the world's ills on Price, the man would go after Price and kill him. Or die trying.

The idea for the drug came from a secret facility in the Ural Mountains east of Moscow. The Soviets were in power at the time, and they were trying to locate the area in the brain where belief-in-God resided. When Krocker heard about this from a Russian scientist, he hired the man to examine religious fanatics with a functional PET scan machine. That device located the current brain activity in the patient. And when the fanatics where on the last limb of being tortured, begging God to spare their lives from the mad scientists, the Pet scan recorded what part of the mind got hottest – used the most glucose. After much work, the scientist believed he had located the exact area in the forebrain bundle where people experienced God.

Krocker knew otherwise. People who where facing immanent death were moved to a state of total suggestibility. They would believe in anything that remotely could save them, and while in that frame of mind, they were totally in a position to be brainwashed.

After paying off the scientist, Krocker got a new team to develop a site-specific drug which would activate the God center of the brain on demand. The scientists experimented until they found a chemical prescription that worked. It was a hormone which caused the release of a neurotransmitter that fully potentiated the brain site for suggestibility. Sure, the drug took a person to that same exact place where the believers went, but it didn't have anything to do with God. Cynically, Krocker named it the God Prescription, or God Rx, and in the lab, people who took the drug reported feeling they had touched heaven.

Hogwash, Krocker had responded. God was simply a person's experience of being jacked-up on the brain's neurotransmitters. That put a person in a state of mind similar to an LSD rush, where you thought you could read one-another's minds, which was as idiotic as thinking you could talk in tongues. And while people might argue about this for the next fifty years, they would miss the important point. If you could use a drug to create a God-like experience in another person, you could use the same drug to control people. For Krocker that meant brainwashing a group of recruits to believe only in him and the Company.

29

"Oh, God, baby, I didn't think I'd ever see you again."

"Marty, is that you?" came Lisa's voice over the phone.

Marty pulled the I.V. pole with him as he moved towards the hospital room window. "Yes, are you okay?"

"They say I had a seizure," she replied. "I'm getting ready to go down and check out. What about you? I heard you got into a fight."

"Yeah, dumb luck called on me again. Are you okay?"

"Yes, I want to come up and see you. What room are you in?"

"361."

"You sure you're ready to see me?"

"I need to talk to you, go over our future. Honey, do we still have a future?"

"Oh, Martin, I wouldn't walk out on you" – she giggled – "not until you learned to protect yourself."

"You can be my bodyguard," he joked.

"You would need an army."

While she chuckled, he said, "I've had time to think about us, about everything."

"Uh-huh."

"I want to talk marriage and kids."

"Before we leave the hospital?"

He guffawed. "C'mon up, and we'll leave together."

"See you in a few minutes," Lisa said, clicking off.

He stared over the parking lot until the intercom in his room blared, "*Wadaya want?*"

It was the nurse. He had flipped the *help* switch a few minutes ago, hoping they would come and take his vitals so he could check out.

He said, "I want out of here as soon as possible, okay?"

"*You'll have to wait until your doctor makes her rounds.*"

"How long will that be?" Marty asked.

"*Who knows?*"

"I've got to get back to work. Is there any way to page her?"

"*You don't page a doc in this business, Mister Price, unless it's an emergency.*"

"Great. Maybe you could get me the pastor."

"*If you can't wait, pull out the I.V. and head out the door.*"

"Fine, thank you," Marty said, walking away from the intercom, cursing the nurse, telling himself no way was he going to sit there waiting for a doctor. No, he vowed, he wasn't going to wait on anyone again. He had seen death in Krocker's eyes, and he had made the decision that he was going to spend the rest of his life fighting against the control that people exercised over him. Like Derek Walker. Marty damn near wrote the computer fraud bill, but Walker was getting credit for it from the Senator. Oh, sure, Marty got the best contractor award for providing technical information. But did Walker ever mention that Marty stayed up late at the Senate office building, when everyone had gone home – fixing the mistakes, the typos, the incongruities? No.

He saw Krocker's picture flash on the TV screen, and he hit the volume control, turning it up. The news made him queasy. Krocker had been appointed acting director of the FBI. Franklin was dead.

He stomped the floor. That meant the meeting was off with the president.

He turned off the TV, and looked at the stainless-steel, I.V. needle jammed into his vein.

Was he going to sit around and wait for Krocker to catch up with him, or was he going to track down Krocker?

Track the bastard down.

Was he going tough, or going wimp?

Tough.

He pulled back the tape and looked at the needle sticking into his arms. A tube ran out of it up to the I.V. pole. He gripped the needle and jerked it out of his arm.

Blood spurt.

He ripped off a piece of the bandage that circled his chest and wrapped it around the area where the I.V. had left a bleeding hole.

Under the guise he wanted to say goodbye to the guy he had met up the hall, Marty led Lisa away from the nurse's station. At a room near the exit sign, he glanced in, told Lisa he guessed the guy had already left, then opened the door to the stairs and headed down, Lisa in tow.

"Where are you going?" she said.

"Out the back way. If I go out the front, people will want to talk to me.

You know, the hero who saved Washington. I don't need that, I need to talk to you."

"Don't you have to take care of your bill?"

"I want to talk, and I want to do it now," he said, stopping to pull her tight against his body.

They kissed.

Lisa pulled back. "Maybe we should negotiate a contract about living together before we get any closer."

He chuckled. "I can see it. Article One: no cell phones at the dinner table."

"No computers either."

He started down the stairs. "No guns at the Riverview."

"The Riverview?" She stopped him on the landing at the next floor. "Something happened there, didn't it?"

He nodded.

"My memory is like a fog."

"It'll get better."

Sibley Memorial Hospital was a small complex of buildings in the northwest side of the District. It sat on a hill and was nestled in shade trees and surrounded by exclusive upper-middle-class homes. When they approached the Mustang, Lisa saw that the car was extensively damaged.

"What happened?" she asked.

"The police rammed it during the chase."

"Then it was as wild as they made it out to be on the news."

"Yeah. They were going to hang me with contrived evidence."

"Are you going to talk to them about paying for the damages?"

"To be honest, I haven't thought about it. Not after the fight with Krocker."

"Krocker?"

"Head of the FBI."

The car door was hung up, and he jerked it open to so that she could get inside. When he saw the palm top computer sitting on the passenger seat, he picked it up. Then, face-to-face with Lisa, he said, "Could I take you over to Cher's until this blows over?"

"What blows over?"

"Krocker is trying to kill me. If we went to Cher's –"

"We're going to the FBI headquarters," she yelped, mad enough to spit. "And you're going to file a complaint. You're the hero, you should be telling

Krocker what to do."

"No, we can't go there. They could take us both –"

"Martin, stop it!" she raved. "We have to go to the FBI and complain. It's just that simple."

He sulked for a moment, then said, "I'm a little nervous about walking into the J. Edgar Hoover building."

"Ha!" she boasted.

"What?"

"A real man would swallow his pride and forget the grudge match he had going with the idiotic Feebie commander. He would go to the FBI headquarters, march in the door, head up, shoulders back, find the officer in charge, and tell the whole story. Tell it over and over until they got so sick of you they did something about it."

"Okay…"

She plopped into the seat and he shut the door. Walking around the car, he looked at the palmtop. There was a message on the screen: *ENTER PASSWORD.*

He stopped behind the car and stared at the PDA, not knowing what to think of it. He had put a command into the programmer's file at Widewater for Heaven to respond only to orders from *Stargazer*. If she had indeed downloaded onto the federal network and was still operable, maybe she would respond to that password. He entered it and Heaven came online.

"She downloaded! I've got her back!"

Jumping into the car and starting it up, he held out the PDA and glanced at Lisa. "This is the palmtop I was telling you about. It interfaces with Heaven, remember? I moved Heaven's files to the basement of the Pentagon, and I can use her to protect us." He looked at her blank face. "I'm sorry, with the seizure, you don't remember any of this."

"Maybe I should take a taxi. You go to the FBI by yourself."

"Wait a second, honey, look. This is the screen that shows where the federal agents are located. I was going out H Street, and I saw I was surrounded –"

"You're not surrounded now. Let's go."

He changed the background map to the northwest side of the District and saw that two FBI cruisers were at Sibley Memorial.

"They're here!" he wailed, cramming the car into gear.

30

"Stop!" Lisa yelled. "I want out!"

Marty hit the brakes, swung in front of the traffic, and exited the George Washington Parkway. "I'm sorry, but it's life or death."

"Why? Because a computer says so?"

"It's more than a computer."

"You and your gadgets."

"Heaven is a complex system. She monitors the FBI, Secret Service, Metro, everything. If she says Krocker is following us, Krocker is following us."

She scoffed.

"He is."

"Why would people be after you?" Lisa said. "They told me at the hospital that you're a hero. And you said you're going to meet the President."

"You had the seizure and you don't remember, but they've been after me since Jack got here." He pulled the car off the road, stopped, and looked at the palmtop. Its screen was lit up with a map of the Metro area. Blue, white, and orange circles blinked, representing vehicles from different agencies. Marty pointed out the Arlington Cemetery. "We're here," he said. "See the blue circle? That's one of the vehicles that was ordered to follow us."

"We were going a hundred miles an hour. Sure they're going follow you if you don't stop doing these dumb stunts."

He set up the laptop to intercept audio communications between the pursuit cars and the dispatcher. When he hit the *play* command, the computer relayed the radio transmission:

– (pursuit car) "*We lost him … driving like a manic.*"

– (base) "*I thought you had the hospital surrounded.*"

– (pursuit car) "*We did.*"

– (base) "*Find him.*"

– (pursuit car) "*If he breaks so many laws, why can't we pick him up?*"

– (base) "*It's a surveillance operation. That's all I have on it…*"

Lisa's face rippled with fine lines of perplexity. "Are they talking about you?"

"Yes."

"If this is one of your pranks, I'm going to kill you."

Marty's phone rang. He pulled it off his belt. "Marty here," he said.

"This is Tanya," said the voice on the line.

"My god," Marty exclaimed, "I can't believe we're both alive."

Tanya sounded bleak. "He got Rolland."

"Rolland's dead?" Marty hadn't met the man, but he still felt awful. "I'm sorry."

"He covered it up," Tanya said. "He's going to get away with it."

"I'm really, really sorry."

"That's not half of it. Franklin died last night. Krocker's been appointed acting director."

"I know. He used the END device to stimulate a heart attack. It was his heart, right? That's how Franklin died?"

"That's the media report."

He leaned back into the seat. "We were just released from the hospital. Krocker had agents in the parking lot. They're running a surveillance operation on us, but we got away. We're at the Arlington Cemetery, trying to figure out what to do next."

A voice of concern came over the line. "Is Lisa okay?"

"Krocker was at Lisa's house last night. He shot me, but she's okay."

"Shot you?"

"Well, hey – I smashed his nose, the jack ass."

"I knew something had happened. We were there. The guards were passed out, and we couldn't wake Lisa up."

"Did you call 911?"

"Uh-huh."

"Thank you," Marty said. "What do we do now?"

"Stake out his ranch and kill him. That's where I'm going. You have Lisa to think about, so you might consider leaving until this blows over."

"It won't blow over. Where's his ranch?"

"Ashland."

"Okay."

"If you're thinking about dropping Lisa at home, don't. It's surrounded."

"That's what I figured. Do you know where we can get some automatic weapons?"

"Yes."

"I've got to get rid of the Mustang. Can you pick us up?"

"Head south on Highway One. There's a Roy Rogers Restaurant. I'll meet you there."

"See you."

Marty clicked off.

Lisa asked, "What did you mean saying Krocker was at my house?"

Marty made an exasperated sigh. "Krocker kidnapped me from your bedroom."

"Why didn't you tell me?"

"When was there time?"

"Did you tell the emergency room doctor?"

"I did, but they had me pumped me full of painkillers so I wasn't making much sense."

She reached out and held his face in her hands. "All I was told was that you were in a fight. What happened to me?"

A tear slid down his cheek. "We were asleep. Krocker hit you with an electroshock device, kind of like a cattle prod. That's what caused you to have a seizure."

Her face wrinkled up into a sad, shameful expression. "That's awful."

"I know. I had to leave you there, not knowing what would happen. The woman on the phone, Tanya, she showed up and called for an ambulance."

"Why was she there?"

"Krocker is trying to shut her up too. She thought she could catch him at your house."

"If the FBI is reporting our location to Krocker, we can't go home, can we?"

He shook his head.

The phone on Krocker's desk rang. He picked it up. "Krocker here."

It was his secretary. "The package you asked about has arrived," she reported.

"I'll be there in a second."

Sauntering across the room, he went to the secretary's office and retrieved the parcel. Putting it on his desk, he pulled out his pocket knife and slashed the tape surrounding the box. Digging through the Styrofoam packing, he latched onto a translucent plastic box. "C'mon, baby!" he said.

Lifting the plastic case out and setting it on his desk, he pulled off the top and looked inside. There were a dozen vials of clear liquid God Rx and a couple bottles of the antidote.

He pulled out a vial and held it up to the light coming in the window.

"Washington is mine!" he said.

31

The Roy Rogers Restaurant was a friendly place to have a real American meal. Or to stop for coffee and pie. For Marty and Lisa, it was a place to catch up with themselves.

Sitting in a booth, he asked her, "Are we going to make it through this?"

"I feel as if you tossed our lives out the window … so worried about Jack, you couldn't hear me. Couldn't hear the warnings."

"You remember that?"

"Now I do."

"I'm sorry," he said. "I didn't know what else to do. It looked like a cold-blooded murder."

"We'll lose everything … if they don't kill us. If you would have called Franklin the moment this started, we –"

The first police car slammed into the parking lot with such force that it was still bouncing on it suspension when it screeched to a stop in the back of the lot, blocking the Mustang in its space. The cop jumped out of the car, his gun drawn.

"Get up," Marty ordered.

There were exits on both sides of the restaurant. Marty pulled Lisa out the door opposite the police car, then headed to the highway. They had crossed the street, going for the mini-mall, when a second police car streaked up the street and came to a crushing stop, blocking the driveway of the restaurant.

"Act like you're shopping." He pointed at a stuffed Teddy bear in the window. "We need one of those. C'mon."

They were headed in the door to the shop when a gold-colored SUV raced up behind them and hit the brakes. Marty turned, ready to pull his gun. When the woman waved at him, he realized it was Tanya.

"That's her," he said. "Somebody might be watching. Greet her like you're meeting an old friend. I'll get in back."

When they got into the car, Tanya asked, "What the hell is going on here?"

"Smile," Marty said, "we don't know who is watching."

Tanya laughed, put the car in gear. "Lovely to see you today. Perhaps you can tell me about the police cars."

"I know what happened," Lisa said. "They heard your conversation with Marty, telling us to meet you at the restaurant."

"Then Krocker called the Alexandria police," Marty said.

Tanya pulled out on Jefferson Davis Highway and headed south. Glancing at Lisa, she asked, "How are you holding up?"

"Okay, I suppose," Lisa said. She studied Tanya for a moment. "Do you really believe Krocker is going to kill you?"

Tanya nodded. "He killed my boss."

"I'm sorry," Lisa said. "What is so important that he would kill you to keep it quiet?"

"He has a machine that will erase people's memories," Tanya said. "He plans to use it to take over Washington."

Lisa nodded. "Okay, but if we all have information that can be used against Krocker, why can't we go to the Hoover Building and tell our stories?"

"Right now, Krocker is in charge of the FBI," Tanya said. "I'm not taking the chance of being thrown into a holding cell and having him torture me." She glanced at Lisa. "You were really lucky he didn't kill you."

Marty's cell rang, and he took the call, saying, "Marty here."

It was Mike Greene, Marty's lawyer. "How's the hero doing?" he said.

Marty wasn't happy. "Where the hell did you get those useless guards?"

"Huh?"

"They were asleep when Krocker came in and pulled the gun on me!"

"What?"

"Yes, we should be dead, but we're lucky. He only sent us to the hospital."

"The hospital?"

"Yes, he nearly killed us."

"Marty, I, ah … don't know what to say."

"Sorry would be a start. But you have to understand, he shot me yesterday."

"Shot you? With the guards there?"

"Yes, he drugged them. Then he hit Lisa with an electroshock tool, and took me to Tidal Basin to drown me."

"Oh, my god…"

"Yeah, I kicked the sonofabitch's ass and got away."

"I couldn't have imagined this guy was so crazy."

"He's at wit's end. He'll try anything to protect his position."

"Where are you?" Mike asked over the line.

"Alexandria. He has the city cops after me."

"The police? How?"

"Krocker has a wiretap on my phone. When he got my location, he called them to send out the troops. I suppose he was going to have them pick me up on speeding violations."

"You're saying this call is bugged?"

"Yes, it's going straight to Krocker."

"Dammit, I can't believe this," Mike said. "The president's people don't know anything about it. They're really cordial. I'll call them. They will get Krocker off your back. Can you stay out of the way until I get it fixed?"

"We'll see. But Krocker is desperate and will take any chance whatsoever to kill me. Do you understand?"

"I got it," Mike said. "You need protection – now."

"Right, and he's undoubtedly listening to this. So how do we plan protection with him listening?"

"I'll call the White House."

"I wouldn't expect him to listen to anyone in the Administration. If they get in his way, he will kill them. That means everyone is in danger, and that all our lives are at risk."

"Okay, I'll hurry it up."

"You'd better. But remember, the Administration benefits if Krocker kills me and plugs the leak on Oilgate. So if they don't take full responsibility for him, I'm going to track him down and kill him myself. That's my only choice." Marty changed tone, blaring into the phone, "*Krocker, you hear me, you goddamned asshole? I'm coming to get you.*"

"Hang on, okay?" Mike said. "Don't try to handle this yourself. I'll get the president's people to fix it."

"Fine, but look. I need a pretty strong guarantee that they are really doing something this time."

"Let me make some calls and get back to you. We really do negotiate in Washington."

Marty didn't answer.

Mike said, "I want you to meet me tonight at six. The place we had lunch together last time. The fish 'n chips and the draft. Remember?"

"Yeah."

"Be dressed for an interview."

"Huh?"

"You heard me."

"Okay. I'll see you at six."

32

The Watergate Apartment Building was circled with rows of spiked pilings – actually, balusters without railings – that collectively formed balcony safety-guards. At a distance, they looked like a post-modern architectural interpretation of *Jaws*. On a top-floor patio, feet up, an imported bottle of beer in his hand, Buddy Young sat on a cushioned chair and looked beyond the spikes at the boats plying the sparkling waters of the Potomac.

The door bell chimed.

Wearing a pair of swim trunks and sweat shirt, Buddy slipped inside and waded barefoot though the thick carpet. Guessing it was something he had ordered on the Internet, he looked into the peephole and saw a curious sight. The uniformed concierge was standing next to a fully decked out FBI patrol officer, one of the cops who guarded the J. Edgar Hoover Building. There was a handcart loaded with several document cartons parked next to them. Buddy reasoned that the concierge would have called the FBI to double-check the authenticity of the agent's identification, so he wasn't a danger. He opened the door.

"Excuse us, Mr. Young," said the concierge. "The FBI has sent over the documents you requested."

Buddy pulled the door open. "I don't remember requesting anything from them."

The concierge gave the Bureau cop an I-told-you-so look.

The FBI man said, "I have orders from the acting director to deliver this in person. He said that you would know what to do with it."

Buddy had been drinking when Mack left last night to help Krocker, and he was feeling extremely wary since neither man had given him a call today. He and Mack were supposed to meet a couple of women for dinner in the French restaurant downstairs. But where was he? And who the hell was the acting director, anyway? Speaking to the concierge, he said, "You didn't ring up. How did you know I was here?"

The concierge forced back a smile. "The women, sir. They know when you are in the building."

Buddy made a rubber-faced smile. "Is that right?"

The concierge nodded.

Buddy moved into the Watergate with doctored references which reported that he represented a gun-manufacturer's lobby. He chose this place because he needed normal people to balance out the untamed nihilism of his heart. Once he'd settled in, it felt like home. Despite their cultivated differences, no one was snappish or haughty with him, but rather helpful and encouraging. Momentarily, he trained his attention on the cartons and gave a smirk. "Looks more like something that you should be delivering to one of the judges."

"I've got orders to give this to you," said the FBI agent.

Buddy sighed. "If I have to read all of these documents, you're going to pay for this." The trooper didn't flinch, but rather, he pulled the cart inside and tipped it out from under the stack of boxes. When the man headed out the door, Buddy said, "No signature, no nothing?"

"I was told it was a private matter," said the agent.

Buddy looked at the concierge. "The gun liability hearings…"

The concierge nodded, and Buddy shut the door.

He stood there for a full minute thinking about the possibilities inherent in the stack of cartons. Believing that no one would send a bomb to the Watergate, not even a drug lord, he jerked the top box off the pile and hauled it into the kitchen and set it on the table. Pulling out a butcher knife, he slit the tape, then pulled off the lid.

The box was full of stacked hundred-dollar bills. A long white envelope sat on top.

Buddy wondered what the fuck was going on. Nobody owed him this much money.

He grabbed the envelope, took it out on the patio, tossed it on the glass table and picked up the beer. He didn't have to read it. Krocker had got his ass promoted. That's all it could be. Now he was asking him a big favor. A favor so big that it would cover the trail of bodies Krocker left killing his way up the ladder.

Hmmm.

It was obvious that Mack wasn't coming back. Krocker never let go of the money unless there was bad news to go with it. Could he work for him again, or should he kill him for what he did to Mack and Harrington?

Buddy picked up his phone and dialed a number. When the party came on the line, he said, "This is the man at the Watergate…"

"Yes, sir," said the voice on the line.

"I've got a pickup. You'll need an armored van to move it."

"A little something for the misses, is that it?"

"Yeah, that's where I want it to go."

"What time should we call?"

"I'm waiting for you now."

"We'll be at the Virginia Street entrance in fifteen minutes."

Buddy clicked off and tossed the phone onto the table. He took the note out of the envelope and read:

NEED SOME HELP, K.

33

In the director's office at the Hoover Building, Krocker took off the earphones and pushed back the chair from the computer. He had been listening to the conversation between Price and his attorney, but he wasn't sure where to go with the information. If the president didn't know about the OPEC deal, and thought Price was a hero, Krocker would get hell if he stopped him from making it to the interview. Yet Price might be right. No one was really going to interfere with Krocker and him until there was some guarantee that Price wouldn't snitch about the election rigging. That bought Krocker some precious time.

Krocker got up from the mahogany desk and gazed off towards the dome on the Capitol building. Why hadn't Buddy called? The agent reported that he gave him the money.

Better go to plan B. Put a trooper on Mike Greene. That would lead to Price. Then he could have someone tracking Price. Double tracking. Quadruple tracking. Hell, put a dozen men on it. Just tell them it was another surveillance operation.

Krocker snickered. No two-bit computer hacker was going to stop him in his bid to control Washington. When Price made a mistake, Krocker would go in and take care of the bastard.

Without warning, the office door flew open, and Krocker reflexively threw up his arms and took a step forward, ready to fight.

"How the hell are you, Mister Director?" It was Buddy Young.

Krocker faked a big grin. "I'm in the most secure office in Washington. How did you get in here?"

Ignoring the question, Buddy shut the door and walked to the window and looked across the Capitol Mall. "Nice view."

"I'm glad you like it."

Buddy pulled an automatic from his gold-colored, leather coat and pointed it at Krocker. "Where's Mack?"

"Archer shot him."

"Yeah, right."

"Look, I paid you a bonus for work well done. And you had the choice, just like Mack, to take it and run. But no, here you are. You want more. And I've got more work for you, more money, and more responsibility if you want it. Somebody is going to have to help me keep this place nailed onto the ground."

"You're saying Mack is dead?"

Hands on his hips, Krocker turned. "I'm saying this is dangerous business."

"Where's Mack?"

"You can read the goddamned account in the paper."

Buddy stepped up close to Krocker and pressed the cold gun barrel into his nose. "I want it from you."

"Archer killed him going into my condo."

"And Archer waltzed away?"

"I shot him. He'd dead."

"An old, white-haired man killed Mack. Is that believable? Get out of here."

"Look up the record. Archer was a dangerous individual. A Ranger in Nam. It wasn't until he got back that he studied medicine."

Buddy pointed the gun at the computer workstation. "Show me." While Krocker headed for the computer, he continued. "How did you get to be boss?"

"Franklin had a heart attack."

"Yeah, right."

"The vice president was here when it happened. By the time the paramedics arrived, it was pretty obvious there was nothing we could do. He made me acting director. He and I go back a ways."

"You and Clark – that's a good one."

"Here, look," Krocker said.

Buddy went up to the computer and clicked through the records and read the FBI background check. It showed that Rolland Archer had a purple heart. "I want to see Archer's Army record."

"I've only been here a day. This system isn't set up to do that."

"Do it now," Buddy ordered.

Krocker pushed the chair up close to the table. He opened the same program he had used that morning to doctor Archer's Army record. But now, he played with it like the Army record was hard to find and he hadn't done this before.

Buddy held the gun to Krocker's back as he read the file over his shoulder.

Krocker could see he had Buddy hooked. Now the challenge would be to jerk in the line tight. Real tight. He pushed back the chair and headed into the snack room. “If you’re going to shoot me, get it over with. Otherwise, I’m going to have a drink.”

Buddy followed him to the next room. A small refrigerator was built into the wall above a counter top with microwave and sink. Krocker pulled out a glass, tossed in some ice, gave it a big shot of mixer, then dumped in a splash of tequila. He started to put it to his lips when Buddy grabbed it from him.

“I’ll take this one,” Buddy said. “Tell me about you and Clark.”

Krocker poured another drink, then went in the other room and plunked into the brown leather sofa. “We plotted to rig the election.”

“You can’t rig an election.”

“We sure tried.”

Following Krocker, Buddy went to the window and looked towards the Mall. The big, globular, red sun was behind Crystal City, heralding in the night. “You killed the whole team to cover your own ass. But you missed me. What happened?”

“I could ask you the same thing about the job in Arizona. Why did you walk, and no one else?”

“Don’t flick shit in my face. Tell me why you didn’t kill me?”

“From my point of view, I hire people to do some very dangerous jobs, and some folks inevitably get killed. You, you’re smarter than the rest. You stay out of the way, don’t get in a hurry. That’s why you’re alive. It has nothing to do with me.”

Buddy took a swig on the drink, set it on the ledge of window, pulled a silencer out of his pocket, and screwed it on the end of his weapon. “I want the truth before you die.”

Krocker rolled his tongue inside the cheek of his mouth. “The story doesn’t change, and I still need you for a job. You’re the only one in the States I can count on. Don’t give me this crap that you’re going paranoid because your partner got killed. We have to face these things. It comes with the job. You should be proud. You’re one of ten men on the planet who can do what you do.”

“Yeah-yeah-yeah…” Buddy said, sick of the shit. He glared off in space until he mumbled, “What’s the crisis this time?”

Krocker leaned back into the sofa. “You know the perp who set up Harrington?”

“Price?”

“He has enough information to lock me away; I’ve got to stop him.”

“Same story, different day.”

“Not for me. I have to get him before Thursday night. That’s when he meets with the president and comes onboard the team. If he makes it that far, I'm kicked off."

Buddy belly-laughed. Then he flipped up the back of his coat and stuck the revolver in the back of his jeans.

Krocker laughed too. He hadn't seen the humor in it up to now, but it was funny. He held up his drink. "Touché," he said as the two of them drank to the irony of life.

Buddy said, "They're using you like you're using me."

"Look at it anyway you want, the job still has to be done."

Krocker watched Buddy for any noticeable change of behavior. Earlier, Krocker had laced the alcoholic beverages in the snack room with the God Rx. The drug was clear and tasteless, and his idea was that he was going have a drink with the next agent who came through the door, then convert the person to the Church of Krocker. But serendipity called, and Buddy was here, now, drinking on a loaded drink. Krocker himself had taken the antidote, an agonist that filled the receptor site in the brain, making it so the drug would have no effect on him. But still he was worried. Buddy had trained under Lieutenant "Wild Bill" Jackson in the 82nd Airborne. Krocker knew the lieutenant from his days at Bragg. He taught his men to *wear their armor,* so to speak. That meant being able to concentrate so thoroughly on the operation at hand that a trooper would be impervious to pain. And nearly impervious to brainwashing. He set his eyes on the other man. "The truth is, you're the only man in Washington who can do the job."

"Where's Price going to be?" Buddy asked.

Krocker stood and went to the window. "He is meeting with his lawyer. Name's Michael Greene. They're having dinner downtown at a place where they had fish and chips with draft beer the last time they met. I don't know where it is. Then they're going somewhere for an interview. The big problem is that the lawyer was talking like he was going to get Secret Service protection."

"What the hell do you mean calling me for something like that!" Buddy roared. "It would take a goddamned Oswald to kill a guy who had Secret Service protection."

"I'd bet on you over him any day."

"That's sure a chicken-shit complement."

"I didn't mean any harm."

"Well, *thank you.*"

Krocker noticed that Buddy's eyes had dilated, and he was following Krocker's every move, something Buddy never did. Krocker wished he could reach over and take the gun out of Buddy's belt, but hey, like he said, this was dangerous business. “I’ll put another million in your account.” Krocker went to the computer. “I’ll set up the transfer page with my numbers. You fill in your information, then hit enter. A million, she’s yours, sent to anyplace on the planet. With the money I gave you this afternoon, you won’t have to work again. Just finish this job. One little asshole – dead.”

“Why don’t you do the job yourself?” Buddy asked.

Krocker swallowed hard and decided to head on into his new song and dance. “I’ve got to be here and protect the others. Hold down the Bureau. You know what it means for the Company to have the FBI under our belt? That means we’ll be hiring agents who will believe in the individual’s rights. In the freedom to own guns. There’s eleven-thousand agents. Think about them fighting to get the wimps off the street and out of politics. Think about making automatic weapons legal. You understand? I’ve got to get them to shape up, kick the sissies out of this building. How else can we protect America? How else can we protect ourselves? Our guns?”

Bitting his lip, Buddy placed his hand behind his back on the gun in his belt. “Nobody’s taking my gun; I’d die first.”

“That’s right. And I feel the same way. But this fucking Marty Price wants to ban guns in the District. From all of us. The FBI, even Metro. Now he has an appointment to talk it over with the president.”

With uncharacteristic innocence, Buddy said, “How would we protect ourselves from criminals if we didn’t have guns?”

“Price says we’re going to do it with our fists. Like England. Rollerblading bobbies.”

Buddy bent back and howled with laughter. When he caught his breath, he looked Krocker in the eye and said, “I never heard of anything so stupid.”

Krocker nodded. “That’s why we have to take control of the Capitol.”

“I hear that.”

Krocker stepped close and whispered. “It’s him, or us. They’re going to take our guns if he takes over. And we don’t have long.”

Buddy glanced around the room until he saw the clock. “At what time?”

“He’s going to the White House at six tomorrow.”

“Twenty-four hours.”

“Right. Twenty-four hours to save democracy.” Krocker glared at the other man. “I know it’s a great time to be alive and that the world is full of opportunity, but sometimes we’ve got to take the garbage pail and dump it. Doesn’t matter what the cost.”

Buddy pulled out the weapon and held it up with both hands, aiming past Krocker at an imagined target. “Okay, Price, you little perp. This is what a weapon is for … To dump the garbage.”

"Yes, that's it." Krocker said, knuckling his fists. "A weapon is used to get rid of the garbage." He went to the window. "Think about it. We'll be able to carry our rifles when we cross the Mall. Hell, George Washington carried a rifle here. Why can't we?"

"He did, didn't he?"

"Washington knew what a man had to do in the name of America –"

"Dump the garbage!" Buddy roared.

"That's it, yes. He did it to the British, and he would do it again if he was here now ... Well, he's not here, but we're going to stand in for him." Krocker inhaled audibly and let his chest swell. "It only takes a few good men to change the course of a nation. A few proud individuals who believe the I.R.S. has no authority to tell us what to do. Men who march in step to a different drummer. Men who believe in themselves. You believe in yourself, don't you?"

"Yes, I do."

"I believe in you too. We'll work together. I'll guard the Bureau and recruit a few good men, and you –"

"I'll dump the garbage."

"Yeah." Krocker studied the other man for a moment, startled by the profound effect the God Rx had on his behavior. When Buddy glanced around like he was nervous, Krocker said, "What's wrong?"

"We gotta plan this right."

Krocker nodded.

"I'll get my M-24."

"That's the perfect weapon."

"We'll need beer, too, and body armor."

"Well, yeah." Krocker headed for the refrigerator in the snack room, Buddy on his heels.

"This is going to be fun. A bullet in Price's heart. That'll stop his wee-wee from wagging."

Krocker pulled out a beer and handed it to Buddy. The other man stood there staring at Krocker like something was wrong. When Krocker realized that Buddy wanted to drink with him, he said, "Another day's over." Pulling out a bottle for himself, he twisted off the cap and held up the brew.

Holding his bottle stiff-armed up in the air, Buddy said, "For guns."

"Freedom," Krocker added.

"For men –"

"– and automatic weapons –"

"– in every house –"

"– and a firing range at every school," Buddy said.

Krocker laughed and took a swig on his beer

"What's wrong?" Buddy asked.

"I was laughing because I hadn't thought of it. See how they get to you. I've been working for the government for so long I didn't even think of firing ranges in the schools."

Buddy glanced all around. "You can never be too careful. They might be watching us now."

"No, I ran the de-bugger today."

"Smart move."

The two men worked on the details of Price's assassination until suddenly Buddy stood and headed for the door. "I've got to do it while I'm hot," he said.

When Buddy grabbed the doorknob, Krocker furrowed his brow and glared. "Be careful in the hall. Act straight, like Jesus was coming."

Buddy straightened the collar on his shirt and stood tall and held up a clenched fist. "Dump the garbage," he said.

Krocker held up a clenched fist, too.

When Buddy shut the door behind himself, Krocker blew out his breath. In the morning, he would have to work on headquarters security.

34

Marty had three weapons hidden on his person when Tanya stopped at the men's store on M and 21st. Opening the side door to the van, he stepped out and stood by the front passenger window. "Don't circle the block worrying about me. Go to a public place where Krocker can't harass you. Maybe the Starbucks at Dupont Circle." He stuck his head in the window and kissed Lisa. "If anything happens, I'll look for you at Cher's."

Lisa nodded. "Let your lawyer settle this. Okay?"

He smirked. "Okay."

"I don't want to hear on the news," Lisa said, "that you went from here and attacked Krocker."

"No shootouts," he said.

"Good luck," Tanya said.

He turned and went to the men's store. Inside, he purchased a Franco Uomo double-breasted dark-blue sport coat with six polished-gold buttons. Wearing white shirt and a criss-cross-patterned red tie, he emerged from the street-level store into the pale Wednesday evening twilight. Crossing the road, he watched for shooters, then went inside a shop and had coffee. From there, he walked a few blocks to West 24, James Carville and Mary Matalin's American-style – and ragin' Cajun – restaurant. The last time he had been there was when he and Mike went over the renewal of the contract for his work with the Commerce Committee.

He found the lawyer in the bar, relaxing on an over-stuffed retro sofa. Mid-thirties, with styled, jet-black hair, Mike Greene had a naturally-blush, oval face with prominent black eyebrows. Wearing a grey suit and shirt with gold tie, he had a stack of legal papers in front of him. His cell was on the coffee table. When he saw Marty, he stood straight and held out his hand.

"You made it," Mike exclaimed, a good-natured grin crossing his face.

Marty nodded. "What have you got?"

"C'mon." He led Marty to one of the private executive dining rooms. Flush with cherry-wood furniture and wrapped in rich, jeweled colors, it was one of the more exclusive places to do business in Washington.

The lawyer spread some documents across the dinner table, and they both sat down.

"Everything comes with a guarantee," Mike said. "You do this tonight, someone will do something for you tomorrow. That's what the paperwork is about. Sound okay?"

"You mean the Administration is onboard?" Marty asked.

Mike nodded.

Marty said, "What were you talking about, saying I impressed them?"

"You showed them their vulnerability to computer ... you know, creating a false data-image."

"Data ghosts."

"Yes, that's it. They want to hire you to make the federal systems ghost-proof."

"That would take a billion dollars."

Mike shrugged. "Who cares. The important thing is that they made a deal to call off Krocker. While they are putting it together, I need you to consider doing a TV interview. It's important. It's scheduled for tonight."

"Tonight?" Marty sat back, looked at the ceiling, and laughed.

"It might strike you as funny now, but there's a lot at stake here. It will be the hero interview. Six figures to go on Dean Jones Live."

"No, way, that's a Global station. They work for Krocker."

Lines of impatience wrinkled Mike's face. "That's over, and besides, Dean didn't have anything to do with it. So think of it this way. The interview will give you a chance to blow off some steam. Okay? You know, talking about the big chase and how Harrington set you up. In the meantime, I'll get the president's people to get Krocker out of the Bureau and back into deep space where he came from."

Marty gave a dry scowl.

"What?" Mike said.

"The Administration promoted Krocker to the directorship. It's either him, or me. One of us has got to go down. They know that, that's why they gave him the job. They don't care which one of us dies. But I do. I've got Lisa to think about. And life. I want to live."

"Okay, fine. I'm not saying you can't kill Krocker if he attacks you. I'm only asking that you go on the air and talk about the chase. Can you do that for two-hundred thousand?"

"Two-hundred thousand?"

"Yes, you're the hero."

"But I can't talk about Krocker?"

"No," Mike shook his head. "But remember, you still have the meeting with the president on Thursday."

"The president?"

"Yes, it was his idea to meet with you. Franklin's death didn't matter. He'll be watching the interview with Dean Jones. He's that kind of guy."

"Great," Marty exclaimed. "I'll forget about the goddamned acting director of the FBI trying to kill me. I'll give a namby-pamby interview about Harrington and the chase, and the world will never know the better half of the story how democracy has been ripped off. But everything is fine, right?"

"You'll be a couple-million dollars richer when you've completed the followup on the Morning Show and the Star Review. And you'll be alive. Guaranteed. The president's people will see to it. That in itself makes it worth it."

"Wonderful."

"It is wonderful. I had to sell my soul in order to get a deal out of these people. Your soul too. For our part, we have agreed not to talk about what we know, especially the election scam. For their part, they will let us onto their team. As your lawyer, they expect me to manage the situation. So be cool, and I'll fix it."

Marty stared off into space until Mike said, "Martin, listen to me. I'm your attorney. You can't beat this by yourself. In fact, let's face it. You're outnumbered, and you're dead if you talk about anything you're not authorized to talk about. But you're going to live. Dean Jones will let you show your outrage about being hunted, and that will get you new allies. Millions of Americans. It's the best compromise anybody could make."

Mike picked up a multiple-page document, turned to the last page, and checked off where he wanted Marty to sign. "Date and signature." He handed Marty a pen.

"What does it say?"

"This is Global's contract. They're leery about dealing with us, but they want to be first with the story on the chase."

Marty looked hesitant.

"Sign it. I'll tell you what it says. You're only going to talk about the FBI chase. And Harrington. And about how you discovered they were following you, how you avoided them. Nobody else, no other names. Can you do that?"

Marty scanned the document. "Just Harrington."

"Right. I went over this with the Administration. It's been approved."

Marty signed the document.

"Here's another one." Mike pushed the document at Marty. "The Good Morning Show, tomorrow. Can you get up?"

Marty looked at the attorney. "It's not easy to sleep when you're being hunted."

"We have the presidential suite at Windmar. I know those people. They mean to please. There will be a couple of Secret Service guards in the hall. You'll sleep."

"Krocker is the doctor of destruction. Get six guards. Spread them out. Constant radio contact. Or I'm not going to be there." Mike nodded and he continued. "This game has got to end. What is the Administration doing about Krocker?"

"There's a policy meeting in the morning."

"Great, I can't wait."

Mike gave a stern look. "Didn't you hear me? They're providing presidential protection."

Marty stopped glaring at his lawyer and signed the document. "I want it set up so Tanya Burns – the third in command at the Behavioral Health Division at Quantico – can join Lisa and I at the hotel. Krocker's trying to kill her, too."

Mike scribbled a note, then told Marty that it wasn't time to make the rest of the deals with the media. The story had to ripen in the public's mind first.

The waiter came with a tray of food and drink.

Marty poured a cup of gumbo soup, leaned back in his chair, then took a sip. He felt this was all a pretentious cover, a way of glossing over the obvious, that he was still a hunted man. "Can you explain the arrangement with Krocker? Why does he still have a job? He's working for someone on the president's staff. That's it, isn't it?"

"It's a classical standoff, okay. You give a good interview, and the power will swing in your direction. That's why you have to get it together and do exactly what I tell you to do. When public opinion goes our way, we're safe. The Administration will back us over Krocker."

"But it would be fine for them if somebody killed me … someone who would do it for fun. Like Krocker. Then the Administration wouldn't have to worry about another Watergate."

Mike set down the documents. "That's part of the trust issue. You have to prove you are capable of keeping your mouth shut. If you can't do that, then we're wasting our time." They studied each other until the lawyer continued. "Right now, as a team, you and I are supposed to step forward, out of the midnight shadows, and appear respectable. Not talk about an election that's behind everyone but the diehard liberals." Mike's tongue wet his lips. "Are we on the same page?"

Marty huffed out a dark cloud of suspicion. "Okay, I won't talk about the OPEC deal."

"Scout's honor?"

"Sure."

At six-thirty, Mike got a call. He answered, spoke briefly, then clicked off. "The car's here."

The sun hung on the horizon like a huge pink grapefruit when the chauffeur opened the back door of the black limousine. They got inside. While Mike shuffled through documents, Marty took out the handheld PDA. He sent an instant e-mail to Tanya. She still had Rolland's computer, and she fired a letter right back. He told her about the suite at the Windmar, and she wanted to know when it would be ready. He talked to Mike, then told her that she and Lisa could go to the hotel now if they wanted. But keep the computer on so they could stay in touch. And – stay armed.

He moved into the Interlink Program and hooked into the federal security system. The map on the PDA showed three FBI vehicles on the West End. A couple more sat near Global's television station. They hadn't given up, he realized. They had watched the meeting with Mike and were going to escort him to the TV station. The question was, what did they plan to do to him after the interview?

"I don't like this," Marty said. "There's no presidential guarantee that I get from Global to the Windmar, or that I'm safe there, either. Nor even right now."

"No, it's okay. There's a Secret Service car following us. They will be with us for the next forty-eight hours."

Marty looked at the screen. "Yeah, but there are two FBI cars between the Secret Service vehicle and us. And there are two FBI vehicles at Global. Why? What are they planning?"

Mike looked out the rear window at the cars behind them. "How do you figure a SUV with a Maryland plate and the red coupe are FBI vehicles?"

Marty showed him the palmtop. "Blue lights are FBI. The white light is Secret Service."

Mike's mouth twisted like he was going to growl. "How the hell are you doing this?"

"That's my job. Data management. The car behind us is checked out to Agent Peter Bolero. The one behind that, Andrea Caldera."

Mike wrote it down. "I can see why they don't like you."

When Marty and Mike got out at the industrial-white, concrete, Global building, a woman with a million-dollar smile escorted them though the door and down a hallway. In the bowels of the building, Mike was led to the elevator for the executive offices, while Marty was taken to the recording room. The green light at the door was on – okay to enter.

Inside, Marty encountered a stage with the facade of a small interviewing room built in the middle of it. The room had flashy, blue-and-silver checkered walls. Two chairs were separated by a slick, custom, black table. One side of the booth was open, and a TV camera had been rolled in dead center where the wall would have been. Outside the interviewing room, and out of the way, sat two deep sofas and a stainless steel coffee table.

The smiley-faced woman in the red power suit held out a hand towards the sofas. "Make yourself comfortable. Do you need something to drink before we start?"

"No," Marty said. He glanced around. A man on a camera crane came down from the ceiling, practicing an angled-closeup of the interview table.

"Have you done TV before?" the woman said.

"Thirty seconds worth during a Senate hearing."

"Great. Today, if you have a problem, or if you get anxious – smile. Or laugh. Or give a little anecdote. Whatever you do, be yourself."

"I'll try."

"We will have a few callers. They will either insult you, or they will praise you. Be gracious to them."

Marty nodded.

She studied Marty for a moment, then looked at her watch. "Max!" she yelled.

A thin man in a gold Nehru jacket rushed over. "Oh, I see," he said, pulling out a brush. "Mister Price is starting to perspire." He powered Marty's forehead. "You look perfect. But if you don't mind, can I run a comb through your hair?"

"Sure."

"Dean will come out and greet you," the woman said. "You will go inside and sit down. He will make a pause in the conversation when he sees the count on the wall has begun." The woman pointed. A plastic device near the stage door showed the illuminated number *10*. "You can see it from inside the booth. When it hits zero, we will start taping. Sound okay?"

Marty nodded.

"We're all under contract," she said. "Stick with what your agent told you. Don't vary. Now smile." The woman stood as Dean Jones entered.

Dean was a medium-sized man with an ordinary, round face and black, starting-to-thin hair. Wearing a bow tie and suspenders over a Brooks Brothers-style, red-and-white striped shirt, he could have passed for a country schoolteacher except for his charismatic smile.

"Wow," Dean said, reaching for Marty's hand. "Someone should make that chase into a movie … *Hunted!* That would be a good name for it, wouldn't it?"

The film comment stung, but Marty tried to act to act professional, nonetheless. "Great, but I'll tell you, it wasn't any fun."

Dean's rubbery face twisted into a gigantic frown. "I'm sorry to hear that. Do you live in the District?"

"Well, sure. For the past two years I've worked for the Senate Commerce Committee."

Dean held out a hand, encouraging Marty to enter the interviewing room. "You like your work?"

"Yes. I discover new ways to catch crooks almost every day."

"The Carnivore Program –" Dean grinned. "You invented it, right?"

Sitting in a chair across the table from Dean, Marty cackled. "No way."

The lights at the doors turned red and the countdown started on the device on the wall.

"We are on in a couple seconds," Dean said. "Don't talk until I ask you the first question."

Marty nodded.

When the countdown hit zero, Dean looked into the nearest camera and started talking in a relaxed, resonant voice: "This is Dean Jones Live. Tonight, we're broadcasting from Capital Hill. Our guest is Martin Price, a private detective who works for the Senate Commerce Committee. He is an expert at catching computer crooks. But he says he didn't invent the Carnivore Program. Tell us about that, Marty."

Marty nodded. "The Carnivore Program … that's something the FBI uses to track crime as it moves over the Internet. It looks for mob e-mail and other abuses. But listen, Dean, there has to be a warrant signed by a judge before the government can monitor somebody's e-mail. This program isn't a threat to anyone … except money launderers, dope dealers, mafiosi, terrorists."

Dean nodded. "How did an L.A. private investigator end up working for the Senate?"

"I was doing computer-crime investigations, and I was never happy when other people knew more than I did. So I went to night school … kept taking classes … learning new data tricks. One day I got a call from the Commerce Committee staff. They needed a favorable witness at a computer-fraud hearing. I've been there ever since."

"How do you rate working for the Senate?"

"Best job in the world."

Dean studied him for a moment. "But somehow you got in a mixup with the FBI. Can you tell us about that?"

Marty gave a sad-faced frown. "I ran into an illegal activity. An agent had killed another agent. When the murderer found out I knew what happened, he set me up. Blamed me for the death. Then the full force of the federal government came down. Security vehicles chased me" – he pointed to the west wall of the studio – "right up North Capitol street and across town."

Dean said, "Were you scared?"

"Yes. For my life, and for everyone who knows me. Then there was the ultimate irony. Being chased past the Washington Monument, the symbol of democracy, and there was no place to turn. No one who'd listen to my side of the story."

"Are you bitter?"

"I'm worried about America in an electronic age. There is so much information that no one knows what's going on. That leads to data manipulation. Some people are making a living by spinning the facts, which causes stock prices to rise and fall. Then there is identity theft, where someone steals all your information and assumes your personhood."

"Is that what happened?"

"No, it was identity substitution. My facts where substituted in the federal computers for Agent Harrington's. Then Washington thought I was the murderer. How do you argue with ten thousand computers?"

Brows raised, Dean said, "But you did."

"Yes. I got into the federal programming and switched the information back around. None too soon. There where several agents coming around R.F.K. Stadium. More coming up behind me on Independence Avenue. All thinking I was the number one most wanted man."

"Not a good place for a guy to hide, huh?"

Marty's brow furrowed and he glared at Dean. "Not hardly, and that's the thing. The District is supposed to be a safe place for everybody. This shattered my illusion."

They chatted for a few minutes until the first call was broadcast into the room.

– (Caller) "This is Waco all over again, isn't it?"

Marty looked at Dean and shook his head. "Oh, no, I don't perceive it as that. This was a single, corrupt FBI agent. Power went to his head. If it were otherwise, I'd be locked up. But no, I'm on TV talking about it. That's what America is all about."

– (Next caller) "Are you going to sue the government?"

"My lawyer is here, and I can tell you we haven't even discussed that possibility, and we won't discuss it."

Dean said, "It really doesn't cross your mind?"

Marty said, "What's my tort, and who is it against? A rogue FBI agent tagged me for a murder I didn't commit. He's dead. I can't sue him. And I'm not going to sue the government. I work for the United States, and I'm proud of it."

Dean said, "So it's over, and that's that?"

Marty hesitated. "Well, yes and no."

Dean smiled. "What?"

"I'm still worried that there are people who don't believe the account, or who haven't gotten the message that I didn't do anything. You have to realize that there are still computers here in Washington which contain files wrongly stating that I killed an FBI agent."

"How could someone in the security services not have heard that it was Harrington?"

Marty was silent. He didn't want to whine, not on TV. Then there was the contracts he'd signed, the new team he had joined, the truce Mike had reached with the Administration. He also had Lisa and Tanya to think about. He looked at Dean who was silently studying him. "I am a government contractor," he said. "There are things I can't talk about on TV."

"But you're still worried?"

Marty gripped his hands together. "Yes." He turned to look at the camera. "If you're watching, Mr. President, I'm sorry, but I'm still concerned. Worried about my loved ones."

"What does this have to do with the president?" Dean asked.

"I'm one of his fans, always have been. But it was he who thought I was the hero ... getting away from those who had falsely accused me. He has tried to comfort me. Help me. But I have to say that there were a couple FBI agents following me when I came here tonight. That bothers me."

"They weren't there to protect you?"

"No, the president's staff had arranged for Secret Service protection. But there were these FBI cars, too, stuck in front of the Secret Service, for god's sake. It was unnerving."

"Back to the chase?"

"Who knows?"

Dean looked into a camera. "A posttraumatic sort of reaction, or a real threat? Which is it?"

Marty laughed at Dean's audacity. "Good question," he said. "I'd say I was still wound up from the chase and prone to overreacting, but the security vehicles are real."

"How did you know about them?"

"I'm Marty Price, P.I. It's my job to know these things."

"But you don't know if you're overreacting. Have you been to a doctor?"

Marty winced. He'd nearly broken his contract by what he'd already said on the show tonight, and he didn't want to go all the way and talk about getting shot. That would end his protection. Lisa's too. "No time to see a doc," he said.

Dean smiled and looked around. "Are we safe here?"

"I suppose."

"But you don't know?"

Marty shook his head.

"Getting chased seemed to have turned everything around."

"No, nothing's changed. I work for the Senate. They're the good guys. My job is to track down the bad guys." Marty gasped, "And Harrington's out of the way."

"So you're safe."

"Dean, you're pressuring me. I could look on my palmtop and tell you who is here, tonight, watching us from the street, but that's not my style."

"Your palmtop?"

"Yes, that's how I track people."

"Who? What?"

The lines on Marty's face drew tight with anguish.

Dean prodded. "How can a palmtop provide protection?"

"I'm the Telematics Man. Data is my game."

"Can you show me?"

Marty pulled out the PDA and made up a story. He didn't want to say that he'd downloaded Heaven and was using her. Instead, he said, "I have directional receivers on the outskirts of the District. They scan the microwave traffic. By tuning to a specific broadcast from a particular vehicle, I can pinpoint its location." He looked at the screen on the PDA. "For instance, right now there is one Secret Service car outside on H Street, a block downhill from the bridge. There are also three FBI cars outside on North Capitol." He fiddled with the computer. "In fact, there's an FBI car next to your driveway." He looked at Dean. "Why is there an FBI car outside of Global? Coming in for the next interview?"

"I wouldn't know," Dean said. "Could they be here to protect you?"

"From whom? See my point? If they think I need protection, I should at least know who didn't get the message and is still chasing me."

Dean's lips pressed tight. Finally, he said, "That gadget. Can I see it?"

Marty held the palmtop out, and Dean took it. Dean watched the PDA's screen for a moment, then said, "The blue light at H and North Capitol. You're saying that is an FBI cruiser in our driveway?"

"Yes."

"How do you know that?"

Marty motioned for the host to hand him the palmtop. Dean gave it to him, and Marty punched in some data that turned on the PDA's speaker. Then, he held the palmtop up towards the overhead microphone boom. "Listen," he said.

– (speaker on palmtop, first voice) "*They're on to us?*"
– (speaker on palmtop, second voice) "*Who?*"
– (palmtop, first voice) "*The camera crew!*"
– (palmtop, second voice) "*Ah, geez…*"
– (palmtop, first voice) "*Everyone, get your cars rolling.*"

Dean glanced at the producer who was seated behind a thick, glass window. "Do we have anyone outside?" he said.

The producer nodded, then held a microphone to his mouth like he was miming the interviewer. With the other hand, the producer pointed at the microphone, then pointed at Dean, and finally at the outside wall, trying to tell him that the crew was coming on the line.

A voice from the street team filtered down from the overhead speakers inside the studio:

– (stage sound system, female voice) *"We're out in the driveway, Dean. A white vehicle roared out of here moments ago. We've captured some of the other vehicles on film. They refused to talk to us. They're racing away."*

Momentarily, Dean looked at the camera. "Well, folks, who's tracking who?"

They discussed the implications of the FBI cruisers, then suddenly the show was over.

Mike Greene greeted Marty outside the studio doors. "You sure know how to burn the edges of a contract."

Marty shook his head. "Did I blow it?"

Mike laughed. "I saw you pull out the palmtop, and I screamed: A million dollars down the drain! Did you hear me?"

"No."

He slapped Marty on the back. "Then I guess we're okay."

A group of reporters held microphones and cameras outside the main door.

"Don't say anything," Mike ordered. "We're under contract."

Marty followed Mike, who pushed his way into the crowd.

"Mr. Price," said the reporter behind one of a dozen microphones, "are you going to track them down, find out who is following you?"

Marty laughed. "Maybe you can do that for me."

Mike held a manila binder up in front of a camera. "We can't talk," he said, grabbing Marty by the arm and pulling him though he crowd. When he opened the back door of the limo for Marty to get in, Mike said, "What a perfect setup for the Morning Show."

Krocker was fuming. Now the bastard had the press coming after him. They were already tying up the switchboard, wanting to know why the acting director of the FBI had agents at Global. But that wasn't the half of it. Krocker had promised the vice president that he would shut Price up so that he'd never talk about the rigged election. That was supposed to be done yesterday, but Price got away. Now he couldn't get to the bastard –

Krocker smiled.

Buddy Young could break into anything. Hell, he broke into some computer somewhere and got the code for the lock on the door of the director's office, then walked in and pulled his gun. If he could do that, he would have this little problem with Price fixed by morning.

35

It was early Thursday morning.

Mike Greene glared across the table and spoke with a firm voice. "You can't mention Krocker's name on the show. It will blow our deal with the Administration."

"But he sent the agents to Global last night," Marty exclaimed. "Surely Ally Winters is going to ask me about it."

"Don't mention Krocker's name."

"Okay, I'll pretend Franklin sent them."

The two men sat in the formal dining room inside the presidential suite at the Windmar. Documents were scattered across the table. Breakfast had been brought up at 6:00 a.m., but neither of the men had touched anything but the coffee. Lisa and Tanya were in the next room watching the morning news.

"We have to say we're waiting for the FBI's report just like everybody else." Mike retorted. When Marty didn't respond, he said, "Do this show and do it right, and you won't have to work for the next year. You can travel. Take Lisa. Paris is romantic in the spring."

"I already don't have to work this year, thank you," Marty retorted.

Mike's eyes roved across the ceiling as he chose his words. "Twenty-million Americans are waiting to hear more about the chase. And about your *very* personal digital assistant. They're technically inept. They would listen all day. They love you." He laughed. "Can you see yourself on David Letterman? Your computer reading the list of the five most important things you learned from the chase?"

"Fine. But imagine it from my perspective. I'm in Paris at the Fontaine de Médicis. The water splashes on the statue of the nude couple. Lisa doesn't understand why I'm not romantic. I don't have time, I have to watch for Krocker."

Mike forced a polite smile. "After last night, you know they've got Krocker on a short chain."

Marty tossed the contract on the table and huffed. "I have to settle this thing with Krocker on my own. That's it, isn't it?"

Lisa and Tanya came through the door and giggled their way up to the breakfast buffet. They were dressed in earth-tone morning robes complements of one of the media contractors.

"What's the word on our hero?" Mike asked.

"They love him," Lisa said, "almost as much as I do."

"There are hundreds of pickets at the Hoover Building," Tanya said. "They're chanting, *Bury Krocker!*"

"This early in the morning?" Mike asked.

"It started last night and turned into a street party," Tanya said. "District police are afraid they will set off a riot if they intervene."

Mike held out his hands palms up and stretched his arms across the table towards Marty and whispered, "It's over."

36

...taking away your clip ... counting your bullets ... no automatics ... no concealed weapons ... takes a clean I.D. to buy ammunition ... no big guns ... no stockpiles ... the right to bear arms ... a few good men ... get the wimps out of the Bureau ... the rifle isn't loaded –

What?

Buddy Young came out of his thoughts and realized the rifle wasn't loaded. What the hell was he thinking?

On the roof of a building across the street and down the block from the Windmar, he set down the binoculars and pulled the bullets out of his pocket. He couldn't believe he had nearly blown it, lying here since dawn waiting for Price to leave the hotel when the gun wasn't loaded.

He plugged five 7.62 mm rounds into the internal cartridge of the silencer-equipped sniper rifle. After cocking the weapon, he set it down on the metal bi-pod that attached to the front-end of the stock. Then he sighted the weapon onto the main door to the hotel.

After a few minutes a blond-haired man came out the door and stood in the view-circle of the telescope on Buddy's rifle. As Buddy sighted-in at the man's heart, an extremely tall, black bellhop stepped in front of the target, and the two men started talking.

"Move, fucker, or you both die," Buddy mumbled.

The big man raised an arm, and barked, "Yo!" for a taxi, then stepped out of the circle of what Buddy could see through the scope.

He squeezed the trigger, and the gun popped softly, sending a bullet on its way.

The blond man jerked like he'd had a massive orgasm.

Buddy stuffed the weapon into a golf bag, then glanced at the chaos in front of the hotel. It was a theater of the bizarre. Some people were screaming, and others running, while some simply stopped and stared at the body on the pavement like there was no danger. He couldn't figure it, but it was happening up and down the street in front of the hotel. Motionless people gaping, others screaming and running. No in-between.

37

"They're shooting!" screamed a man, rushing into the Windmar Hotel.

Standing behind the glass wall next to the door, Marty watched an older man on his knees. He held the victim tight to his chest so all that was visible of his head was his blond crop of hair. "That bullet was meant for me," Marty proclaimed.

Mike Greene didn't seem to hear. He grabbed a bellhop by the arm. "Is there another exit?"

The bellhop pointed across the lobby. "It lets out in front of the hotel the same as the main door."

Dressed in dark suit and sunglasses, the Secret Service escort placed a call on his phone.

"Noooo!" wailed a middle-aged woman, bursting out the door and onto the street.

Marty followed her out the door and started towards the victim.

Mike and the Secret Service agent chased after Marty, and grabbing him by the arms, tugging him towards the corner.

"Let go, dammit!" Marty yelled, twisting free.

"They're shooting!" Mike yelled. "Let's get out of here!"

"Who? Where?" Marty said, turning around in a circle.

The agent said, "They're expecting you at the TV station. C'mon."

It was nearly 8:00 a.m., and Good Morning Show host Ally Winters sat on a tan sofa. She wore a sleek, white-chiffon dress with black patterns such that the effect closely imitated dark flowers sketched on silk. Her long, red hair was pulled up in a bun. When Marty entered the room, she flashed her vivacious smile and said, "Telematics Man, I presume?"

Taking a seat on the sofa, Marty gave a faint-hearted smile. "That's me."

"Telematics could be the Internet, right?" she said.

He nodded.

She watched him for a moment. "Is something wrong?"

"There was a shooting on the street."

"Oh, my … I'm sorry. You just don't know anymore, do you?"

Marty huffed out an ocean of frustration. "Where were we?"

"Telematics…"

"You probably do that, experiment with your email … larger font, stationary, something to get the reader's attention. It's telematics when you try to move data more efficiently."

"I need to learn more about that."

The door light turned red.

"Are we on?" Marty asked.

"I like to warm up on the air," Ally said. "That's what the viewers are doing. You can do it, can't you?"

He nodded.

The camera rolled in close.

"Good morning, America. I'm Ally Winters here in Washington with the man from the great chase, Marty Price." She turned to Marty. "How does it feel to be the new kid on the block in DC?"

"A little scary, Ally," Marty said. "But God and Starbucks willing, I'll make it."

"Did you hear about the protests on Pennsylvania Avenue?" Ally asked.

"Yes. And I have to say, it's empowering to know people care." He looked at the camera. "I don't know your names, but thank you. There were times when I was close to giving up, that I … I can't tell you how much it means that you are out there protesting against acting director –"

Marty gulped a quick breath of air. He wasn't supposed to mention Krocker.

"– acting from your hearts, supporting my cause, freedom for everyone. Thank you, I deeply appreciate it."

Ally took a serious tone. "The world will want to know who is watching us? You brought your palmtop, didn't you?"

Marty chuckled. "I've been so busy," he said, reaching into his coat pocket, "that I don't know what agencies are here. Will you give me a second?"

"Yes. Can you tell us more about how that machine works? Did you write the programs yourself?"

"The components are off the shelf programs, but I rewrote them. Nothing complex. Everyone is going to be doing stuff like this on a handheld in a couple years." Looking at the computer, Marty said, "There's a District patrol unit parked in front of the shop across the street. I saw them on the way in. They really are having coffee … There is also a Secret Service unit over on Massachusetts Avenue. It probably has something to do with the

Philippine Embassy, considering the hostage situation in Mindanao." He glanced at Ally. "That's it on the West End."

"You look relieved."

"I can't tell you how comforting it is when the whole screen doesn't light up."

"Did you have the computer with you during the chase?"

"That's why I beat them."

"What's it like being the number one most wanted man in the free world?"

"I never thought of it that way. It was too personal, too immediate, too frightening."

"If it happened again, what would you do differently?"

"I'd call my lawyer before I called my Senator ... before I tried to track down the murderers on my own. That was too risky. At any moment Harrington could have pulled up next to my car and cut me down. He was a pro, a hitman par excellence. He would have figured a way to cover it up, too." Marty frowned for a long, hard moment.

"What's going on?"

Marty shook his head.

Ally studied him a moment. "Is there something you haven't told us?"

"I had a shootout with Harrington. He had the windows blown out on my car and was holding a full automatic to my head before I knew what was happening."

"You have got to be kidding?"

"No."

"Why haven't we heard about it? Another FBI coverup?"

"No. I didn't tell anyone."

"What?"

"I was being chased. There wasn't time to talk."

"Where did the shootout happen?" Ally said.

"Virginia."

"How did you get away?"

He put the computer in his pocket. "Something I learned from Rambo."

"You know Sly Stalone?"

Musing over his situation, Marty chuckled. He had a killer on his tail, and no one seemed to care, but they'd all grope to hear a Rambo joke. He leaned forward and raised a brow. "For me, time had stopped. That was when I listened to my inner voice telling me –" Squint-eyed, he looked at Ally. "You are Telematics Man. Kill him with data."

Ally roared.

With the show over, Mike and Marty headed back to the hotel.

"Krocker's going to assassinate me if I stay in town," Marty said.

"No," Mike said, "we have a truce."

"The bullet that killed the kid – that was meant for me."

"No, it's over."

"The hitman saw blond hair and fired."

"The news is saying it's a drive-by … a drug thing."

"In the heart of the District? C'mon."

They went into the hotel without speaking. Coming out of the elevator on the top floor of the Windmar, they a found a photographer and a reporter leaving Marty's suite. Lisa was bidding them goodbye. A couple of guards watched the proceedings.

"What's this?" Marty asked.

While the photographer snapped away, Mike escorted Marty into the room.

"The Star Review," Mike said, shutting the door. "You signed a carte blanche contract. They used it with Lisa."

Marty could imagine the headline: *Telematics Mate Tells All.*

38

Lisa didn't think there was any danger staying another day at the Windmar. She told Marty that he was being paranoid, thinking the assassin's bullet was meant for him. And besides, Cher had come over, and they were enjoying themselves.

Marty laughed. Everyone would be wondering from now on, asking if it was his post traumatic stress from the chase, or whether he had new enemies. While Lisa and her friend chatted in the front room, he headed for the bedroom, picked up the hotel phone, and dialed.

Commander Nelson at the District Police Department came on the line, saying, "Marty, how the heck are you? I just got back on duty, and would have called immediately, but we had a shooting at the Windmar, and everyone is at my desk demanding action. Did you hear about it?"

"Yes, I'm staying at the Windmar."

"What?"

"It's not safe at my home. The big chase is still on."

"I knew something was happening. When I watched you and Ally, I told Helen, Marty's holding out, not telling us something. Who is after you? I'll have my men track them down. I don't care if they're feds or not."

Marty swallowed. "It's a difficult problem discussing this on a non-secure line."

"Why's that?"

"You've been knowing me how long?"

"Marty, get it out. Who is chasing you?"

"The acting director of the FBI."

"Holy hell. So the pickets at the Hoover Building are legitimate?"

"You got it. So listen. The blond-haired kid took the bullet for me this morning."

"Yeah?"

"He zipped out the door sixty seconds in front of me, when it was all set for me to go around the corner and do the Good Morning Show. Coincidence? I don't think so. The bullet was meant for me. Sure, I can't prove it, but look. A lot more is happening here than is being reported.

What's the department's take on the shooting?"

"We're thinking it was a drive-by, that maybe the kid's family or friends were doing something with drugs. But that's totally unsubstantiated."

"What does ballistics say?"

"Looks like it was a deer rifle. A .308 Winchester slug."

"How many shots were fired?"

"We found one slug, but we had reports that there was up to five shots. Others say they didn't hear a thing."

Marty looked out the hotel window at the surrounding roof tops. "What did Terry Washington say?"

"The bellhop?"

"Yeah."

"He had just turned from the victim and was shouting for a taxi. The cab was down the street, no cars in front of the hotel. He said he didn't hear the sound of a gun, and when he looked back at the kid, he was falling. How do you know Terry?"

"I was working on a crime bill, and I met a consultant here in the restaurant. We got talking to Terry while we waited for the valet to bring the cars around. He's a keen observer. If he says there wasn't a sound of a gun, I believe him. My guess is that it was a sniper with a silencer, probably using a military rifle. Did you guys check the tops of the buildings?"

"I don't think we did."

"Don't bother. You won't find anything."

"No?"

"It was a professional. That's all it could have been. I mean, how else could there be no witnesses in broad daylight? Listen. I've got to get going. Can you get back to me if anything turns up?"

"Well, yeah, but tell me what the Secret Service is doing over there."

"I have presidential protection until we figure out who is trying to kill me. It's obviously John Krocker trying to protect his fiefdom, but no one is willing to go over and lock him up."

"I've never heard of such a thing."

"He has a secret operation. I exposed it. That was covered up. Now the government is too embarrassed to tell the public what Krocker has done. So I'm stuck in the middle." When Ken didn't respond, Marty said, "What are you thinking?"

"I'm stunned. Do you want some more help out there at the hotel?"

"A few more cops on the beat would be great."

"You got it. Call me if there's anything I can do."

"I will. See you later."

Marty clicked off. He didn't expect to get much protection from Nelson. His people were no match for Krocker. But at least he had the lowdown on the shooting. No doubt now it was a professional assassin. The information fit with what he had learned earlier when he hacked into the FBI main computer. During that data search, he inspected the Bureau's computer link with the DC telephone network. Searching though that system, he proved what he believed all along. Krocker had a tap on his new cell phone. That meant Krocker had someone enter into the wiretap program and rewrite it after Marty had messed with it earlier, cutting off the wiretap. This demonstrated that the Administration had not reined in Krocker. No, they were simply waiting for the acting director to kill Marty. Then they could stop worrying about the election being exposed.

Wanting to be alone to think through a new strategy, Marty went into the livingroom and told Lisa he would be back in a few minutes. Then he packed one of Tanya's automatics into a gym bag and called the Secret Service chauffeur to bring the limo around. He should be safe in it, he figured. It was bulletproof and the driver was armed. When the car arrived, he told the chauffeur to head towards Virginia.

Sitting in the back seat, Marty recalled the disturbing notion he had earlier. He decided to test it now. Taking out the palmtop, he brought up the Interlink Program and used it to dig into the Crays at the Pentagon where parts of Heaven were stored. Making a search by time and date, he looked at Heaven's files for listings made during the break-in at Krocker's office. There were hundreds of files listed, way beyond the amount of files he had searched.

He sat back and considered what he had discovered. Heaven not only copied every file she read, she copied the entire folder from which the file had been extracted. This meant that Heaven had stored a copy of Krocker's hard drive.

Amazed at the discovery, he searched through the files until he bumped into one Krocker had made on the Russians. Reading through it, he discovered that the foreigners had built the palmtop which acted like a remote keyboard for Heaven. And yes, they'd constructed the electro neuron disruptor. He also noted a pattern here. Krocker had gotten rid of each group of scientists after they had completed a project. His latest firing included a group of Russians in Azerbaidzhan.

Marty read further, discovering something that inspired his curiosity and his fear: Krocker had fired the crew who had refined the drug for the *God Rx*.

A prescription for belief?

Huh?

Marty scanned through the file. Krocker had been in Asia two weeks ago and had used the portable Eraser on the whole scientific-development team, liquidating their memories of the belief project. That left him in charge of a drug which activated the belief system in the brain.

Fine, but what did this mean?

Marty guessed it meant that Krocker had the power to use the drug to make people join the Company and take an oath to kill for its principles.

Marty considered similar cases. While living in L.A., he had studied the workings of the Charles Manson cult. Manson had used drugs when he indoctrinated the members of his clan. After that, they would obey his orders religiously. They killed for him. Comparing Manson's action to Krocker and his God drug, Marty discounted the idea that someone could locate God. The Lord was everywhere. What Krocker had discovered was a chemical method which could induce hypnosis. Not natural hypnosis, which precludes getting people to do things that could damage themselves. But rather Manson-style cult hypnosis. In other words, chemical brainwashing. Putting it all together, it meant that Krocker had discovered not God, but the devil.

Marty knew that he had to kill this man. He was Doctor Death turned guru. Soon he would have a cult following who would carry out his death orders with religious fervor. Regardless of what good meaning people like Mike Greene did to try and stop Krocker, the acting director would kill until he himself was killed.

Looking out the limousine window, he noted that they had crossed the Loop at Springfield. Marty asked the driver to pull off the freeway and take him into the forest.

On a side road in the boondocks, they parked in the area devoid of development. Marty got out. Leaving the driver to attend the car, he walked through the brush and into the trees. In his mind, he saw a vision of Lisa flopping in the bed after Krocker had hit her with the END device. All that had saved her life was dumb luck. Well, dumb luck wasn't good enough now. He had to go get Krocker. Walk into the FBI office and shoot him.

Marty took off his tie and slung it around a tree at neck's height. He tied it so it hung down as if it were around a man's neck – Krocker's. Then he took a few deep breaths. Backing up ten paces, he turned and bowed behind himself. Then, spinning around, he pointed his right arm at the tree at the same moment he hit his right wrist with his other hand.

The wrist-gun fired. It was the non-metalic weapon he'd taken from Harrington's office.

Going back to the tree, Marty looked at the tie. There was a hole in the knot.

Marty emerged from the trees and opened the back door of the limo. Not seeing the driver, he looked up front of the vehicle. Wearing a black suit, the driver stood in a thicket thirty or forty yards away. His back was turned to Marty. The guy was taking a leak on a tree, apparently.

Marty got in the car and waited, but the driver didn't move, hadn't moved, actually, not since Marty noticed him. That made Marty suspicious.

He opened the door and got out. Pulling the gun from his shoulder holster, he cocked it and went to see what was going on.

Don't fall into your opponent's trap.

Marty stopped. In his mind, he heard his weapons instructor's voice. He could see the man standing in front of the classroom. He was wearing a green camouflage shirt, saying the number one rule of war is to call the time and place of the battle yourself. Don't rush onto your opponent's field of battle thinking there is a crisis. Usually it's no more than a trap, and your opponent has set it in such a way to make you believe you can win. But you won't.

Marty glanced at the chauffeur. He still hadn't moved.

Then Marty saw what looked to be a strand of rope coming out from under the driver's coat. He'd been strung up to the tree limbs.

A foreboding chill shot down Marty's spine, and he dove to the ground.

Immediately, an automatic strafed the limo. Then a burst of God-awful laughter rang though the forest. Finally, a voice yelled, "What's a matter, pretty boy?"

Marty scrambled into the brush, away from the direction of the shouting. When another bust of weapon's fire sounded, he ran straight into the trees, the branches whacking him on his face as he went.

The insane laughter followed him, and when he'd run wildly for over a half-mile, the crazy voice rang out, not more than a couple-hundred yards behind, "You're making it too easy, pretty-boy!"

His instinct was to fire in the direction of the sound. Instead, he ran, knowing now that it had to be Buddy Young. He also knew the sound of the weapon Buddy had fired at him. It had the distinctive *pop-pa pop-pa* of an AK-47. Marty couldn't fight a man with that kind of an assault rifle, not with a semiautomatic pistol.

But there was something else going on here too. Buddy sounded insane. No professional killer would yell *pretty boy*, for Christ's sake.

Marty raced to the edge of the oaks and stopped before a tall grass meadow. Knowing he would be dead out there, he skirted the edge of the trees, turning occasionally to see if Buddy had emerged from the woods. Not challenging fate, he headed back into the thick cover of the forest, and breaking his way through the woods, he realized that he was leaving a noticeable trail for Buddy to follow, and tiring himself out while he did it.

He looked up and caught the position of the sun in the sky. Remembering that the limo was parked in a direction that pointed towards the golden orb, and that the car was parked perpendicular to the road, he turned and ran away from the sun. That should get him to the street.

The plan worked. When he broke through the bush and came to the blacktop, he had to make a quick choice. The highway was two or three miles east; the limo about a half-mile west.

Seeing the image of the dashboard in his mind, he realized that when he looked inside the limo and hadn't seen the driver, he had seen the keys hanging on the steering column. That had given him the thought that the chauffeur would be right back. Then he had seen the driver standing in the distance, not moving at all. What it meant to Marty now was that if he got to the car before Buddy, he'd be home free.

He turned west and raced towards the vehicle, sprinting as fast as he could go. When he looked back, he saw that Buddy had abandoned the rifle and was chasing after him.

He thought about turning and fighting. After all, he had the pistol. But seeing he was outdistancing the man, he kept going.

When he reached the vehicle, he dove inside and slammed the door. With a cold determination, he fiddled with the key and fired up the vehicle. Seeing Buddy at the window, he hit the lock.

The man howled with hideous laughter and gave a quick blow with his foot, kicking the driver's side window.

Chunks of glass went everywhere.

Marty picked the pistol off the seat and fired it at Buddy, but he was already on the ground, rolling out of the way.

Marty crammed the limo into reverse and floored the gas.

The big, black car shot backwards, Buddy racing to keep up with it.

When Marty stopped to put the car in forward, Buddy pulled a small pistol from his pocket, cocked it, and fired.

Ducking down, Marty raced towards Buddy, trying to run him over. When he dove out of the way, Marty headed towards the freeway cursing at the fools who marketed the limo as a bullet-proof vehicle.

Around a bend, Marty slammed on the brakes.

Why not set his own trap?

He had the automatic in the bag in back, and he was out of Buddy's line of sight.

Taking the car straight into a thicket of bush, he let the vehicle stop by its own inertia.

Jumping out, he took the MP-5 automatic Tanya had given him and jammed in the fifty-round clip. Lying in the bushes, he waited.

Momentarily, a red Cherokee raced up the road from the direction Mary had come. The SUV was twenty yards away when he stepped out and pulled the trigger, plugging the car with bullets from one end to the other.

The car went wild, turning a hard left and rolling over and over, shedding cracked glass and doors as it spun. When it came to a halt upside down, Marty charged towards it and fired another blast of bullets. He was bending down, looking inside, when heavy breathing came from the back of the vehicle.

Marty turned.

It was Buddy. Blood streaming down from the crack in his forehead, he raced towards Marty with a hunting knife slashing in front of him.

Marty fired, then jumped out of the way as the man ran past him and fell blindly into the street.

Marty walked over to look at the body.

Buddy screamed and grabbed at him.

Marty emptied the clip into his head, splattering his brains across the blacktop.

Walking back to the limo, Marty stared into the distance. He remembered how Buddy was so quick to adapt that he survived the fight at the airport. He wasn't crazy like this. Maybe he acted differently now because Krocker had used the God Rx on him. That had to be it. He didn't know whether to thank Krocker for the mistake, or to curse him. But if Krocker was willing to turn a professional killer into a mindless thug, it showed one thing. Krocker was getting desperate.

39

Under a balmy afternoon sky, a black limousine approached the Naval Observatory checkpoint at Northwest Massachusetts Avenue and 34th Street. The guard in the winter-blue uniform stepped out to greet the car. He talked to the driver, made a quick phone call, then saluted, letting the vehicle enter.

In the back seat of the limo Lisa exclaimed, "Isn't this exciting?"

Marty was less enthused. Laconic, actually. He knew he should have told Lisa about killing Buddy. But instead, he went home, took a shower, got dressed, and called Commander Nelson. He told him about what had happened. Nelson said to bring the limo to headquarters. Marty said, no, it was parked in front of his house. He was going to keep his schedule to meet the president – keep his life going forward, not sit the rest of the day at police headquarters. After he clicked off in the middle of Nelson's tart reply, he called a taxi and headed back to the hotel. On the way, he called Mike Greene. The lawyer wanted to know where the hell Marty had been; he was going to be late for his appointment with Vice President Russell Clark, and that might give the White House enough reason to cancel his meeting with the president.

Mulling the whole thing over now, Marty wondered if the Administration was going to keep their agreement and get Krocker off his back. He doubted it, but he was in a real bind. Krocker could send a dozen fanatics like Buddy after him. Get them high on the God Rx, tell them Marty was the devil's disciple.

But maybe if he smiled through the whole thing, Marty might get a chance to see the president alone for a moment. Then he would tell him the whole story and plead for mercy. What choice did he have? He was in a trap set by men who controlled forces so vast he was no more than a pawn in their game.

He glanced around the verdant grounds of the naval base. What would happen if Krocker had gotten through to the vice president's staff? Hell, the Naval Observatory could already have been converted to the cult of Herr Krocker.

"Marty, look!" Lisa said. The limo had pulled into the parking circle behind the vice-presidential mansion. Margarete Clark and a bunch of kids were playing croquet on the lawn.

"Cool," he said.

The vice president's wife looked young for her years. And vivacious – wearing a bright-yellow sun dress and white, wide-brimmed hat.

Seeing the limo, Margarete Clark and a couple of the kids headed in that direction.

The driver stopped and waited for orders.

Lisa hit the button for the window.

Margarete approached and looked inside. "Lisa, come join us. Let the men catch up with us later."

"Well, sure," Lisa said.

"Are you Data Man?" asked the boy.

Marty cackled. "That's me."

"I have a new digital assistant. Will you help me set it up?"

"I sure will," Marty said, wondering what the hell he had been thinking earlier – bringing a weapon here.

Margarete said, "Russ is in a meeting. You can wait with us, or go inside."

"I'll go in," Marty said. He looked at Lisa. "See you in a few."

Marty sat on an antique sofa in a stark, white room that was an add-on to the original mansion. He fiddled with the palmtop to pass the time.

Suddenly, the door opened and closed.

Time stopped for Marty when he looked up and saw the tall man aiming a pistol at him.

It was Krocker.

"Set the computer on the sofa," the FBI director ordered.

Listening to his own breath, Marty slowly exhaled, then let go of the handheld.

"Stand."

His eyes tracking the gun, Marty stood. For him, Krocker looked surreal. Wearing white gloves to keep his prints off things, he could have been the Marquis de Sade, ready for a magical day of debauched torture.

"Hold out your arms and come to me," Krocker said.

Krocker was on the far side of the room. Marty took a step forward.

"C'mon," Krocker said.

Staring at the silencer on the weapon, Marty realized that the further back he was when Krocker fired, the more likely Krocker would miss him.

"Move it," Krocker said.

Dressed in a dark-blue, three piece suit, Marty was in the middle of the next step when he saw Krocker pull an aluminum tube from his pocket. He wasn't planning to frisk him for a gun, but to hit him with the END device. Stimulate a seizure, or more likely, a killer stroke. Then Krocker could sneak back out of the mansion, and no one would no the difference.

Instead of going to Krocker, Marty leaped sideways.

Krocker pushed the gun forward.

Marty pointed his right hand towards Krocker's head while swinging his left hand towards the bulge under his coat sleeve.

Krocker fired.

Marty hit the wrist-gun on its firing button … then fell to the floor.

The sound of the Marty's gun echoed in the building even as Vice President Russell Clark burst through the door saying, "What is going on here?"

He glanced at Krocker, wobbling on his feet, blood dripping from the dark hole in his neck. His eyes blank, ghostlike, as he pointed the pistol at Marty.

Marty stood on-guard, fists up, ready to fight, staring at Krocker, not turning to look at Clark.

The ghost of death hovered in the room.

No one spoke.

A hand hanging at his side, Krocker dropped the END device.

It bounced on the floor.

Motionless, Marty stared at Krocker's gun.

Suddenly, Krocker fell forward, flat on his face.

Clark rushed forward, sighing with relief. "Were you hit?" he asked.

"No."

"I can't believe this," Clark said.

"You knew he would try to kill me."

With the barrel of an automatic rifle leading the way, a burly man came through the door. He had a radio plug in his ear. "What is this, Russ?" he said, looking at Krocker, face down on the floor.

Clark said, "An intruder broke through security. Mr. Price killed him."

"Are there more of them?" the agent said.

"I don't know," Clark said. "Get some guards out in the yard with the children, then search the house."

A wiry man in a sport coat, jeans, and loafers burst through the door. It was the V.P.'s press spokesman, Akki Cohen."What the hell happened?" he exclaimed.

Clark said, "The acting director of the FBI discovered that Martin Price had information implicating him in Tucker Johnston's death." He looked Marty in the eye, and Marty nodded. "He used his office to break though the security at the Naval Observatory."

"He was going to kill me and cover it up," Marty said.

"Unbelievable," said Akki.

40

"They acted like an ordinary couple," Lisa said. "Wasn't that incredible?"

"Yes," Marty replied.

It was Thursday night. They were at the luxurious bar at West 24. Half the tables were empty. Soft jazz filtered through the room.

"What were you doing with the president's laptop?" she asked.

Marty smiled and leaned back into the overstuffed sofa. "Showing him how to send self-erasing messages."

"What is that?"

"They self-destruct after ten days. Doesn't matter if they're read or not. They have an attachment that gobbles them up, and then they are gone."

"I need that when I send a stupid letter and want it back before someone reads it."

"A recall program."

"Yeah."

He reached for her smooth white hand. "Can you handle being with me when people will always stop and want me to fix their computers? Do investigations? Manipulate the data?"

Smug-faced, she said, "You don't have to do computers anymore, you can do interviews."

He chuckled. If Akki Cohen was allowed to spin his version of the Krocker story, the vice president and Marty would become national heros. "I was hoping this would be a special evening," he said, "something we'd want to remember ... meeting the First Family and all. So I brought a surprise."

She smiled. "That's what you stopped at home to pick up, right?"

"Well, yeah. I was thinking it was time to go all the way –" He pulled out a small white box, flipped it open, and showed her the humongous, sparkling diamond. "Will you marry me?"

"Marty!" she exclaimed.

He smiled. The timing was perfect. "You like it?"

Enamored, she slipped it on. "It's beautiful."

"You don't have to decide right now, but I am giving you the ring anyway. It's yours forever." He held her hand and looked into her eyes until a quick movement at the door caught his attention.

He mumbled, "Please, God, nooo..."

Lisa turned to look.

Leather coat, and in a hurry – it was Jack.

*